*For David Rapalee —
in appreciation —
Franklin Bakun*

DEATH OF A
MARIONETTE

FRANK M. ROBINSON AND PAUL HULL

DEATH OF A
MARIONETTE

A TOM DOHERTY ASSOCIATES BOOK
NEW YORK

This is a work of fiction. All the characters and events portrayed in this novel are either fictitious or are used fictitiously.

DEATH OF A MARIONETTE

Copyright © 1995 by Frank M. Robinson and Paul Hull

All rights reserved, including the right to reproduce this book, or portions thereof, in any form.

This book is printed on acid-free paper.

A Forge Book
Published by Tom Doherty Associates, Inc.
175 Fifth Avenue
New York, N.Y. 10010

Forge® is a registered trademark of Tom Doherty Associates, Inc.

Library of Congress Cataloging-in-Publication Data

Robinson, Frank M.
    Death of a marionette / Frank M. Robinson and Paul Hull.
        p.   cm.
    "A Tom Doherty Associates book."
    ISBN 0-312-85967-8
    1. Intelligence service—United States—Fiction.   2. American—
Belgium—Brussels—Fiction.   I. Hull, Paul, 1939–   . II. Title.
PS3568.02888D43   1995   95-34747
813'.54—dc20   CIP

First Edition: November 1995

Printed in the United States of America

0 9 8 7 6 5 4 3 2 1

For Gene Klinger

To the tables down at Mory's. . . .

one

"SOMEBODY GOT FALK," Louis said, loud enough to be heard over the squeal of wet tires and a loose fan belt. "A bomb in his Fiat. Tindemans is interim Chief." There was a pause while he tugged at the steering wheel and they skidded around a corner. "It's in the papers."

"Too bad," Morley said, keeping his voice casual. Louis obviously didn't consider it the greatest of all possible tragedies, but then he had never been overly fond of the other Bureau employees. "When?"

"Last night. He was on his way home."

Falk had been Morley's liaison. The beefy man had been in his early fifties, with gravy stains on his tie and trouser legs that flapped when he walked. But unlike many Belgians he knew how to laugh, and it hadn't taken Morley long to discover that behind the smiling eyes had lurked a first-rate mind.

Falk could have been useful.

Morley cracked the window slightly, ignoring the cold air that leaked in. Anything to get rid of the smell of the greasy paper in which Louis's *frites* had been wrapped—the odor of fried potatoes and mayonnaise was as pervasive in Brussels as that of strong coffee. Louis's cab was his home away from home—complete with the greasy wrappers, a stack of Danish skin magazines on the front seat, crumpled packs of Caballeros and Marlboros along with the *Manneken-Pis* on the dash, and a small coffee cup that Louis had liberated from some sidewalk cafe.

Morley cursed his failure to check out the cab at the airport. He should have realized the Bureau would have been notified to pick him up. He liked Louis, but hadn't been prepared either for him or his Grand Prix driving style. It's what came from being laid up in bed for six months.

The memory of the secure medical unit in Mayfair chilled him, and he settled his briefcase on his lap, thumbed the catches and started sorting through its contents. There was damned little to go on—nobody seemed to know much about Serge Cailleau. Not that it mattered; Cailleau was hardly the real reason why he had wanted to get back to Brussels. In London, the counterterrorist commander known only as Simon had suspected as much and said so.

"I thought you hated the city, Neal—hardly blame you, of course. I'm delighted that you're willing to go back, but you don't need to volunteer; our assets in Brussels should be able to handle it easily enough. An hour's talk with the old man should make him happy."

It was Simon who had suggested going back to Brussels in the first place.

"I think there might be more to it than smuggling," Morley had said, trying to keep his voice casual.

"You really think so?" The two of them were alone in the small patients' lounge. Simon had leaned back in the white plastic chair and carefully crossed one leg over the other, rearranging the crease in his trousers. Simon was a relatively new man, careful to hide his opinion that Morley was a necessary evil. Or perhaps not so necessary. Not anymore.

"It's sort of like climbing back on the horse again once you've fallen off." Simon had smiled slightly. "Terrible analogy, but I think you follow me."

"It's not like that," he'd lied.

"Sorry," Simon had said, not sorry at all. He had leaned forward to tap Morley on the knee, careful to touch him gingerly.

"Neal, don't go off on your own." There was a distinct warning note in his voice. "The drug ring was broken, and you certainly played the key role. But it would be a shame to waste time covering old ground. While you've been here, we investigated it pretty thoroughly." A smug look flickered across his face. "Once the distribution channels were cleaned up, that was it. There weren't any others involved."

Morley had stared at him. "The ones I hit had diplomatic immunity. I can understand why it would be sensitive."

Simon had frowned, annoyed at his stubbornness. "There were Pierre Faure, Edgar Mollett and Leon Lavaisse." He ticked them off on his fingers. "Thanks to you, they were eliminated. A few minor accomplices were rounded up while you've been here, but that's all there were. We had our own difficulties with the French Embassy, but by then you were gone and we and the Belgians worked it out with the French." A note of reproof crept into his voice. "They would, of course, have preferred a trial—after all, the three were French nationals. It wasn't quite an incident, but it came close."

It was also something Morley knew Simon would never forgive him for. He had closed his eyes. "I knew them personally," he said quietly.

"From your days in Vietnam—you told us." Simon's voice had turned edgy.

"They dealt in heroin," Morley had continued. "It was bad shit. I had a lot of friends who died."

Simon was silent for a moment. "That was a long time ago, Neal."

It still seemed like yesterday to him, Morley had thought. "There had to be a banker," he said stubbornly. "There was too much money involved, we don't know where it went."

Simon had stood up, shaking out the creases in his pants. "You really don't need to go, Neal. If you'd like, I can have you transferred back to the States."

It was a threat, not an offer. Morley hadn't been back to the States since 'Nam. If he ever went back, chances were he'd never be assigned out of country again.

"I'd like to return to Brussels," Morley had said, not meeting Simon's eyes.

"You were badly injured there," Simon continued in a low voice. "You think the people who did it are still there and you would like revenge. I don't agree with your assessment. And we can't afford a rogue agent. Understand me, Neal—the first indication I have that you're pursuing a personal vendetta and you'll be recalled immediately. The assignment's a simple one. Cailleau won't talk over the phone and he won't talk to the Brussels Bureau. He will talk to an agent from this department. In person. Do you want to go or not? On our terms, not yours."

There was no point in arguing further. Once in Brussels, he would do as he wished.

Before he left the patients' lounge, Simon had hesitated and said: "You have a problem with the past, Neal. Some day you'll have to come to terms with it, you know."

"I'll watch myself in Brussels," Morley had reassured him.

Simon had shrugged, then said: "I wasn't referring to Brussels, Neal."

Louis swerved to miss two nuns pedaling a tandem, then fought to regain control on the rain-swept street, fishtailing for a hundred meters before straightening out. Morley suddenly realized that Louis had asked a question and was waiting for an answer. He cleared his throat.

"It's good to be back, Louis."

The face in the rearview mirror looked doubtful. "You're glad?"

Morley looked through the streaked window at the gray skies and the rainwater running in the gutters. "Not really, no."

"We didn't expect you so soon, Neal."

"I booked an earlier flight. I wanted to talk to Cailleau before he opened his act."

"Tindemans was unhappy."

"I don't work for Tindemans, Louis. You do."

He caught Louis's face in the mirror again and realized that the big man was inspecting him as well. Louis's face was pocked and heavyset, with a black watch cap pulled low over the forehead, almost touching his ears. The ears themselves were outsized, even for such a large head, and networked with purple veins. Thick, matted eyebrows matched the ears for size; below them a dark thicket of a moustache hid coarse lips. A strong face, brutal, and one that was studying him now with a certain caution. He relaxed. Louis didn't realize how badly he'd been hurt.

Then his own sense of irritation at Louis's inspection faded. Louis was the reason he had been yanked out-of-country and sent to intensive care instead of the morgue.

His own face had been through some changes since Louis had seen it last. It was thinner now, and pale, with fatigue lines permanently etched in the cheeks. Add a slightly receding hairline with a telltale crinkling at the edges of the eyes, and you had the face of a worn executive in his mid-forties, or perhaps that of a tired schoolteacher.

For his purposes, it was the perfect face—you'd have to

look twice to connect it with the face he'd worn in Brussels before.

From his expression in the mirror, Louis was having trouble weighing the differences between the old Morley and the new. He wanted desperately to have something to take back to the Bureau. His new keeper, Tindemans, was probably waiting anxiously for his report.

Morley shifted awkwardly—Louis was a huge man and had pushed the front seat as far back as it would go—and turned to look out at the street again. He had driven down it frequently enough in the past, but during the months he'd been away some of the familiar bars and clubs had undergone a sea change; their facades had been remodeled and new names hung over the doors. Others had disappeared completely, replaced by huge excavations and crane booms pointing stiffly at the sky.

What little color the city possessed had been washed away by the downpour, the dullness of the boulevards matching the clouds overhead—even the bicycle riders had turned on their lamps. Brussels on a rainy mid-November morning: beech trees stripped bare of their leaves with their limbs a wet and ugly gray; stuccoed walls with tattered circus posters slowly being peeled away by the rain; pedestrians huddling under spidery umbrellas; slicker-clad schoolchildren trailing after their teacher like so many yellow ducklings . . .

The bleak clinic tucked away in London had been just as bleached of color. White walls, white sheets and white uniforms. The only hues had been in the clear plastic bags that held blood or intravenous solutions tinted by a dozen different exotic medicines.

On the drive to Heathrow that morning, the riot of color along the road had been almost more than he could take; the dullness of Brussels had come as a relief.

Louis slid through a pack of honking Volvos, Citröens

and Peugeots to squeal to a stop at a crosswalk. Morley closed the lid of his case and studied the faces in the crowd waiting impatiently at the light. You really couldn't tell the right-wingers from the left, or the ITT executive from the rising young man in the Naples-Montreal narcotics ring. But then, there really wasn't any difference. In Brussels, it was all a matter of style or semantics.

"How was the airplane food?"

He pulled back from the glass, a faint smile easing the lines of his face. "Best I've had in months." His mind slipped back to the last time in Brussels. The memories were vivid up to a point and then grayed out. Like the city itself.

"You showed up just in time, Louis." He paused, embarrassed because he was being so obvious. "I'm talking about six months ago." He had never really thanked the big man, but that wasn't the point. Louis remembered what had happened that night. *He* didn't. His last memories were of being tailed and then cornered in an alley, his last image that of a man lumbering toward him, silhouetted by the streetlamp at his back. It was Louis who had saved his life, though not before he'd nearly been killed.

In the mirror, Louis's face was blank. "I did what I could, Neal."

"It couldn't have been easy." Morley watched the face in the mirror. "And the Bureau let you go it alone." He was careful to show some sympathy, a trace of you-and-me-against-the-world, and waited for Louis to pick up on it.

"The hospital, Neal. How was it?"

Morley hid his disappointment. "I wouldn't recommend any of it."

Louis winked. "Not even the nurses?"

"Only on their nights off." You talked about women when you couldn't bring yourself to talk about death. It was the great

15

emotional anesthetic. Louis didn't really want to hear about his punctured guts or the internal hemorrhaging nobody could stop or the nights he woke up screaming for them to give him something, anything, for the pain.

You know how I feel about you—now tell me about the blonde with the big tits.

He changed the subject. "What else did the papers say?"

"The Bureau's blown. The reporters are calling it a front for spooks. They listed the personnel. Almost everybody was named."

"But not you."

Louis grinned. "I'm not important enough."

He should have been, Morley thought. For a local hire, Louis was at least as useful as Tindemans. But Louis preferred running errands. He was chauffeur, strong-arm and gopher—and when the call for his services was slack, he passed himself off as a real cab driver, picking up the young girls who flocked to see the Grand'Place. The cab itself, despite the fact that it was of the right model and color, with all the right equipment and lettering, had never been in a private garage and never would be. Its two-way radio was connected to the Bureau, not any taxi cooperative.

Morley suspected that the cab also served as Louis' mobile bedroom as well as his lunch pail.

"The papers really play it up?"

A broad smile. "It's bigger than the European Union meeting."

Ordinarily the loss of the Bureau wouldn't affect him that much, but somewhere in the files lay the report on what had happened to him six months ago, the report that would fill in what he couldn't remember. Simon was wrong; the death of the two consulate officials and the head of the import-export company hadn't been the end of it. Somebody had been the banker. And the consulate officials had been too plugged in; they had known too much about him. And he'd been too slow; if it hadn't been for Louis, he would have died in the alley.

A motorcyclist plunged through a puddle just ahead of them, the spray misting the windows. Then a tram came clanging out of the grayness and they veered off at the last second, the tram sliding past them in the gloom. The street ahead was tangled with traffic, and Louis swung the battered Mercedes into the rue de L'Ecuyler, chasing several pedestrians back to the safety of the sidewalks. Morley suspected that was why Louis liked the cab so much—the sense of power. In Brussels, the driver had the right-of-way. Always.

"I keep wondering where Falk was that night." He said it while still looking out the window.

There was an undertow in Louis' voice. "Where he always was, Neal. Back at the Bureau going over reports."

Which didn't feel right at all. Falk had been concerned about him—aside from Louis, the only man in the Brussels Bureau who had been. Had Falk really ignored the setup, hung around doing paperwork far into the night? Maybe Falk had, he couldn't remember. He couldn't remember a goddamned thing about that night, what he had done—or failed to do, and Louis wasn't about to tell him.

"Want me to come along, Neal?"

Louis was watching him in the rearview mirror, waiting for his answer. Morley finally said, "Not this time, Louis. Thanks."

In London they had all agreed that this temporary duty was a minor assignment at best, a bit of occupational therapy while the doctors and Simon decided what to do with him. Cailleau had admitted to smuggling people through borders and into Belgium and then had refused to say more over the phone. There was nothing new about smuggling refugees—trafficking in people had been heroic during World War II, and had continued with the advent of the Cold War and the Berlin Wall. The Cold War had thawed, the Wall had come tumbling down and borders had been open for a few years. Then the wave of immigrants fleeing poverty and chaos in Eastern Europe, and Arabs and North Africans desperate for any foothold, had swamped the NATO countries. National walls had gone back up, even higher this time. But there would always be new barriers, new reasons to flee one's homeland. The traffic in refugees would always be profitable, and the people who dealt in it continue to be a mix of patriot and profiteer.

Maybe Cailleau was feeling pangs of guilt and wanted to confess all to London. . . .

Louis squealed around another corner and swung over to the curb in a wave of muddy water. "The theater is up that street, just inside those wooden doors—it's part of the *galerie*. What time do you see him?"

Morley ignored him, opening the briefcase again and checking the background notes.

"What time, Neal?" Louis repeated. He seemed anxious, and Morley wondered if Louis was under orders to play nursemaid.

"As soon as I can, Louis."

Louis reached for the small coffee cup in its homemade holder on the dash. "Want some?"

Morley had thought it was empty; the smell of the coffee had been lost in the stink of the *frites* and mayonnaise.

"No." He took out the long-barreled Beretta from its recess in the case and slipped it into a pocket of his mackintosh. He snapped the lid of the briefcase shut.

Louis nodded at the stores. "Business has been off; the shopkeepers are hungry."

"Don't let them kid you—they're making money." Brussels was single-minded in that respect. If it weren't for the buck, Morley thought, nobody would stay here.

Louis patted the meter. "I'll drop your stuff off."

"Hold on to it." Morley hunched his shoulders against the drizzle and got out.

"Neal." Louis was holding out something in his hand. "You'll need these. *Jetons* for the telephone." Morley pocketed them and then shook hands. It wasn't until his hand was almost in Louis's that he remembered the big man's grip, that this was going to be Louis's subtle way of judging if he still deserved his reputation. A quick squeeze, a wince, and Louis would have his report for the Bureau.

His palm met Louis's, his thumb firmly against Louis's thumb. He pressed hard, caught the brief look of surprise, smiled and said: "I'll tell you about the marionettes later."

Louis gunned the motor. "Be careful, Neal." He sounded cool.

The cab rattled off down the street and Morley suddenly felt defenseless. Two days out of the hospital, and he wasn't sure he could handle anything, not even the piece of cake Cailleau was supposed to be. Even questioning Louis had turned out to be more difficult than it should have been. He wondered if Brussels was still an unlucky city for him and felt a brief buzz of panic. He didn't want to wind up back in Mayfair with the tubes up his nose and the clear plastic bags slowly leaking their contents into his veins.

He turned and searched the street for Louis's Mercedes but the rain hid everything except the reddish glow of its one tail light and then it, too, was swallowed up in the grayness.

He shivered, not only from the cold but because of Brussels itself. It was a pale, cheerless city whose streets were named after failed kings or battles that had bled the country white. What little charm it once possessed, what illusions its people

19

might have entertained, had long since vanished. Now it existed only for the sake of the international corporations that made their headquarters there, the European Union and everyone's lobbies, NATO, and all the political refugees, East and West.

It was a city where the locals chose up sides depending on whether they spoke Walloon, the French dialect of Belgium, or Flemish and the result was a Brussels that bred hatred and vice like a farmer's pond bred mosquitoes. The city wrung out everybody who lived there. The last time it had almost killed him; this time, it might succeed.

He pulled the collar of his mackintosh closer around his neck and turned toward the *galerie*. There was unfinished business in Brussels, and he took a sour pride in knowing that he had succeeded in doing what he'd once doubted he ever could.

He had come back to finish it.

two

THE RAIN WAS heavier and colder than Morley remembered. He shifted his briefcase to his other hand and walked toward the *galerie*, trying not to favor his left leg. The feel of the cobblestones beneath his feet was as much a signature of Brussels as the smell of coffee and *frites* or the broken line of trenches that had been gouged out of the narrow street in front of him. On either side little mounds of clay gradually dissolved into yellow puddles that hid the few unturned cobblestones. The muddy water trickled toward the gutters, slicking the stones with an oily film.

He stepped carefully over them, amazed that the streets were still so torn up, then realized that he had never seen them any other way. Brussels mythology had it that they had been working on the streets ever since the city was liberated in 1944, and they'd be working on them until Judgment Day.

He balanced for a moment on a shaky plank that bridged another ditch, almost lost his footing on the slippery stones on the other side, then sloshed toward the *galerie*'s double doors. Just before pushing through, he paused to study the reflections of the street behind him in the rain-streaked glass: The usual anonymous noon crowd, thinned down by the rain. No cars idled at the curb, and nobody was making a show of studying the plumber's window brightened by a display of stainless-steel faucets and a tank of sickly goldfish. A street sign, printed in both Flemish and French, the two languages of Belgium, caught his eye and he grimaced. Maybe it would have been better if the country had split in two a long time ago. . . .

Inside, the *galerie* was enormous, its stone walls and high glass ceiling reminding him of a train depot or an immense aviary. A block away, another set of double doors opened onto the next street while in between was a broad plaza lined on both sides by dozens of shops. Outside one of them was a small push-cart heaped with *waffles d'bruxelles*. Above, the rain was a drum-roll against the panes of the roof, with water seeping through a dozen gaps to spatter on the floor below or into a rusting oil drum next to a nearby pillar.

It was nearly deserted. A newsgirl, almost lost against the shop fronts in the distance, hawked copies of the *International Tribune*; an old woman hobbled slowly toward the far exit and a few lonely pensioners browsed through the bookstalls and fingered the blooms on the cart outside a flower store.

He watched the scene for a moment, then tucked his brief-case under his arm and walked slowly across the flagstones. It was hard to ignore the pain in his left leg. The other annoyance, the light rub of the Smith & Wesson in its shoulder holster, was easier to take. It wasn't as powerful as the Beretta but it was just as accurate; it was also lighter and easier to conceal. It was as much a part of him as his addiction to strong black coffee.

Outside the bookstall, he stopped to read the headlines in the morning paper. The European Union meeting got two columns. Most of the rest of the front page was devoted to the blown Bureau, topped with a blurred photograph of Falk. He scanned a few paragraphs, then turned to a table piled high with second-hand books. He picked one at random, a late-nineteenth century volume on dueling pistols, and idly thumbed through the pages, occasionally looking up to study the square. Directly across the way was a narrow facade set off by black ornamental ironwork with the florid lettering, Théâtre de Vaudeville. Every minute or so, another theatergoer hurried up—usually a woman old enough to be his grandmother.

There was a sudden flurry of customers, then nobody. Morley glanced at his watch—the show had probably begun. He picked up his briefcase and walked over to the theater. Before going in, he paused to study the smiling faces in the glossies tacked to the corkboard behind a sheet of plastic. Some of the photographs were yellowed and must have been there for years; none of them looked like the portrait of an aging puppeteer.

The lobby was small and smelled of smoke and stale chocolates. Except for the woman squinting at him through the tiny window in the pay booth, it was empty. The inner lobby, beyond the cashier's box, housed a cloakroom and several tables set in a half-circle around a small bar. There was a hot plate with a pot of coffee and a bucket that held chunks of ice, a pick and a dozen small ice-cream cups. Behind that was a shelf with several bottles of Wiels among the lemon tonics and mineral waters. At the far end of the lobby, a raucous recorded version of "Hold That Tiger!" floated out from behind closed doors, followed by muffled laughter.

The ancient redhead selling tickets didn't like him—even with his tired schoolteacher's face he was still too young to be a regular and, adding insult to injury, he was a foreigner. "Four hundred francs!" she piped in a thin voice.

He pushed the franc notes through the hole in the window, hanging onto the ends. "I want to see Monsieur Cailleau."

There was a brief tug-of-war over the bills. Morley flipped down another note. "Cailleau," he repeated. "He's expecting me."

She staged a strategic retreat. "Downstairs—third door on

your right." The francs disappeared and Morley started across the carpet, its faded gold turning to green. There was a sharp rap on the glass and he turned. The redhead was glaring at him. She shoved a pasteboard through the wicket-shaped opening in the glass. *"D'entrée,"* she chirped, holding out her other hand for more money. *"D'entrée!"*

Backstage was dimly lit and hectic. A two-dimensional plywood mock-up of a double-decker bus was jammed in the wings. It had been painted bright yellow and red with the words Fun Bus printed on its side in English. A song-and-dance team balanced the prop between them and gossiped as they waited for their cue. Morley slipped past them and threaded his way through a snarl of parasols and trained dogs toward a flight of narrow stairs. He waited a moment while a rouged young man in a bellhop's uniform raced past, then started down the sagging steps.

A piece of paper had been tacked on the third door. Scrawled on it in red ink was the name Cailleau. Morley knocked twice and waited. There was a shuffling of footsteps, a muttering as someone tugged on a bolt, and then the rattle of a chain. A sliver of face peered out at him.

"Monsieur Cailleau? Neal Morley."

The man who opened the door was slight and stooped, with a head of gray close-cropped hair and thickly-muscled arms and shoulders. Well-preserved for . . . what? His mid-seventies? His green undershirt was rumpled, his suspenders and tan corduroys faded but clean. There was a dull red splotch on his forehead and Morley guessed he had been sitting at his dressing table, resting his head on his arms, when he'd heard the knock. He looked like he needed sleep; his eyes were red and swollen. Something about Cailleau suggested he was more at home with French than Flemish and Morley felt a minor sense of relief. He'd picked up some French in Vietnam, though both the Belgian and the Vietnamese strains were bastards of the French spoken in Paris.

Cailleau gripped his hand tightly. "You came quickly, Monsieur." His voice was gravel, the words spoken with a drunk's too-careful precision. He closed the door and slid the bolt, then gestured to a hook alongside the loden coat hanging on the wall.

Morley hung up his mac and set his briefcase on a corner of a table. It was barely large enough for the half-bottle of wine, the morning paper and the old Luger that were already on it. The automatic looked like it had recently been oiled, and Morley assumed that it was loaded.

The room itself was small and crowded. Marionettes hung on the four walls and over the dressing-table mirror and slumped across the trunk on the floor. Unlike the marionettes that hung from the ceilings or behind the bars in many of Brussels's cafes and brasseries, these were of superb craftsmanship. Their tiny hands and faces were extraordinarily lifelike, even close up. Morley knelt down to take a closer look at one that hung off the end of the table. It was a miniature Don Quixote, with stainless-steel armor and copper sword, its face a portrait of saintly madness with staring, painted eyes.

He turned back to Cailleau, freezing when he caught a glimpse of somebody standing in the shadows. Half-hidden in the other corner was an exquisite, life-sized ballerina in tutu and silken slippers.

"London said you were good with marionettes." He didn't try to disguise the admiration in his voice. Some of the puppets in the local bars were more than a hundred years old and others were excellent reproductions, but none of them displayed the attention to detail, the care that Cailleau had obviously lavished on his.

Cailleau nodded stiffly. "I am good with illusions, Monsier." There was a barely perceptible slur to his words. He fumbled for a pack of Caporals on the window sill and shook one out to offer it. He didn't take one for himself, and Morley realized they were only for guests—otherwise the cubbyhole would have reeked even more of cigarette smoke. As it was, the air was gamey from too much wine and sweat—Cailleau's grip was slippery and his face had a sheen to it.

Cailleau sat down at the dressing table and stared at him with growing disapproval. "You've been ill, Monsieur? Perhaps hospitalized for a while?" He didn't give Morley a chance to answer. "It's not hard to tell—a man's skin fits him differently after a long illness. You can see in the eyes how badly the soul has been hurt."

Morley regretted his earlier admiration. "I've been in Brussels before; this time I'll be more careful."

Cailleau abruptly shook his head. "No, no, no." His voice was tinged with contempt. "What possible good can you be? I was in the War." He said it as if there had been only one, and it took Morley a moment to realize Cailleau was talking about World War II, the only one that mattered to him. "A man who has been badly wounded loses his edge." He looked down at the table and traced the wine rings with a stubby forefinger. "Once you lose your confidence, Monsieur, you have lost everything."

Morley felt the back of his neck grow warm. He didn't need to be reminded that he wasn't the man he had once been, that returning to Brussels had been bravado. Cailleau was a shrewder judge of him than Louis had been, but he wasn't about to thank him for it. He stared at Cailleau through a light haze of cigarette smoke. "You're the one who asked for help, Monsieur, not me."

Cailleau's slur was more pronounced. "They should have sent somebody else. The situation is too dangerous for anyone who is not . . . well."

Morley stubbed out his cigarette in an ashtray, took the Luger from the table and inspected it. "More dangerous for you than me—try firing this and you'll blow your own brains out." He picked up his briefcase, slipped his coat off the hook and opened the door. "You drink too much and think too little, Monsieur," he said casually. "They won't send anybody else."

Cailleau grew sullen. "I didn't mean offense."

Morley let the door swing shut. "You have something you want to tell me?" A two-foot-tall Henry VIII caught his eye, and he dropped his briefcase on a chair and stepped over to look at it.

The silence thickened. Cailleau finally said cautiously, "I've done more than just manipulate wooden dolls."

Morley didn't bother to turn around. "Such as?"

With a touch of pride: "I used to smuggle."

Henry VIII was left to dangle from its strings. "What? Kif? Cocaine? Bibles? Dirty pictures?" He smiled without humor. "We don't judge."

Cailleau reddened. "Your people told you nothing?"

"They never tell you enough."

Cailleau nodded, wise with wine. "Of course, you must hear it all from me." He refilled his own glass, glanced at the level in the bottle and reluctantly offered it to Morley. He looked relieved when Morley shook his head. "I was a *fluchthelfer*, an escape-helper, during the War. And for some time after, when people wanted to flee the Iron Curtain. I smuggled many people across frontiers."

Morley sat down in the other chair and straightened his leg to take the weight off it. He felt faintly bored. First they boasted of being a patriot, then admitted to being a profiteer.

"A man could get rich being helpful."

Cailleau slammed down his glass. "You goad me, Monsieur! It was an honorable thing to do, even though later the politicians found it embarrassing."

Old men never stopped fighting old wars. Morley thought of the weathered elderly man who had been Simon's predecessor and who had first shaped the London-based counterterrorist unit. He had been a legend in his day, and when he chose "Moses" as his code name, biblical names for Command had become instant tradition. It was Moses who had convinced Simon to send Morley to the clinic rather than a military hospital in Frankfurt, who realized Morley had lost his faith in the military years ago. Moses was the one Cailleau had called for help and who had passed the request on to Simon. Nobody had told the puppet master that his friend had retired, or maybe Cailleau couldn't accept it. Who could blame him if he wanted to believe the world was safely in the hands of old friends?

"World War Two is ancient history, Monsieur. So many chapters in a textbook." Morley picked up Don Quixote to inspect the fragile costume, then noticed the expression on Cailleau's face. He had seen the same look on overprotective parents when they watched their children play. He flipped open the toy vest to inspect a tiny shirt of mail.

"I was never a hero," Cailleau continued, his eyes riveted on the puppet. "But I was never so afraid that I wouldn't try to help. I have always believed in freedom."

"So do we all." Morley worked a tiny arm, marvelling at the smooth articulation.

Cailleau's forehead was wet. He leaned across the table with his hands outstretched. "Monsieur, I beg you! You'll break him! *Please!*"

Morley handed him the marionette. "Not everybody had noble motives for fleeing, Monsieur. Not the petty criminals nor the black marketeers afraid they'd be caught, nor the whores lured across a border by the promise of becoming somebody's

28

mistress . . . am I right? I'm sure they paid handsomely." Despite the words, he kept his voice gentle.

Cailleau glared at him, eyes glittering with anger, clutching Henry VIII against his undershirt with both hands. "Not all of them were angels. If you want me to admit that, then yes, I admit it."

"They all wanted out. And somehow they got their hands on the money to pay you. You always got your fee, didn't you?" Morley said it like one con man confiding in another. He'd be wasting his time if he let Cailleau wrap himself in a patriotic flag and gild the truth.

Cailleau's voice shook. "Are you a judge, Monsieur? I saved our mutual friend in London several times during the war. There was never a charge."

Morley refilled Cailleau's glass. "Our friend has always been grateful." He leaned back, his voice soft, hiding his impatience. "Tell me what happened."

Cailleau looked suspicious. "You are suddenly friendly, Monsieur. You have interrogated prisoners, perhaps? Maybe in Vietnam? Pakistan?" He smiled slightly when Morley's expression froze. "No matter. Recently . . . I was asked to help once again. A big load from Bucharest. I said I would do it."

For the first time, Morley felt uneasy. "Who were they?"

A shrug. "I was told they were seven refugees who wanted to find a home."

"But you didn't believe it."

Cailleau looked nervous. "They all knew each other. That had never happened before. A few might know each other, a small family—but not everybody in a big load. Especially not this one." He hesitated. "One was a Japanese woman, the rest were Egyptian or Sudanese men, several Iraqis, one Slav. And they carried newspaper clippings about the European Union meeting." Morley stiffened in his chair. "I wondered why—"

There were footsteps in the hall and a rap on the door. *"Oui! Oui!"* Cailleau shouted. "I know!" The footsteps retreated and he turned back, his eyes wide. "They hardly wanted a home, Monsieur. And I don't believe they wanted to enter the West to look for work. They were terrorists, I'm sure of it." The words were coming very fast now, and Morley had no doubt Cailleau was telling the truth, or at least thought he was. "They had guns!"

Cailleau had realized they hadn't been refugees at first glance. So why had he agreed to smuggle them across all those borders of half-a-dozen countries into Belgium? Strictly for the money? And how had he managed it? There was no way the old man would have been up to it.

Then Morley had a brief flash of panic. If Cailleau had actually done what he said, his own simple assignment would become a major operation, and he would be replaced by somebody who hadn't spent six months buried in bed.

The glass trembled in Cailleau's hand. "I do not know who they thought I was, or what they thought I believed in." He shook his head. "But then they discovered that I was only Cailleau, the puppeteer, and two of them tried to kill me. Outside, in the street." He pointed at the Luger. "I didn't have the gun with me then, but the concierge and several of the troupe heard my shouts—they came out and the men ran." He reached for the bottle again, pushing it aside when he realized it was empty. "I think they will be back." He sounded as though his teeth might start chattering at any moment.

Cailleau was an old man who had drunk one bottle too many that night, Morley thought. A terrorist team depending on Cailleau to smuggle them across half of Europe? He wasn't about to believe it.

"Why didn't you go to the police?"

Cailleau looked offended. "The police? I am not naive, like the concierge. You saw him—the old man with the ribbon in his lapel? It's a decoration for fighting with the Resistance." His eyes misted with memory. "After the War, we were told to sign our names in a book and turn in our pistols. Anyone foolish enough to do so got a piece of ribbon. Then we were told, 'Pay for the bridges you destroyed.' Those who couldn't went to jail. No thank you, Monsieur, I'll keep my gun. And I'll stay away from the *flics.*"

Morley frowned. "You didn't have to call long distance to contact our friends."

Cailleau looked at him once more with disapproval. "I wanted help, not my name in the headlines." He poked at the newspapers on the table. "I never trusted *them*. I do trust *him.*" Morley reminded himself that Cailleau was talking about a feeble old man back in London, long retired. A fading legend.

Footsteps sounded in the hall again. This time the knock was more insistent. *"Merde!"* Cailleau yanked open the door.

"You're late for the setup, Serge." The young man in the bellhop's uniform looked at Morley curiously, then turned and took the stairs two at a time.

"They've waited this long to see talent!" Cailleau shouted after him. "They can wait a minute longer!" He put the empty wine glass on the window sill, then turned back to Morley and studied him again. "There's more—much more. I'll tell you after the show." Cailleau had finally made up his mind to trust him. "It's a mad world, Monsieur. Each of us is the enemy of someone, someone we don't even know."

He suddenly brightened and clapped Morley on the back. "Have you ever seen a really good puppet show?" He waved his hand at the marionettes in the room. "Watch our little play and see these come alive!"

Morley followed Cailleau up the stairs. Anywhere Cailleau would go, the borders these days were porous. Few countries welcomed refugees any more. But if you wanted to badly enough, and had money or sold yourself, you could get across.

Nobody in his right mind would have relied on the old puppeteer.

In the wings, the noise was deafening. Other performers dressed in marching uniforms had joined the song-and-dance team and were prancing around in circles, banging on drums and cymbals and blowing horns in some absurd finale. Morley lost sight of Cailleau for a moment, then spotted him climbing a ladder to a catwalk hidden by a drop curtain hanging several meters above the stage. Cailleau would be working the marionettes from the walk.

The puppet master drank too much and had an active imagination, Morley thought with distaste. After the show, he'd listen to the rest and then make whatever Cailleau told him just interesting enough for London. Cailleau was his justification for being there. He couldn't let London think he was chasing a will-of-the-wisp, or they'd recall him—just as they would if they thought there was any truth to Cailleau's fantasy.

Either way, he'd lose the one opportunity he desperately wanted. To kill whoever had almost killed him.

three

THE MATRONLY USHERETTE resented Morley as much as the cashier had, showing him to a seat in the last row. Once his eyes had adjusted to the gloom, he glanced around the theater. At one time, it had had pretensions of grandeur. The interior was similar to the plaster-and-paint rococo of American theaters of the twenties, with a small balcony at the back and tiny boxes on each side. The seats were red velvet and so, in the distant past, had been the dirty ropes at the rear. Over the years, a thousand clutching hands had crushed the velvet to a black scab.

The stage itself was tiny, though anything larger would have dwarfed the acts. It took him several minutes to realize that the actor who played the midget policeman in the cops-and-robbers routine was the same one who sang a duet in Italian with the brunette who had just finished balancing atop a stack of chairs. He was taller than she but he played the policeman by stumping around on his knees, like José Ferrer playing Toulouse-Lautrec.

By the third act, Morley was bored and glanced frequently at his watch. It shouldn't be taking Cailleau this long to set up his act.

He studied the audience while he waited. They were all even older than he felt. A few male pensioners nodded in the comfortable seats; the remainder were gray-haired old ladies with funny hats and sad faces who had probably been coming here for years and knew the acts by heart. He had always wondered what the women did when they weren't walking their dogs or feeding them biscuits in some cafe. The air in the theater was humid with the moisture generated by full-length winter coats thrown over the backs of their seats; even the poorest woman in Brussels had a thick wool coat, or one of rabbit—it didn't matter how old or how faded they were, or how little money they had.

The actors knew the ladies, too, and flirted with them across the footlights. At intermission, they probably met in the lobby, the performers gallantly pretending that their fans were, at best, no more than middle-aged, and the ladies convinced that their favorites hadn't changed since first they met, that the rosy bloom of powder and paint was the real thing.

Then Morley realized that not everybody in the audience was an antique. Directly in front of him was a girl, about twenty. As far as he could tell in the dark, she was wearing a beige business suit and had long sable hair combed up on her head. He watched her, interested—everything about her seemed out of place. It was too late in the afternoon for her to be on her lunch hour, and it was unlikely, even if she were, that she would be spending it at the Théâtre de Vaudeville. She was staring at the stage with a bemused expression, apparently entranced by a stout actor in a white suit standing on a small pedestal playing a statue of Churchill. He was smoking a very real cigar and striking a V for Victory pose while two other actors took turns reciting a soliloquy about the Great Man.

The "blood, sweat and tears" bit brought down the house. Morley scanned the theater once more; the Keep Smiling sign that hung from the balcony reminded him of an enormous get-well card. The smell of chocolate and violet scent was suffocating, and he felt claustrophobic. He wished that the show was over so he could finish up with Cailleau.

On stage, Winston flicked the ash from his cigar and strode off, once again flashing the Victory sign at the audience. He was replaced by a dog act featuring two poodles pedaling unicycles. The dogs and the couple who trained them finally finished by leaping off the stage and riding up the aisles. A Belgian version of an English music-hall quartet took their place. The songs were old, with risqué asides, and the women around Morley nudged each other and giggled.

After that, he lost track of the skits. There were half-a-dozen resident performers—the "boys and girls," the emcee called them—who popped in and out of costume as quickly as the worn velvet curtain could close and reopen. In between were the acrobats and jugglers and finally Electro, the magician, who pulled lit light bulbs out of his mouth and doves from a seemingly empty cage. He made the doves disappear again by stuffing them back inside the collapsible cage and flattening it with a loud crack between his hands, much to the dismay of the ladies in the audience.

There was a muttered *"Merci"* and Morley was distracted by the sound of a slight scuffle from the next row up. A fat Belgian smelling of wet wool and clutching a haversack blocked the view as he struggled toward a seat. Morley found himself resenting the intruder as much as did the rest of the audience.

Then there was a drum roll, and Morley watched the magician's assistant haul an old steamer trunk from the wings. Together they raised the top and tipped the trunk so everybody could see inside. Without a word, the magician climbed in and closed the lid behind him.

It happened so fast, even the assistant had vanished, stepping into the wings as soon as the magician had climbed into the footlocker. The stage was bare now except for the closed trunk. A minute ticked by. Another. The audience began to fidget, the women whispering among themselves.

A low voice behind Morley suddenly muttered: "Watch."

Morley turned. A man was standing by the rear wall, buttoned up in a greatcoat, the sort who looked like he might expose himself any minute. He lurched up the aisle, apparently drunk, climbed the few steps from the orchestra pit to the stage and inspected the trunk, ignoring the low murmur of protests from the audience. He thumped the footlocker once or twice, circled it several times, then lifted the lid. He leaned over and peered inside, finally tipping the trunk so everyone could see it was empty. Then he suddenly threw off his coat and cap to stand revealed as the now-triumphant magician, smirking at his startled audience.

A switch, Morley thought, intrigued. It was the assistant, disguised as the magician, who had originally climbed into the secret compartment. The magician himself had ducked into the wings to reappear in the back of the theater. It was a good act. In the States, it would have rated cheers. But here there was only a cool patter of applause. Maybe it was because the ladies hadn't forgiven what the magician had done to the doves. Or perhaps because he was a new performer, an outsider—and this audience didn't like outsiders, nor did it care for surprises.

It was the regulars whom the ladies loved the most, the familiar faces who made love to them from the safety of the footlights.

Now the emcee was introducing "François," mentioning the cities where he had played last. Morley caught "Bucharest" and "Sofia" and then the velvet curtains parted once more. There was no applause, just an expectant hush.

With the previous acts, it had been a simple flirtation. This time, it was going to be a love affair.

A second, darker curtain rose part way. There were another few taps on the drum and a cheerful, handsome François strolled out to meet his admirers. He looked relaxed and debonair, every inch the handsome aristocrat with his boots and ascot and riding crop. His smiling, carefully painted face turned from side to side as he beamed at his audience. Then he bowed low, hanging limply from his strings a moment, and blew them all a kiss.

Morley glanced around the theater again, noting the glazed eyes and the half-open mouths. He had been right: the ladies were passionately in love with the life-sized marionette. He looked back at François. It was startling in its appearance, in its movements. There was an occasional jerkiness, but the overall effect was astonishingly real, and there was one bit of business so thoroughly *human* that it made the puppet completely convincing. It was a small thing, but you couldn't miss it: the smacking of the riding crop into the left palm as Cailleau manipulated the marionette into strutting back and forth across the stage. The slight rotation and snap of the wrist—how many hours of practice had it taken?

> *"You che-ri up-on my knee*
> *No strings for you no strings for me*
> *Just me for* tu *and* tu *for me a-lone. . . ."*

A happy, carefree François slowly tap-danced across the stage to the ghostly tune. The sense of reality again was overwhelming.

The women around Morley were ecstatic. They'd probably faint, he thought, if the immense butterfly that hovered over François's left shoulder should flap its wings in time to the music. But Cailleau would need two more hands to bring off that miracle.

And then, of course, he did just that. Both wings, fragile

kaleidoscopes of rainbow colors, pulsated in perfect time.

The applause started then and Morley guessed there wasn't a grandmother present who wouldn't have cuckolded the memory of her husband to spend a few minutes alone with the marionette that clopped across the stage.

> *"No-bod-y near us to scold us or jeer us*
> *No one'll ev-er 'gain pup-pet-eer us*
> *We'll stand on our own, dear and we'llll. . . ."*

The applause was so deafening that he almost didn't hear it when the phonograph arm slid across the record's face. François abruptly stopped dancing and *something* plummeted down from behind the curtain to sprawl on the stage.

There was a gasp and a sudden, shocked silence. For a moment Morley thought that Cailleau had slipped on the catwalk and knocked another life-sized puppet to the stage. Then he struggled to his feet and plunged down the aisle, ignoring the sudden pain in his side. The faded greens and browns were too distinctive—it was Cailleau himself who had fallen.

There was no sound or movement on stage. Then François slowly crumpled over the body of his master. If there was a gasp when Cailleau had fallen, a moan now swept the theater at the "death" of François. The marionette must have been balanced just right to have remained standing for so long. . . .

Morley was halfway down the aisle when he realized the theater had suddenly lost several of its paying customers as well as two members of its cast. Both the girl and the fat businessman with the haversack had disappeared.

four

BACKSTAGE THEY HAD dropped the curtain while out front a dance team did its sweaty best to distract the audience from the sudden appearance of Cailleau and, worse, the apparent death of François. The distraught stage manager was shouting in French at the frightened performers huddled in the wings, staring blank-faced at Cailleau lying on the boards. Close up, the "boys and girls" looked even older than Morley had suspected, the greasepaint only emphasizing their lines and pallor.

He glanced down at Cailleau. It wasn't the fall, it *couldn't* have been the fall. Or chance.

He started towards the body and was brushed aside by the fat man with the haversack. "I'm a doctor, please move back." The fat man knelt and lifted Cailleau by the shoulder, rolling him over. The brunette who had sung in Italian muffled a scream.

Death had been instantaneous. Whoever got to Cailleau had known what they were doing. The handle of an ice pick jutted from behind Cailleau's left ear where it had been jabbed upward into the brain. The pick had been forced deep within the skull; there were few signs of bleeding and no indications that there had been a struggle.

Cailleau would have been preoccupied with what was happening onstage below. And probably none of the stage crew had seen anything—everyone would have been caught up in the magic onstage; they wouldn't have been watching the man who pulled the strings.

"He's dead," the fat man said unnecessarily.

The stage manager mopped his face. "I've called the police, there's no need to panic, I've called the police."

The young man in the bellhop's uniform hurried out of the wings carrying a painted backdrop; his face was pale and his hands shook slightly. Morley guessed that he intended to use the canvas as a stretcher. Now he noticed the ice pick and looked sick. The actor who had played Churchill stepped up to help, and they spread the canvas over the body. Morley stared at the still figure a moment longer, doing his best to memorize Cailleau's face. The eyes were still open in shocked surprise, staring blindly at the iridescent two-foot-wide butterfly that lay crumpled near the curtain, its gauzy wings as limp and lifeless as Cailleau himself.

Whatever Cailleau had been going to tell him, it must have been important enough for his "terrorists" to want to shut him up. And then Morley thought that if Cailleau really had smuggled in terrorists, he had probably been killed because he could identify them. And then he caught himself shivering. He had a pretty good idea just whom Cailleau might have brought in.

But there could be other explanations for Cailleau's murder. There had to be if Simon wasn't going to pull him out of Brussels.

There was the bleat of a siren on the street outside, and Morley drifted offstage toward the lobby bar. For perhaps the first time in years, it was doing a healthy business. He watched the sweets girl use the knife kept for scraping the foam off glasses of beer to chop at the ice around the paper cups. The pick he had noticed before was now nestled deep in Cailleau's brain.

A small ring of elderly women had gathered around the tables, some of them gossiping in scandalized whispers, others dabbing at their eyes. They mourned the marionette more than Cailleau. Morley glanced around at the others crowding into the lobby and wondered if the hit man had vanished or was still there among the elderly patrons.

He had edged over to the bar for a better view when somebody tried to squeeze past him. It was the petite, fresh-looking girl who had been sitting in front of him—only she didn't look so fresh anymore. Her face was tight, pale, and she was trying to hold back tears.

"*Pardon.*" She glanced up at him and her French changed smoothly into English. "I didn't mean to bash you."

He smiled. "I rather enjoyed it."

Her face frosted over. "Did you now." She took a step to edge past him and he blocked her.

"You knew Monsieur Cailleau?"

She paused, the little muscles at the corner of her jaw tensing. Of course she had known him, Morley decided. He leaned closer to make himself heard over the buzz of the crowd. "The puppeteer. You knew him?"

She looked trapped. "If you don't mind—"

He was going to lose her. He fumbled with his briefcase, pulling it free of the crowd and making sure she saw it. Businessmen with briefcases had more on their minds than pickups. "Great show! He would have been fantastic in the States. I'd hoped . . ."

Her face mirrored a moment's shock and then disgust.

41

"Really, I must . . ." He didn't budge and she gave up. "Yes, I knew him. Now, *if* you please—

He held out his hand. "Morley, Neal Morley. Mademoiselle—"

"Hannie de Vries, if you must know."

"Your English is very good." He beamed. "You're—"

"Dutch." She was frantically searching the crowd for an opening she could squeeze through. Morley edged past her again. "You've lived in England?"

"Zurich, actually."

"You go to school there?"

She turned on him, her face flushed. "Look, for the present I work in London as an assistant financial analyst and it's just as boring as it sounds. And that's all I've got to say, Mister Morley. I don't like you and I don't want to talk to you. Now, *please*—"

"Pardon me," a thick, nasal voice interrupted. Morley had sensed the man's presence even before he saw him. The doctor, like many Belgians, was swollen to twice the size of other Europeans, and his bulk broadcast an acrid perspiration you could smell three meters away. Short and squat, with pale watery eyes and the sniffles, he had been standing nearby, hanging on every word. "Is this man bothering you, Mademoiselle?"

Hannie bit her upper lip. "Please, leave me alone, *both* of you. I don't want to talk to anybody and I don't need anybody's help!"

Morley feigned surprise and then regret. "I apologize. Really." He hesitated as if the thought had just occurred to him. "You weren't related, were you?"

She had trouble keeping her voice steady. "He was my father," she said, and then quickly amended it. "The closest I ever came to one."

Morley shifted slightly, taking advantage of the crowd to

wedge himself between them. "You look pale. The least we can do is get you a drink." He couldn't afford to let her slip away. He turned to the fat man, again working on a hunch. "The name's Morley, Neal Morley. You'll join us, Doctor?"

"Taca," the fat man said reluctantly, blinking at him from behind thick lenses. "I already have a reservation at a nearby restaurant—but they'll accept dollars."

He held out his hand and Morley pumped it. It wasn't the handful of flab he had expected—it was tough and surprisingly firm, and he had the fleeting impression of an aging weightlifter whose fat only covered the surface.

"The young lady has given every indication that she wants to be left alone," the doctor said, reluctantly, glancing at Hannie.

"You're right, Doctor, but after what just happened, we could all use a drink. My editor will buy. He'd like to know about Monsieur Cailleau and the girl."

Hannie glanced at him sharply, but it was Taca who took the bait.

"What girl?"

"The girl who played François, the marionette," he said innocently. "She's disappeared."

five

BOTH OF THEM stared at him: Hannie, her mouth slightly open as if she had been interrupted in mid-sentence, and Taca, caught completely off guard and uncertain, his pale eyes blinking furiously.

Morley shook his head in sympathy. "It's a shame, a once-great act and then . . ." He sighed. "You grow old, and there comes a day when you can no longer handle the big puppets so you hire some young girl to play the part. She was really the star, you know."

"That's not true," Hannie protested angrily. "Serge—"

"—was a great man, a great artist," Taca interrupted in a wheezy voice. "On stage, François was as much his creation as if the strings were real. You're an American, Monsieur Morley, there's no way you could understand."

Morley turned to Hannie and flashed another smile. "You could convince me over a drink. I wouldn't want to write anything that would do Cailleau an injustice." He wasn't sure either of them was what they claimed—a twenty-year-old girl who said Cailleau was her "father" and a doctor who apparently had nothing better to do than attend the theater that afternoon.

Hannie reddened. "Meaning if I don't come along, you will?"

He spread his hands helplessly. "What do I know about marionettes? I have a story to write, and right now all I have are questions."

It was Taca who wavered. "Comme chez Soi is close by, we can get a drink there. It's also Europe's finest restaurant this side of the Champs d'Elysees." His voice became condescending. "But I'm not certain you'd appreciate it."

Morley struggled to keep the warmth in his voice. "Please be my guests."

Hannie hung back, still furious. "I can't believe I'm hearing any of this."

The doors to the lobby suddenly burst open and the commune police stalked in. The crowd surged back to make room, momentarily separating Taca from Morley and Hannie. Morley took advantage of it to drop his role for a moment. "You could stand that drink."

Before Hannie could reply, Taca had forced his way back to them. "As your guests," he repeated firmly, taking Hannie by the arm.

The restaurant was everything Taca had implied, a standout even in Brussels which, despite its drabness, had the reputation of being a city where no one ever made a bad cup of coffee or drank second-rate champagne. The table sparkled with crystal and pale linen. Morley speculated on the probable size of the bill and understood Taca's haste to accept his offer.

Taca ordered an *apéritif la maison* for all and proposed a toast when it came: "To Serge Cailleau—a true artist and one of the last great Europeans!"

Morley leaned back in his chair, shifting slightly to ease the pain in his leg. He savored the subtle taste of the aperitif and studied the two of them. Taca was somewhere in his late forties, with a wispy brown moustache and pale blue eyes that looked enormous behind his glasses. His face was flushed, with the broken blood vessels typical of so many proud Belgians determined to help Wiels outsell Guinness. Like the rest of him, Taca's neck and head were outsized, a suitable turret for his tanklike body.

Hannie had recovered most of her color—the chill air, the brisk walk to the restaurant and her anger at both of them for shanghaiing her all had helped. Morley guessed that she was naturally vivacious, though now she was withdrawn. Both Hannie and the fat doctor had given him reasons for being at the theater in the middle of the day; he didn't believe either one. Paranoia, he thought irritably. The occupational hazard of the trade.

"Comme chez Soi is an heirloom," Taca was saying, gesturing proudly around the room. "Family owned, in the grand tradition." He jabbed a finger at a far corner. "I'm told Churchill sat over there, and I, for one, like to believe the story that *that* was Goering's favorite table. And over there, Margaret Thatcher's . . ."

Morley fussed with a small notebook. "I ought to mention that—"

"For God's sake!" Hannie shot them both an incredulous glance, then focussed on Morley. "How did you know that François wasn't a marionette?"

"I didn't, not during the show. But when Cailleau fell, François didn't collapse—not right away, it took a few seconds. And then, backstage, she was gone."

She was still suspicious. "You said François was a woman. What gave her away?"

He wondered if she were setting a trap. "Size. It was either a child or a woman, and I doubt that a child could have aped the mannerisms as well."

Hannie fell silent, staring at him. Then, defiantly: "It took you a while before you suspected, didn't it?"

"Whoever played François was really very good."

"You mean Serge was really very good." Her eyes were teary again, and Morley decided she was probably telling the truth about her relationship with Cailleau.

The fat doctor, on the other hand, had forgotten the puppeteer with his first whiff of the kitchen.

"The finance ministers always dine here when they're in Brussels." Taca opened the large menu and studied it. "I happen to know that the minister from Egypt loves *la terrine de foie de canard frais aux raisins sultanes.* Ireland's religiously orders *les filets de sole mousseline au Riesling,* while England's is torn between *le homard Cardinal* and *le pigeonneau à notre façon.*" He took another sip of aperitif and smacked his lips, then looked up at Hannie. "It seems our ministers can't even agree about entrees. What would you like?"

"Scotch and tonic," Hannie said, still defiant.

Taca was appalled. He took off his gold-rimmed glasses and polished them on his napkin. "My dear," he said feebly, "a restaurant of this quality, you can't possibly . . ." He looked at the expression on her face, gave up and turned to Morley. "You can't order it this afternoon but if you ever get the chance, try *pintaceleau Cervoisière,* it's one of the most famous of Belgium's dishes—a superb wild fowl in a sauce made with beer instead of wine. To be precise, with Cervoise, the brew drunk by the Gauls seven centuries ago."

While he talked, Taca's chubby fingers fondled the white-on-white linen, caressed the freshly cut roses and traced the pattern on the silver. They were powerful, stubby fingers that didn't seem to belong to the doctor—they were too neatly manicured, too much care had been lavished on the cuticle and the nails. They flashed in the candlelight, and Morley realized they had been lacquered with a plain polish. He studied them over the rim of his glass. Taca's fingers lived a life independent of their master. Like François.

"Well, Monsieur Morley?"

"You order for me." He finished his aperitif and signaled for another. "You both knew Cailleau rather well, then."

"He was like a father," Hannie said curtly. "I told you."

Morley turned to Taca, who sighed and took a mini-Schimmelpennick from its gold case. He lit it with a matching lighter, inhaled deeply several times and made a show of letting the smoke curl slowly past a mouthful of porcelain teeth.

"No one really knew Serge, Monsieur. But no one who saw his creatures come alive will ever forget them. *That* was his genius." He knocked a quarter inch of ash off the end of his cigar. "Personally, and as a critic for *Hier*, Serge intrigued me." He looked hopefully at Morley. "You've heard of *Yesterday?*"

Morley shook his head and Taca frowned. "It's dedicated to preserving the old ways before all of Europe gets swallowed up in your Coke culture. If you had seen Europe before your skyscrapers and your hamburger stands and your Levis had conquered all, you would know what I mean."

Morley did know. European cities had become as indistinguishable from one another as Cleveland was from Cincinnati or Indianapolis. Moscow had its McDonald's and even Sarajevo probably still got Coca-Cola.

"Mademoiselle, M'sieurs." Their chef greeted them. Marie-Therese, his wife, was smiling and watching steaming dishes being set on their table.

"*Bon appétit,*" Taca sniffed, tucking a napkin under his tight collar. "It looks as good as usual."

Marie-Therese saw to it that their wine glasses were filled

and motioned for a waiter to bring more butter. "It *is* good, *Docteur.*" There was a hint of disapproval in her voice, and Morley wondered if everyone found the fat man objectionable.

Taca recommended *la cervelle de veau citronnette* and urged Morley to try *pates urtyp* before he left Brussels, assuring him that—just as in the good old days—the pork had been soaked in beer for forty-eight hours. "You know, Monsieur Morley, you're one of the few Americans I know who has spent an afternoon at the Théâtre de Vaudeville." He paused to wash down the calf's brains with wine. "I find it hard to believe you're really interested in marionettes. You Americans seem to go for the . . . spectacle, the *extravaganza.*"

Morley tried the dish. It was exceptional, and he took another bite, then paused, afraid he would lose everything in his stomach. The food was too rich after six months on a hospital diet. "I was following up a lead."

Taca glanced up, a hunk of brioche in his mouth. "What sort of lead?" The words were muffled by the bread.

"For my article." Morley toyed for a moment with the *bouillon du jardinier*, letting Taca flounder. His stomach settled down and he concentrated again on the plate before him. The situation had its grotesque side—his first real meal outside the hospital, in a five-star restaurant at that, and he was sharing it with a beautiful woman who couldn't stomach it any more than he could, and another doctor just as arrogant as those who'd worked on him in Mayfair.

Taca raised an eyebrow. "I had forgotten—who is our host?"

"The *Enquirer.*" They were both listening closely now and he took his time, sipping the wine. "I'm looking for unusual European acts to hang a story on. Our readers like something different." He made the appropriate face. "Live in suburbia and you lead a pretty vicarious life."

"And you'll bring joy into their lives by titillating them with a little scandal," Hannie said coolly. "How bloody decent of you."

Morley half-smiled, thinking of the skin magazines on the front seat of Louis' taxi. "I take it you don't read the London tabloids or the nightstanders published in Amsterdam, Miss de Vries." He turned to Taca. "I'm surprised a medical man would be writing for *Hier*."

Taca finished off the last of the *cervelle*. "I'm sorry if I unintentionally deceived you. My doctorate's in library science. Professionally, I'm a librarian and computer analyst."

Morley wasn't at all sure the deception had been unintentional. Hannie said sharply, "But in the theater, you—"

"—did what I could. As a friend, Mademoiselle. I'm afraid no physician could have done more." He signaled the waiter and ordered another bottle of wine, then glanced sharply at Morley. "This lead of yours . . ."

They were fencing, Morley thought. He wasn't the only one who was curious about his dinner companions. He bought Hannie's story—with reservations—but he wasn't about to believe the librarian. "A friend in London told me about Cailleau." He glanced at Hannie. "He didn't say anything about the girl. Who is she?"

Hannie made a show of being disinterested. "I don't know, probably one of the regular performers." She was lying, Morley thought. She knew damned well who played François.

Taca looked amused. "Why the interest in François, Monsieur Morley? I don't deny her talent, but Serge was the true genius." He steered the conversation back to Hannie. "And you, my dear? You're hardly one of Théâtre de Vaudeville's grandmamas—you hadn't seen your 'father' for a long time, perhaps?" He placed a chubby hand on hers. She stiffened and pulled quickly away.

"Serge looked after me when my parents died. That was a long time ago. Now I'm on holiday and . . ." She almost broke, her voice starting to tremble. "I saw him for a few minutes this morning. He was busy. He had the matinee and an appointment—we were to have the evening to ourselves."

"What a fortunate, unfortunate man!"

Her voice chilled. "He was my . . . father."

She had kept her purse in her lap ever since sitting down, and now she was clutching it and reaching for her folded umbrella on the empty chair. She was going to leave, Morley thought, and if she got away, his best chance of finding out more about Cailleau, his friends and his enemies, would leave with her. "If Serge was so good," he demanded, "what was he doing in that broken-down music hall? No disrespect, of course."

Hannie threw her purse down on the table, furious. "Of course!"

Taca leaped to Cailleau's defense, even foregoing another bite of brioche. "Théâtre de Vaudeville is a national treasure. He played out of nostalgia—he began there." He leaned back in his chair, hooking his thumbs in his vest. "Serge wasn't merely good, he was extraordinary. The last time he played the Casino de Paris, the city was his. His marionettes were the toast of Prague, Vienna, Rome—of every capital on the Continent." He managed a labored wink. "You saw coats of rabbit fur at the matinee—tonight you would have seen sable."

"The women in the lobby talked about Cailleau's 'return'," Morley said. "From where?"

Hannie cut in. "He retired last year. His hands had started to tremble—only a little, the audiences never knew. But he did. He was as much a realist as he was a perfectionist."

"But he came back to the theater," Morley persisted.

Hannie shrugged. "He grew lonely. Nothing really mattered anymore except performing. And so he created François to—"

"Illusions were his life and he missed them, a simple enough reason," Taca interrupted. "Your readers should be able to understand that. One hopes, at least."

How long ago did Cailleau play Prague and Vienna? Morley wondered. Twenty years? Thirty? He doubted that he would have seen sable coats at the evening show. The only thing he would grant Taca was that illusions had been Cailleau's life.

But the biggest illusion of all was the one Taca and Hannie were trying to create for him now. What he had seen at the Théâtre de Vaudeville was an aging puppeteer whose hands trembled so badly he'd had to fake the show, performing in a third-rate club before an audience of ancient nostalgia buffs. The act had been good; it had also been pathetic.

Taca wiped the perspiration from his face and buttoned his jacket as he hauled himself up from the table. "You'll excuse me, but I must telephone *Hier* before it goes to press. Serge's death will certainly come as a shock to our readers."

After Taca had left, Morley said simply: "I'm sorry about Cailleau."

"You never knew—" Hannie stared at him.

"I'm the one he was supposed to meet this afternoon."

Her face went blank. "Who *are* you?"

She was more than attractive, he thought. In six months she was the only woman he'd been close to who wasn't wearing a nurse's uniform. "Cailleau wanted to tell me something," he said, aware that she realized he had sidestepped the question. "Somebody got to him before he could."

She looked bitter. "Why would he confide in you?"

"You don't have to believe me. But you better believe that whoever killed him thinks he talked to you, too."

She paled. "Only briefly."

"Nobody knows that." He didn't know if she were in danger, but it would be easier to get her away from the fat librarian and by herself if she thought she were. Unfortunately, she didn't trust him any more than she did Taca. He kept his voice low. "When I leave, Hannie, leave with me. Just listen to what I have to say. *Just listen,*" he repeated. "Then do whatever you want."

He started to say more, read a warning in her eyes and turned to smile amiably at Taca, who was lumbering back across the crowded room.

"Did you make your deadline?"

Taca nodded, breathless, and eased into his chair. He seemed almost jovial as he dug into the remains of his squab.

"You wanted to know about marionettes, Monsieur Morley, and the role they've played in the arts. Let me assure you, they've survived better here in Belgium than anywhere else on earth. At one time puppets were so popular there were some thirty marionette theaters in Liège alone. Tiji Vilenspiegal—you're familiar with Strauss's *Till Eulenspiegel?*—is to Flanders what Punch is to England. Of course, we Walloons have him, too, only we call him 'Tchantehes.' "

Another brioche followed a mouthful of squab to be joined moments later by a gulp of wine.

"We can trace them back to the cathedrals and monasteries where divine petite Madonnas and saints rolled pleading eyes upward and genuflected. David and Goliath, devils and angels and martyrs—they were all favorites of seventeenth-century puppet shows."

He signaled the waiter to pour more coffee. "I'm not boring you, am I, Monsieur?" He didn't wait for an answer. "Eventually, the little dolls became *too* popular. In Rome, wooden ballerinas were ordered to wear tights to conform to a papal ruling on decency. The proprietor of a puppet theater in this very province was convicted of spreading heretical doctrines. He and his marionettes were burned." He sugared his coffee and blew on it. "It's not insignificant that during the French Revolution, marionettes were the drawing room's second most popular diversion."

"What was the first?" Hannie asked, playing innocent.

"Miniature guillotines," Taca continued, with no trace of a smile. "A highlight of the marionette performances was when Polichinelle was guillotined on his little stage at the same time as real executions were carried out on the larger one."

A waiter brought dessert: *la pêche de vigne de Gascogne caramelisée et flambée au Kirsch*. Taca dug into it delicately, the spoon almost lost between his thick fingers. "Punch or a close cousin—Kasper or Kasparek or Karagoz, Guignol or Petrushka, depending on one's country—was every European's folk hero. His audiences loved him as much as the ladies this afternoon loved François. After every show they would shake his hand and offer to stand him to a round. 'For He's a Jolly Good Fellow'— you know the tune?"

Morley nodded. Taca was stalling and he suspected why. He motioned to Marie-Therese for the check.

"It was written especially for Punch, Monsieur. And of course you know Gounod's 'Funeral March of a Marionette.' But composers weren't the only ones inspired. Goethe conceived Doctor Faust for the marionettes. In turn, Shakespeare lifted the idea for *Julius Caesar* from a glove puppet performance he saw near the Tower of London; Milton borrowed his poetic arguments from an Italian string puppet; and Byron plucked Don Juan from Punch's 'The Libertine Destroyed.' "

The plate had been wiped clean, and Taca dried his hands with his napkin. "George Sand was particularly fond of a hand puppet that could be manipulated with three fingers. She said that when she thrust her hand under its skirt, she felt the puppet come alive with her soul, that they were one. An interesting insight when you consider she was Chopin's mistress."

He dropped the crumpled napkin on the table and stifled a belch, then took a sip of cold coffee. Morley prompted: "And Cailleau?"

Taca sighed. "Serge knew more about the little creatures than anyone living or dead. When you watched, you *knew* they were real, that it was the people around you who were the illusions. For Serge, they came alive and danced and sang and made love. So you see, Monsieur, you should not feel contempt for the grandmamas this afternoon. They loved François and he loved them. A safe and harmless love, no? This girl you mentioned may have been on the stage, but it was Serge's soul you actually saw up there."

Morley looked at the check and took out a wad of franc notes and arranged them neatly on the check plate.

Taca lurched to his feet. "I'll be glad to drop the young lady off."

"Mister Morley has already offered, thank you just the same." She didn't seem delighted, Morley thought.

"I lose to a stranger." Taca said it with just the proper emphasis, his face darkening. For a fleeting moment, Morley glimpsed the soul within and then Taca's pale eyes had lidded over and he was caged once more behind his thick, tinted lenses. He wondered if Taca had wanted to question Hannie alone or just isolate *him*. He reached out and squeezed the damp hand in farewell.

Taca was suddenly curious. "Where are you staying, Monsieur? I know some clubs you might enjoy—Brussels has the most unique on the Continent." The lewd wink behind the thick glasses was grotesque. "As a fellow journalist, I'll be glad to take you." The mouthful of artificial teeth gaped open in a desperate smile.

"The Hilton," Morley said, taking Hannie's arm. Then he was nodding at Marie-Therese and assuring her that the meal had been superb.

It had been, even if he couldn't remember what he'd eaten.

Outside, the rain had dwindled to an uneven dripping from awnings and ironwork. Across the square, drying windows had begun to gleam in the fading light. Morley waved for a taxi and they rode two blocks in silence. Then he picked an argument with the driver and insisted on taking another cab. He handed the second driver some folded francs, holding the door open for Hannie. "Hotel Metropole."

Hannie froze. "You said the Hilton."

"I'll meet you in the lobby. Go on—get in."

"Why the bloody hell should I?"

"Taca didn't spend all that time on my education for nothing. He was waiting for someone to catch up with him. Now go on while I have a word with our new friend."

He pushed her in, slammed the door and motioned for the driver to take off. He didn't know what Taca's game was, but he would soon find out.

He turned and walked slowly down the street, pausing to admire the pastries and cakes in a bakery window. It was already late afternoon and the shadows were thickening in the narrow streets.

It wouldn't do to walk too fast, he thought. He didn't want Taca's friend to lose him.

six

MORLEY TOOK A side street that was crowded with mothers pushing prams. He climbed a steep, cobbled hill, cursing the throbbing in his side where half a hundred stitches were still a recent memory, then turned into a narrow street filled with pigeons and the sound of canaries singing behind slatted wooden shutters. Stella Artois beer signs hung over the tavern doors, creaking in the late afternoon wind that had suddenly sprung up. It was going to rain again, reminding him even more of the last time he had been on the run in Brussels.

Schoolgirls, look-alikes in dark-blue sweaters and skirts, skipped down the short flight of steps, forcing him to hug the stone wall. The younger ones swung book bags and chased each other; their older sisters shot him half-hidden glances and passed by whispering and giggling. He was near the top of the steep stairs now, the aroma of freshly brewed coffee growing heavier as he reached the last step.

He paused to catch his breath, watching while a scowling concierge washed down her sidewalk, trying to erase a red and blue sailboat that had been chalked on it. The sky was growing darker, and here and there in the city below a light twinkled on.

Turning, he glanced back down the hill. The man in the tight-fitting blue leather jacket was easy to spot. He was taking his time on the stairs, acting like any other citizen out giving his dog a chance to piss on the cobblestones. He had paused, too, both fists sunk deep in his trouser pockets, idly studying the flower boxes on the balconies overhead. Every now and then, he stuck two fingers in his mouth and whistled low for Fido.

Morley had been watching him for several blocks now. He was sure that Leather Jacket didn't have a dog.

He hesitated at the corner, then turned down the narrower rue des Pigeons. A cobbler glanced up as he passed his cellar window, then looked behind him as they both heard other footsteps in the narrow passageway. Morley could feel his muscles tighten in his chest. Leather Jacket would probably be carrying a knife. He'd have to surprise him; he'd have to count on Leather Jacket being overconfident.

Morley was sweating now, his thoughts running wild. Leather Jacket didn't have to be Taca's man, there were other possibilities. He'd been involved in too many operations— someone might have doubts about letting him retire. And the most logical way to terminate him would be while he was in Brussels.

He swore under his breath; the months in bed had preyed on his mind. More than likely, somebody had heard he was back and his past was catching up with him. It was as simple as that. He wasn't the only one who had unfinished business in Brussels.

Christ!

The only thing that mattered right now was taking out Leather Jacket. He would have to pick a spot, but it couldn't be here; it would have to be somewhere quieter and more deserted. And he would have to handle Leather Jacket quickly; he didn't have the strength for anything that took time.

58

The flood of adrenalin started then and the pain in his side was suddenly muffled.

Halfway down the sloping street he stopped and lit a cigarette. The windows here were blank, sightless. Rue des Chandeliers, which emptied into the narrow street at the corner, was also deserted except for an underfed wolfhound watering a Fiat's front tire. As good a place as any, he decided. Then the door to a bistro flew open and two pensioners stumbled out, arguing over which pub to go to next.

He dragged on his cigarette, flipped it into a puddle and moved on. Midway down another street he stopped to unwrap a sheet of damp newsprint that had blown around his leg. He glanced back and caught another glimpse of Leather Jacket.

His shy friend was standing under a still-dripping awning, engrossed in a shop window, his collar turned up and his nose pressed against the dirty glass. Another window would have been more convincing—that one was cluttered with dusty hearing aids, batteries and ear molds.

It was beyond the magic store, beyond the stamp collectors' boutique and the shop where a barber was massaging the scalp of his last customer for the day that he found what he was looking for.

The sign on the four-story building said Hotel. A placard over the locked door added, Hotel Cafe. Drink Coca-Cola and English Spoken Here decals had been stuck on the windows. The rest of the panes were smeared with paint and torn shreds of circus posters.

Along one side of the crumbling building was the alley.

Morley didn't bother checking the reflections in the one clear pane of glass that caught them. Leather Jacket would still be there. But there was only Leather Jacket: nobody else had been following, there had been no cars cruising slowly behind them.

Just a slender young man in a cheap jacket, somebody who looked vaguely familiar, though he hadn't caught a clear glimpse of his face. Probably somebody he had noticed in the crowd before, somebody who had been following him since he'd come to Brussels.

He turned into the alley as if he had been heading there all along. A stout woman was working just inside the open back door of a dry cleaner's, and he nodded to her as he passed. A dozen steps farther on, the narrow alley made several sharp turns. Now he was in a cul-de-sac, and the few windows that looked down on it were closed and thick with soot.

He stopped, his heart suddenly trip-hammering. It had been in an alley like this where he had almost died the last time, and he was terrified. He had been with somebody and . . . and . . . He forced the image from his mind. Leather Jacket was only seconds behind him.

It would have to be quick. His leg was hurting again, and he knew he didn't have the wind to go for more than a minute or two.

He put down his briefcase and flattened himself into a doorway. He was ready now, his shirt wet with sweat, his breathing ragged and his heart racing. The cobblestones, the narrow streets with their brick-walled buildings . . . at night the residents could hear the echo of footsteps behind their closed and shuttered windows, but it was a section of Brussels where nobody would look out if somebody yelled.

Far away there was the honking of a lorry and the sound of a couple arguing. There was also a low whistle and the quiet rattle of shoes on gravel thirty or forty meters up the alley.

Morley watched, listening, as the air turned a chill, twilight purple. The alley was growing darker as he stood there; half an hour more and it would be lost in blackness. But he didn't need more than a few minutes. Any longer than that . . .

He caught his breath, sweating. Maybe that was what Louis hadn't wanted to tell him, that he had made mistakes the last time he had been in Brussels, that he wasn't up to the work anymore. That it was time for him to bow out and spend the rest of his life shuffling papers and bullshitting with one or two close friends about the operations they had been on and how they had once saved Democracy. Only that would never happen—he didn't have the one or two close friends.

A shadow suddenly profiled itself in front of him and his world exploded.

He shot out of the doorway. He wrapped one arm around a slender neck and jabbed four stiff fingers into Leather Jacket's gut. There was a *whoof* of air and a strangled sound. A boot flailed back and he kicked out with his right foot and caught the ankle. He twisted the shadow's left arm behind its back, jamming it upwards.

Leather Jacket catapulted onto the cobblestones, then tried to get to his feet and run. Morley caught him once in the rib cage with his shoe and Leather Jacket rolled into a tight ball, instinctively trying to cover his groin.

Morley kicked him again, half-lifting Leather Jacket off the stones. The slender body snapped flat onto its belly. Morley dropped to his knees, grabbing Leather Jacket by the hair and smashing his face into the bricks. Leather Jacket's hands flew to his face, trying to protect his already mashed lips and nose. He doubled and kicked out, catching Morley in the side. Morley gasped, the pain blanketing the fatigue that had set in seconds after he had lunged from the doorway.

Leather Jacket fumbled in his pants pocket, then rolled to his knees. There was a *snick* and his right hand sprouted a blade. He waved it weakly at Morley, his left hand still shielding his bloodied face.

He couldn't afford to make a mistake now. Morley cursed

his own body that moved slower than he wanted and was already screaming with pain and exhaustion. He gasped for a second wind and batted at the hand that held the knife, grabbing the fingers and bending them back. The knife clattered into the alley.

He ducked behind Leather Jacket, held him by the collar and hauled him into the small pool of light cast by a flickering bulb over one of the alley's doorways. Leather Jacket jerked away, almost pulling out of his grasp, and Morley whirled him around and kneed him in the groin. Leather Jacket doubled up and Morley slipped behind him again, still clutching his collar. Leather Jacket was surprisingly limp—the standard trick, go limp and then come back to life when it's least expected. He rammed Leather Jacket into a nearby wall, then twisted him around for a good look at his face.

The kid had left his bellhop's uniform at the theater, but there was still a smear of greasepaint under his chin, not quite covered by the blood oozing from his nose and eyebrows. Morley automatically took in the damage: a broken nose, probable fractures to the small bones of the face, several broken front teeth, with two of them jutting through a torn lip.

The tide of adrenalin receded and Morley felt weak; his leg hurt and his side had developed a searing pain. *"Who sent you?"* The words came out as short, angry puffs of vapor in the chill night air.

Leather Jacket's eyes rolled back in his head, and it was only Morley's fading strength that held him upright. He let him go, and the kid slumped to the ground. "Who sent you?" he repeated dully. Leather Jacket didn't answer, and Morley knelt and felt for a pulse. It was erratic, weak.

His head felt foggy. Leather Jacket hadn't been sent to snuff him. It had been a simple assignment, like his own. Find out where he was staying. Nothing dangerous—just follow him and report back.

Whoever sent Leather Jacket had sent a boy to do a boy's job. He could have lost him any time.

He stood there staring, trying to control his heavy breathing and thinking that if Leather Jacket had put up any fight at all, the contact could easily have ended the other way around. He watched as the blood pulsed slowly from the boy's nose and ran down the side of his face to drip onto the damp cobblestones.

He should call an ambulance, he thought. He turned to leave, then froze at a shadow just beyond the circle of yellow light from the doorway.

A small dachshund had run into the alley and was somberly blinking up at him. It whimpered tentatively, then ran over to nose its master.

Morley bent down for a final look. Leather Jacket had been almost pretty. And he couldn't have weighed more than seventy kilos.

He was suddenly furious. "You're an asshole," he croaked at the still figure. "You know that? A real goddamned asshole!"

seven

MORLEY TURNED THE key in the lock and pushed the door open, groping for the table lamp in the darkness. He clicked it on and placed the key with its loop and heavy metal ball on the lamp table. The room looked drab after the gilt of the lobby. It also smelled musty and felt vaguely chilly— the radiator must have been turned off when the last tenant had checked out. He reached for the wooden knob, wrenched it and was rewarded by a soft hiss.

It was the first time he had seen this particular room, but he knew it by heart: the anonymous room in the old-fashioned Continental hotel—the bland rug, the rickety writing desk, the overstuffed chair with the lumpy cushion and a dent worn at head height in the back . . .

The white-tiled floor of the bathroom was a ghostly gleam through the doorway to the left, and he could hear a sullen drip from one of the faucets. That was familiar, too, along with the soap wrapped in embossed paper and the orange stain in the porcelain wash bowl.

The writing desk was in front of two narrow windows overlooking a blind alley, while an arm's reach away, headboard hard against the rose wallpaper, was the double bed with its graying chenille spread. Almost everything in the room was brown or beige; what wasn't was faded rose or dun-tinted green.

Hannie was not impressed. "I suppose if you want a view, you can always turn on the telly."

Morley set his briefcase on the writing desk. "It has one advantage—nobody knows we're here."

She was still standing in the doorway. "All my luggage is at the Ravenstein."

"So? They won't give it away."

She walked into the room. "This isn't very smart of me."

Who was she, really? Morley wondered. Not who she said she was, at least not *just* who she said she was.

There was a spatter of rain against the windows and he could feel a draft of cold air around his feet. He pulled the thick drapes shut to keep the chill out and prevent anyone from seeing in. "Serge Cailleau is dead. You're still alive and so am I. It would be nice to stay that way until morning." He was deliberately frightening her, but there was no other way to begin what would eventually turn into his . . . interrogation.

Hannie bit her lip at the mention of Cailleau's name, and he guessed she felt guilty at having forgotten him, no matter how briefly. She glanced around the room and he said offhandedly, "You can have the bed." He couldn't tell whether she was relieved or not.

"And you?"

"The easy chair. I've had enough of beds." He took off his mac and hung it in the armoire, then picked up the desk phone and dialed. A woman's voice finally crackled in his ear and he ordered a pot of coffee. *Grand.* He replaced the phone and sank into the chair. Once he was sitting down, the muscles in his legs started to tremble. He had pushed himself too hard.

Hannie slipped out of her coat and dropped it on the bed.

"You took a long time. I began to feel awkward waiting in the lobby."

"We were followed. I told you."

"Did you kill him?" she asked sarcastically. "I think there's blood on your cuff."

It took an effort to keep from conjuring up the image of Leather Jacket. "Not quite." He concentrated for a moment on the small sounds of life around him: The occasional tram rattling by in the streets below, the faint sounds of a commode being flushed somewhere above him, the muffled sounds of a woman laughing.

"What do you tell people you do?" Her voice was cool and impersonal but he could sense the uneasiness running through it.

"I don't hand out business cards." He stretched out his legs, trying for the position that hurt the least. "If you're going to spend the night, Hannie, you might as well get undressed and go to bed."

She gave him a hard glance, then began matter-of-factly to undress. He thought of looking away, of granting her that much privacy, but didn't. When it came to morals, she was obviously your young European liberal.

He lit a cigarette and watched her clinically. She was petite, with a slightly chubby face, a halo of ebony hair and skin as smooth as a bar of soap. Her complexion gave away her age; she couldn't be much more than twenty. She still wore traces of last summer's tan, but she had none of the dimpling in the backs of her legs that even very young girls seemed to have nowadays. Her bra and panties were colorful, designed to be looked at, and from what he saw of the rest of her, she at least had the spirit for nude beaches.

There was a quiet knock on the door and Hannie scrambled for the bed. Morley tensed, then, remembering the coffee he had

66

ordered, edged open the door. A smiling, elderly bellman brought in the tray and left as quietly as he had come. Morley handed a cup to Hannie, buried in the feather bed with the covers drawn up primly around her neck. He settled back in the chair, letting the warm aroma of the coffee wash over him.

"Where's home, Hannie?"

She scooted up against the headboard, fishing the pillows out from under the blankets and propping them behind her. "London, I suppose. Switzerland feels that way, too. I was there longer, but I'm happier in London."

Her accent was a surprisingly soft mixture of Dutch and English, and once again he found himself listening as much to the sound of her voice as to the sense of what she was saying.

"What do you do?"

"I told you—I'm an assistant financial analyst." She fluffed the pillows, restacking them. "I also dance, ski, go to the races and curl up with a good book now and then."

He smiled. "Just a book?"

There was a sudden hint of laughter in her voice. "You're not bad looking when you smile, you know. You should do it more often."

"I'll keep that in mind." He poured himself more coffee, wondering who was toying with whom. "How did you get to know Cailleau?"

"My parents were high-wire people. There was an accident." Her voice was flat and he guessed that she had explained all this more than once. "They didn't fall—the tent caught fire. After that, Serge took care of me. He was a widower and very much alone."

Maybe he believed her, maybe not. "How old were you?"

"Six. I traveled with Serge until I was thirteen. Then he sent me to boarding school in Lucerne."

"You said Cailleau mentioned our meeting. Exactly what did he say?"

"Only that he was anxious to spend some time with me afterwards." Her voice sounded shadowed.

"How long had he been in Brussels?" Cailleau had been an old man who drank too much. How much of what Cailleau had told him was true and how much had spilled out of his wine glass?

"Four days."

"Before that?"

"Berlin."

"Where?"

"A tiny cabaret in what had been the East sector, I forget the name. The owner was an old friend." She yawned. "Do you smoke hash? I have some in the bottom of the cigarette pack in my bag."

He didn't answer. He handed her the bag and watched while she took out the cigarette papers, moistened them with her tongue and pieced them together, then split open two cigarettes and heaped the tobacco on the new wrapper. The small piece of hash was hard and almost black. Indian. She crumbled it over the tobacco, then made a joint using a rolled-up strip of matchbook as a filter.

"And before that?"

"Before what?" Her words came out strangled. She held her breath a moment longer, then offered him the joint. He didn't take it and she said, "Puritan?"

He shook his head. "I smoked in 'Nam. Then one day I figured out half our casualties died because they were stoned out of their minds. It's not a smart thing to do if your life's on the line."

"We're all alone, *Mister* Morley. I don't think our lives are on the line right at the moment."

"That's a comfort to know, Hannie."

She took one more defiant drag, then pinched out the hot

68

tip with the remains of the matchbook cover and carefully slipped what was left into the cigarette pack.

"Before Berlin," Morley repeated.

"Sofia, Bucharest. Sopron."

"Bulgaria, Romania . . ." He wasn't conscious of talking; he was more intent on the sound of elevator doors opening and stealthy footsteps on the hall carpet. There were two of them. Amateurs. Professionals would have walked right up to the door and shot it open with a Sten gun. It would have been over in seconds. "Hungary . . . in that order?"

"Yes. In Sopron—that's about a hundred kilometers east of Vienna—there's an old cabaret, one of the first Serge ever played. He never forgot it, and they never forgot him. He would always play there on his way back."

He had the Smith & Wesson in his hand, hidden from Hannie's view. He edged forward in his chair. It wasn't that he was panicked—he hadn't panicked in years, he just couldn't let go of the drill, not even here. Not even after Leather Jacket. He blinked the sweat from his eyes and began counting silently in Vietnamese—*mot, hai, ba, bon*—waiting for the two in the hall to card the lock and slip in, thinking he and Hannie were in bed making love.

Were you this tense when I crept in, Tran? Were you taken by surprise, too, Daud?

The steps halted. There was the sound of a key turning in a lock, then a giggle and the quiet opening and closing of a door a few rooms away.

"You're not listening," Hannie said.

He fought his nerves for a moment, then said: "Cailleau told me he helped some folks out of Romania. I'm curious what he told you."

She looked surprised. "He didn't tell me anything, not about that."

69

He didn't believe her. He'd ask her again, later. "Let's assume he did. How would he have gotten them across the borders?"

"I have no idea." Then, doubtfully: "Maybe as puppets." Morley watched, poker-faced, waiting. "It was an old family trick. When Serge was young, he and his brothers and sisters had to play they were puppets. They were the same size as the puppets and they wore heavy costumes and beards and wigs. They'd play the leads while their father worked the others. They never made much money so when they came to a country that had a border tax, Serge's father made them put on greasepaint and lie still in the back of the wagon. They became quite good at it."

It couldn't possibly have succeeded, Morley thought. Not now.

"Did the girl travel with him to the East?"

"Yes." Then, bitterly: "Serge added her this year."

"But you don't know her name."

"That's right, he never told me."

"Where did they stay? Serge and the girl?"

She bit her lip. "Serge always stayed at a pensione near boulevard d'Anvers. Maybe they both did. Maybe she had her own place. I wouldn't know."

"Who would have set up the deal for Cailleau?"

She suddenly looked bored. "Who knows? Serge used to help a lot of people during the Second World War and after. That's all I know."

There was very little more about Cailleau and his clients that she could tell him—or would tell him, he thought. At least not now. He'd try again in the morning, with more questions about who Cailleau's friends and enemies had been.

He clicked off the lamp, shifting again in the overstuffed chair. He'd grown tired of rooms like this a long time ago, but the Metropole was close to the Théâtre de Vaudeville and he knew its layout by heart—even in the darkness he could sense the outlines of the room. It reminded him of the first hotel he'd stayed in after the fall of Saigon. . . .

He yawned and the memories came crowding in then . . . memories of his special unit and the parachute flare with its dripping white phosphorus tip jabbing at the Vietnamese woman to make the men in her village talk. And behind that memory was one of the eight frightened villagers condemned to death by the White Mice, the South Vietnamese special police, for being enemy agents. He had photographed the dead, staring faces for the record, then discovered that the village tipster had wiped out a lifetime of debts by feeding his creditors to the police. Finally, behind all of them was the memory of a dark, thatched doorway and the screams of a young girl in pajamas. How old was she when she had died? He didn't know then, he didn't want to know now. . . .

It could have been a sound or just the sense that something was wrong that made him snap awake, the Smith & Wesson jumping in his hand. He didn't know how long it had been, but the pelting rain had dwindled to a quiet drizzle and he could feel the dust settling in the quiet room, disturbed only by Hannie's breathing. He glanced over at her in the huge double bed.

The dim light from a partially draped window left most of her face in shadow. He couldn't tell whether her eyes were closed or open and wondered if she were asleep or just lying in the dark, replaying the afternoon at the theater. He felt for the matches on the table and struck one, the glow briefly flooding her face. She was awake, studying him from the safety of three blankets and two goose-down pillows, her expression wary and tentative.

"You didn't sleep more than ten minutes," she said quietly.

71

"I imagine you worry about things like that."

He felt almost grateful. "Sometimes."

After a moment she said: "I've answered your questions. But you haven't told me anything about you."

Here it came, he thought. He'd been expecting it. Time to go to work.

"There's not much to tell."

"I have a right to know something."

He struck another match, studying her face by the flickering light. He blew it out just before it burned his fingers. "Ask anything you want."

"Neal Morley isn't your real name, is it?"

"Would it make a difference?"

She let it pass. "You were born," she went on from her fortress of linen and wool, "where?"

"Chicago." It was only half a lie; his birthplace was actually near there.

She was quiet for a moment and he guessed she was wondering how far she could press him. "You're forty-something and not married. At least not now."

"That's right." Neither deduction had been difficult; she had seen both his face and his fingers.

"No brothers or sisters?"

"An older brother, an engineer. Two sisters, both younger, both married." His younger brother was in marketing; he had no sisters.

She patted a pillow and leaned up on one elbow. She had decided to press her luck. "What did your father do?"

"He was a priest—he left the Church to marry my mother. It didn't work out and he split when I was ten." He took a perverse pleasure in coming so close to the truth. It was the only way to play the game; skate close to the edge, don't fake everything.

"It doesn't fit," she said.

He yawned. "Would you like the rest of it? I was on the college football team and the varsity debate team. I was in the R.O.T.C. and president of my fraternity. After I graduated, I sold insurance, just like everybody else."

"I don't want to know your resumé, I want to know you."

He found himself wanting to respond to her. It had been a long time since anybody had seen him as anything but a patient. And swapping half-confidences was all part of the game.

He was silent for a moment. "After the old man disappeared, I hung around the carnivals that came to town, trying to get up the courage to run away. I settled for riding the ferris wheel and the Tilt-A-Whirl until closing time, trying to pick up girls." He smiled to himself, putting on hold that part of his mind obsessed with survival. "I was small for my age, I didn't succeed very often. Then one afternoon I was smoking behind a tent with some friends and one of us flicked a butt into the air and it landed on a midway concession—the one where you throw a ball to knock over the milk bottles. It burned a hole in the canvas a yard in diameter."

It was a deliberate lie. He remembered what she'd said about her parents, about the circus tent catching fire. It would make for something they had in common. She didn't say anything. Just when he wondered if she had drifted off to sleep, she said, "You were in Vietnam, weren't you?"

He snapped alert. "Among other places."

And then, too casually: "Special Forces, wasn't it?"

"Who told you that?"

She realized, too late, that she had made a mistake. "Just a guess."

"You didn't approve of Vietnam, did you?" It was a deliberate needle.

"Most Europeans didn't. But it was a long time ago, I was too young to know much about it"

"Most Americans didn't approve of it either, Hannie."

She could have dropped it, but she didn't.

"Only at the end. When you had already lost."

"You're right," he said. "It was Special Forces."

"Were you proud of what you did?"

He sighed.

"Hannie, I didn't have any position on 'Nam except doing whatever I had to do to keep from being wasted." She was picking a fight with him, and he wondered why. He had needled her, but now *she* was overreacting.

"It wasn't your war," she said primly. "It was theirs."

He stood up and crossed over to the window. In the alley below, three figures staggered past the glow spilling from an open doorway. A musician, bent under the weight of a bass fiddle, and two chorus girls from the nearby nightclub, their makeup garish in the harsh light. All three were drunk. The bass player caromed off a wall, then lurched into the street, followed by the giggling girls. Morley watched with professional curiosity.

"I didn't think anybody gave a fuck anymore." Silence. "Shit, it was everybody's war, Hannie, just like Afghanistan was everybody's war, just like Bosnia-Herzegovina. Every war is everybody's war."

"You believed in it." There was surprise in her voice. "You still do."

"Like you said, it was a long time ago, Hannie." He stared out the window as the last of the entertainers left the club and drifted up the darkened street. When the clicking of high heels on cobblestones finally died away, he turned back to the room. He couldn't drop it, either. "Sure, I believed in some of it. Some of the time."

"I'm sorry if I annoyed you." She didn't sound sorry at all, and he realized that she wasn't going to be satisfied with just winning the game. She wanted something more.

"You talk in your sleep," she added after a moment. "You have nightmares."

They'd never mentioned that at the hospital. Not once. He walked over to the bed and looked down at her. He almost felt sorry for what he was going to do to her.

"When did you last see Cailleau? I'm not talking about this morning."

In a muffled tone: "A few years ago."

"You didn't want to go to boarding school, did you? It must have been fun traveling with him, being backstage. You hated him for sending you away. And you couldn't have liked him any better when you heard about his new assistant."

She whirled around in the bed. "That's not true!"

"Of course it's true, Hannie," he said softly. "The English Channel is pretty narrow, you could have visited him any time. But you didn't want to, did you?"

He knew now just who she was and what she was really doing in Brussels.

"I don't want to talk about it."

He sat on the edge of the bed and put his hand on her shoulder. She moved away. "Who sent you, Hannie?"

"Nobody. I—"

He stood up, ripping off the blankets and leaving her a naked, frozen ball on the far edge of the mattress.

"Don't lie, Hannie, it doesn't become you. He looked you up at work, didn't he? A decent sort with trim hair and moustache and old school tie. He was properly patriotic. He didn't want much, merely for you to visit an old friend in Brussels, a friend of his as well as of yours. Serge Cailleau had something he wanted to get off his chest, and your old family friend thought that Cailleau would talk to you rather more fully than he might to me. You hesitated and he played upon your memories of the good old days. Now Serge was in trouble and you could help. And just in case you hesitated, Mother England and Belgium, old allies, would both be grateful. He knew your weaknesses, he knew everything about you. He was a gentleman and a talker. What did he offer, Hannie? A fancy flat? Enough money for a sports car?"

She flattened herself against the wall, arms crossed over her breasts. "You bastard!"

He let the blankets slip from his fingers. Like the fight with Leather Jacket, it was an unequal contest. He limped back to the table for a cup of coffee, lifted the cold pot and slammed it down in frustration.

"You're not bad, Hannie. What you settled for is nothing compared to what they'll offer you if you really work out. The job isn't that difficult, they must have assured you of that. Just keep your lovely eyes and ears open, that's most of it. You'll be well kept, promised everything. All your betrayals will be small and in the name of God, Family, Country and money well spent." His voice was bleak. "Welcome aboard, Hannie—you'll find we're an Equal Opportunity Employer."

"*You* work for them!"

"I'm a true believer. You said so yourself."

"You don't believe in one bloody thing!"

She hadn't resorted to tears, he'd give her points for that. "But I do, Hannie. It's you who don't."

She pulled the blankets around her shoulders. "I think you're over the hill, like some broken-down Hollywood cowboy. I think you're sitting here wondering where the Cold War's gone, and why you've been at it for so long and just what do you have to show for it."

"Dead right," he said quietly.

"When they find out Serge's been killed," she said angrily, "they'll take you off the assignment."

"Sorry, Hannie, that's one thing I can keep as long as I want."

"You don't really believe that," she said, her voice icy. "You know what the doctors will say. They wouldn't risk everything on a sick man."

He ignored her and picked up the phone to talk someone into bringing another pot of coffee. It was two in the morning but it would be even later before either of them would be able to sleep.

When he was through, he turned back to her. "They really sent you to talk to Serge?"

"I wasn't sent, he asked if I'd be willing to go."

For the first time that night he felt shock, not at what he knew she was going to say next but that he hadn't seen it coming.

"Who?"

"Moses," she said, her voice low. "Simon agreed to the assignment as a favor to him."

"Why?"

"They thought you might not get around to talking to Serge. At least, not right away. They were afraid you'd go off on your own."

Old friends were the best friends, he thought, and Cailleau had been one of Moses' oldest. Which meant that nobody had trusted him, but they had let him go anyway. Like almost everything else anymore, it didn't make sense.

"You going to call them in the morning?" he asked quietly.

"I don't know."

"Why not?"

"I don't want you to go off on your own, either. To me, Serge really was a father. I want to know who murdered him."

Her voice shifted. "And you've spent half the day convincing me you don't really give a damn!"

"You want me to find out who killed him. That's quite a vote of confidence, Hannie."

The words came out with an effort. "You have to. I can't."

He shrugged. "Like you said, London would send somebody else."

She stared back at him. "I heard you have a reputation."

He should have been flattered, but wasn't.

"I don't have much choice," she continued, adding, "and I don't care whether I've offended you or not."

"I have my own interests in Brussels," Morley said. He had to know how badly she wanted him.

Her voice was pinched. "I'll call London. Tell them you're not up to it."

"If they recall me, they'll recall you."

For the first time that night she sounded close to tears. "I can be helpful," she said. "You really need help."

Morley glanced toward the window again so she couldn't see his expression. Everybody was good at using. London used him, and it used her and now he was going to use her, too.

He still felt a brief twinge of guilt. She was young and far more innocent than she herself realized, and if she stayed with London, in a few years she'd be just another Sister bedding down with the opposition as part of her patriotic duties. Some other kind gentleman would explain the necessity of it as convincingly as any pimp explaining the necessity of the latest kink to one of his girls.

"You're right," Hannie said, her voice muffled by the blankets again. "I hadn't seen Serge much. I owe him a lot."

Morley had an irrational desire to send her back on the first plane, then smothered it. Nobody had forced her to come.

"What did they tell you about me?"

"That you were a loner, that your specialty was counter-terrorism. . . . That you were almost killed the last time you were in Brussels."

"I meant personally."

"Personally? What makes you think they said anything at all about you?"

"You're not the type who goes to hotel rooms with complete strangers, Hannie." He permitted himself a smile. "They must have told you something."

The laughter edged back into her voice. "They said I could trust you. Up to a point."

They both fell silent then, waiting for the bellman to bring up the coffee. The pain in Morley's leg was coming back and he swore quietly to himself and concentrated for a moment on Cailleau. What he knew wasn't nearly enough. A team of terrorists hardly needed an old man to help them cross frontiers. Belgium, with its coast and open borders, was easy enough to penetrate. Since they hadn't needed Cailleau to get into Belgium, that meant they had needed him to get out of some other country. Or maybe they hadn't needed him at all, but wanted to use him for something else. And when they had, Cailleau had become expendable.

He'd check tomorrow to see what the Bureau had in their files. After that, he'd go back to the Théâtre de Vaudeville. And when he was through there, he'd get down to the real business of Brussels. To find out who had almost killed him the last time he'd been here. And maybe, along the way, find out who had murdered Cailleau.

He shifted in his chair again, impatient for the bellman to show up. He really needed that coffee.

He glanced over at Hannie. The coffee—and a comfortable spot in the bed, curled up beside her. He wanted to feel the animal warmth, to feel the slow breathing of somebody next to him and smell the humid scent of faint perfume and fresh-washed skin.

Perhaps even make love to her, despite the pain.

Or try to.

It hadn't worked out at all with the night nurse. She had reassured him, saying it was just a matter of time before his body would respond once more. But he hadn't believed her. He still didn't.

Just before he fell asleep, he had a brief moment of regret that he'd lied to Hannie. He would like to have confided in her, to have told her everything about himself. He wanted to think she would have understood, that she would have forgiven those things he could never forgive in himself, that she would have loved him for being what he was.

He was still thinking about her when he nodded off.

eight

THE NEEDLE-SHARP SPRAY of the shower gradually brought Morley back to life, the water sluicing down his scarred back and relaxing his knotted muscles. For the last five minutes, he turned off the hot water and stood under the cold until it had become ice water and the spray actually stung.

He dried himself with a thick, graying towel, pausing when he glimpsed himself in the full-length mirror on the back of the bathroom door. He had made a habit of not really looking at himself since one traumatic day in the hospital washroom. He had gained a little weight since then, but he was still twenty pounds shy of his regular one hundred eighty at a height of six feet. His skin was pale, with pinkish scars snaking across his stomach and around his left leg, the stringy muscles standing out as if they had been embossed. The scars would always be with him, even after the doctors pronounced him completely fit. When he got a tan again, they'd stand out a fish-belly white.

He took a final look and shrugged. He tended to be hairy, with a deep brown mat on his chest and below, thinning to a light underbrush on his upper arms and shoulders. Now there were glints of silver among the darker strands.

He hung up the towel, locked his knees and bent over until his fingers touched the floor. He held the position a moment, ignoring the pain in his side, then straightened up and repeated the movement, slowly increasing the tempo of his repetitions. The doctors had recommended the calisthenics to keep his muscles from stiffening. He hated them. Unlike his old workouts, these were a constant reminder of just how weak he was.

Halfway through a set of knee bends, the muscles in his left thigh spasmed. He hobbled over to the toilet bowl and sat on the edge, massaging the rock-hard flesh. He couldn't afford to have his legs go out on him today; there was too much to do. He'd have to try and pick up old leads at the Bureau, then check out Cailleau's fellow artists at the Théâtre de Vaudeville, though that might be more up Hannie's alley. They'd talk to her—she was the bereaved.

And there was still the question of what to do about London, how to feed them Cailleau's story with just enough skepticism so they wouldn't pull him. Hannie could help with that, too.

She was awake when he stepped back into the other room, a towel wrapped around his waist. "Don't you ever sleep?" She was squinting up at him, her face half-hidden in the pillows. He had been right, he thought. She did look good in the morning, even with her eyes still lidded with sleep and her hair in a tangle.

"I've been hibernating since May, that's long enough." He dropped the towel without embarrassment and pulled on his shorts and trousers, then limped over to the chair to put on his socks and shoes.

Hannie looked sympathetic. "I should have let you take the bed."

"You should have offered to share it."

"You should have asked."

He wasn't sure if she meant it or not, then decided she did. He'd been a damn fool. He took his shirt off the back of the chair. "What's she like?"

"Who?"

"The girl who played François." She didn't answer and he said, "Why don't you like her?"

"Did I say I didn't?"

He buttoned his shirt and tucked it into his trousers. "You didn't have to, I could see it in your face."

She sat up, wrapping a blanket around her. "Serge first thought of François when we were together—he knew he'd need somebody to play the part. I guess I considered that mine. When you're thirteen, you do that. So when I heard that he'd finally put François in the show, I suppose I resented her."

Sardonically: "Try again, Hannie."

She reddened. "She wasn't right for Serge."

"You really cared all that much?"

The hurt was heavy in her voice. "I was angry with him for a long time. But not yesterday."

"Was she there when you talked with Cailleau?"

She nodded. "He never introduced us and she ignored me, she wouldn't talk to me. Serge acted like he was ashamed of her or embarrassed."

Morley packed his toilet kit into his briefcase. "Any reason why?"

"Because she's a whore." He looked up at her, startled. There were red spots in her cheeks. "I told you Serge was lonely. I could understand the whore. Even at his age."

"Big of you." He glanced around the room to see if he'd forgotten anything. "What's she look like?"

Hannie yawned and got out of bed. She walked over to the window, trailing the blanket behind her, and pulled the drapes back to let the sun in. In the sunlight, Morley could see that her tan had started to fade. She looked more golden than brown.

"She's tall, trim—you saw that when she was on stage. She has strawberry-blonde hair, close cut. She spends a lot of time making up her face. And she smokes too much."

Morley was only half-listening now, his mind caught up with the Bureau. Usually he'd try and bypass it. He'd check in by phone when he had to, and at other times he'd use Louis as a go-between. Now he wanted something, and it was the worst possible time. The Bureau had been exposed and Tindemans would use that as an excuse not to cooperate.

He glanced up. Hannie was looking at him impatiently.

"I said I was going to see about Serge, arrange for the cremation."

Morley finished strapping on his shoulder holster and sat down at the desk. "I think we ought to talk."

Hannie wrapped the blanket around her shoulders and made herself comfortable on the bed.

"The people Cailleau claimed he smuggled into Belgium," he said. "According to him, they were mixed nationals. He said they were terrorists, that they had tried to kill him."

She went pale.

He smiled without humor. "You're a little too quick, Hannie. If there had been any strangers backstage, we would have heard about it when we were back there ourselves."

"You didn't believe him."

He didn't try to be diplomatic. "Cailleau was upset, he'd been drinking."

Hannie looked indignant. "Somebody bloody well killed him!"

"I'm more inclined to think it was somebody he knew than somebody he smuggled in."

"You want me to ask questions at the funeral service."

84

He shrugged. "I don't think you'll have to ask many. You'll probably hear more than you want to."

She looked uncertain, and he realized she wanted to do more. He thought again of sending her to the Théâtre de Vaudeville but changed his mind. If someone there had murdered Cailleau, it could be dangerous for Hannie to be nosing around.

"And you?" she said.

"Check in with the Bureau. Pay a visit to the Théâtre de Vaudeville, take a look at Cailleau's personal effects and find out what the people at the gendarmerie have on him. Then I'll think up some bone for London." He owed Simon a call, but there was no sense in making it before he had something substantial to offer.

"And I can spend the day worrying about the size and shape of the urn for Serge's ashes. I don't think he'd be much interested. I'm not."

Morley ignored her anger. "After the service, go to the Palais Berlaymont Building—that's headquarters for the European Economic Commission—and talk to the people trying to keep it afloat." He eyed her tan again. "You won't have any trouble getting people to talk to you. Find out why this week's meeting is so important and who's going to be there." It wouldn't be as risky as the theater; she'd be surrounded by ten thousand EEC workers.

"Sounds important," she said sarcastically.

He put his briefcase on the table and snapped open the latches to give the contents a last inspection.

"*If* what Cailleau told me is true, there's a group of terrorists in the city. London will be more than interested. So will I. Question is: Who's the target?" He glanced up at her. "I can't believe it was Serge, Hannie. More likely, it's the finance ministers." He still didn't believe it, but the important thing was, she might.

"I'm sorry," she said stiffly.

He closed the case and put on his mac. He started to say more, then thought better of it. She was twenty years old, she was going to live forever.

"I suppose everything stopped being exciting for you a long time ago." She hesitated. "Was I right last night? That you want to prove yourself?"

She invited more confidences than a psychiatrist. "The last time I was in Brussels somebody almost killed me. I'd like to know who, I'd like to find him."

"You want to die with your boots on," she said. Then she caught the expression on his face. "That was thoughtless of me."

He shrugged. When you were her age, you spent a lot of time being clever.

"You're partly right. I don't want to go on the disability list. I don't want to go out that way." And then he hated himself for being so open with her. It was the hospital Morley talking, the Morley who'd had to be fed, who couldn't go to the bathroom without help.

He stopped at the door. "One more thing—get a room at Cailleau's pensione for tonight—what's its name? The commune police seldom check Dutch and American passports anymore, but somebody might come around here asking about us. I'd just as soon nobody knew where we were. And pick up my flight bag downstairs; I'll have Louis bring it over." He hesitated. "Don't tell Louis where we're going today—he talks."

"Coffee, tea or milk," she mimicked, straight-faced.

"That's right, Hannie," he said gently. "It's all a game—until somebody gets hurt."

Outside in the morning drizzle he realized for the first time that he genuinely liked her.

What was worse, he was worried about her.

nine

$\mathbf{W}$ITHIN A FEW minutes, the drizzle had turned into rain, adding to Morley's impatience. He lingered for a while on the far side of the street, idly glancing in shop windows. The reflections were streaked and watery but he had no difficulty making out the small, four-story brick building that housed the Brussels Bureau. Avenue Louise itself was as fashionable as he remembered, though construction cranes and half-completed highrises spoiled the air of aging chic.

By the second shop window, he had memorized the block: the scattering of hunched, gray buildings that had been old when Louis was still in diapers, the new towers of marble and glass that would have been just as much at home in Manhattan or São Paulo, a few shoppers bundled up against the chill and fat businessmen, red-cheeked and panting, hurrying to catch a tram.

The corner was dominated by the huge world headquarters of ITT. The glass-walled monolith towered in the mist, the symbol of an occupied Brussels, a victim of the new co-prosperity sphere. A maroon Bentley with Community license plates was drawn up in front. Another Eurocrat or foreign minister called up before the chairman of the board, he mused.

For two hundred years, Brussels's most memorable attraction had been the statue of a small boy gleefully pissing in a public fountain. Now it was glass, concrete and steel towers dedicated to foreign corporations. Like God himself, they were everywhere, and they could buy out Belgium with their petty cash.

He paused at a window featuring a display of expensive fur and studied the other buildings across the parkway, their reflections muted by the ermine and sable. The one which housed the Bureau, a somewhat sedate-looking residence, was almost lost in the drizzle. While he watched, a passerby who remembered yesterday's headlines glanced at the building curiously, then bent his head against the rain and scurried past.

Morley started to shiver inside his mac. The dampness was getting to him, his bad leg already stiffening. He started walking to the corner, trying to hide his limp. A movement in the mezzanine window of a fashionable *chasseur* shop two doors down suddenly caught his eye. A heavyset man in an Alpine hat examining a rifle had swung it up to his shoulder. The small hump of the telescopic sight had caught a reflection as he aimed it toward the workers raking wet leaves in the parkway. Now the rifle wavered and rose slightly. It was leading him.

He froze in the middle of the street. For a moment he felt nothing except the tingling in the tip of his own trigger finger, then he caught himself straining to catch any slight movement on the part of the distant marksman.

The customer in the window absently lowered the rifle, waved casually at him and turned away, probably handing the gun to a smiling clerk and commenting on the exquisite engraving on the hand-wrought Belgian stock and barrel.

Morley swore, glanced at his watch and quickened his pace toward the brownstone. He was just another eager businessman who had shown up early for his appointment and spent a few minutes too long with the window displays. Only he didn't feel very convincing. The amateur marksman had thrown him. For a moment he was sure somebody set him up, that he had been followed. Paranoia again. But the anger at finding himself so helpless had also turned out to be useful. It had drowned out the pain in a leg that had threatened to go out from under him completely.

The huge varnished doors were recessed, giving him some slight protection against the downpour. He pressed the top button beside the name Euro Technical Consortium and waited. The speaker finally crackled: *"Qui là?"*

"Morley."

There was a sharp click and he spun the ornate knob and slipped inside. The voice had been lower, curter than he remembered. He wondered if JoJo was having a late breakfast, then changed his mind. The accountant was too cheap to eat out, he probably brown-bagged it.

The empty lobby smelled of disinfectant. He limped across the brown tiles, avoiding the slippery spots, and when the elevator didn't respond to the call button, began slowly climbing the newly carpeted stairs. It was harder walking on a thick rug than it was on tile or concrete.

He paused on the third floor landing to catch his breath, then saw why the lift hadn't responded. The cage's folding gate had been jammed open with an umbrella. The matron who owned it was just coming down the hall, clutching a leash with a whippet straining at the end of it. He smiled a tired *"Bonjour."* She stared through him, yanked the hound into the open cage and slammed the gate shut behind her.

He struggled up the last flight, remembering the long-simmering resentment of the building's other tenants for the strangers who ran the all-hours business on the upper floor. The story in the papers must have been the last straw.

He knocked on the Bureau door and the peephole flipped open, then winked shut. *"Voilà."* The door swung wide and Louis was standing in front of him, a shade too quick to take his briefcase and wrap a welcoming arm around his shoulder. Behind the big man was a laser printer and several computer operators. None of the operators bothered to look up.

"How were the marionettes?"

"As good as everybody says." He shrugged away from Louis and started to unbutton his mac. "Where's JoJo?" The gnome-sized accountant usually answered the buzzer and covered the door. He never said more than " *'Allo,* " but Morley had come to expect him. JoJo was as much a part of the Bureau as the travel posters on the walls or the whisper of the laser printer.

"The gout. He'll be back tomorrow or the next day." Louis's heavy eyebrows arched slightly. "Myself, I think it was the newspapers."

Morley followed Louis down the long hallway to the kitchen. Some things had changed, and then he remembered that he hadn't come around the last time he had been in Brussels. *That* visit had ended too quickly. The Bureau itself was nearly empty: two women busily keyboarding, a thin man in his thirties with a green eyeshade studying the printer output, and several girls packing files and supplies in cartons. They were getting ready to move.

In the kitchen, Louis's unofficial office, Morley sat down at the small table while Louis made coffee. The red enamel pot looked ridiculously dainty in the big man's hands.

"Yesterday was too much for you?" Louis's eyes were as searching as a specialist's, his attitude as professionally solicitous.

"No, yesterday was not too much for me," Morley said sarcastically. He leaned back in his chair, trying to hide his relief at finally being able to take the weight off his left leg.

Louis found two uncracked cups and set them on the table. "Tell me about the marionettes, Neal." He was half-smiling in anticipation.

Morley started to describe François, then found himself reliving the afternoon at the Théâtre de Vaudeville, once again seeing the life-sized dummy stroll casually across the stage.

"And then?" Louis had been hanging on every word.

Morley opened the refrigerator to search of the canned milk, fending off Louis before the big man could help.

"Cailleau never finished." He frowned. "Read something besides comic books and skin magazines, Louis—you'll never get to be Chief if you don't." He lightened his coffee with a trace of milk and swirled a mouthful of it as if he were tasting wine. One of Louis' virtues was his ability to make Belgian coffee so strong that even he had to cut it. "He was five minutes into his act when he caught an ice-pick behind his ear. Nothing very original."

He stretched out his leg, keeping it straight to see if that would help. From where he was sitting, he could see across into the next building where a fat, middle-aged woman was ironing. The board was set up so that she had a good view of the back office.

Louis sat down and stirred four cubes of sugar into his coffee, turning it into a dark-brown syrup. He pointed with his sticky spoon at the window behind him. "She's been at it for weeks. All day, all night—so long as anybody's here."

"She's your competition, Louis—all Belgian and a mile wide." He was suddenly distracted by the flowery silk scarf looped loosely around Louis' thick neck. He had seen it before, a long time ago, but it hadn't been on Louis. It wasn't Louis' style, it didn't go with his old wool cap or ravelling sweater.

Louis noticed his interest and fingered the material proudly. "All silk. Rose Marie gave it to me."

Morley remembered Falk's widow as a thin, apprehensive woman constantly fingering her cameo brooch. She wouldn't have had anything to do with Louis. Besides, Falk hadn't even been cremated yet, and it was too early for Rose Marie to start giving away his clothes.

"Nice."

"He left lots more in his office."

That explained the scarf. Louis had copped it the moment he was sure Falk was cold.

Louis sipped at his coffee and stared innocently at him over the lip of the cup. "Monsieur Cailleau must have had a lot he wanted to get off his chest."

Louis was usually more adept. "Not enough." Morley changed the subject. "How do you like Tindemans?" He realized he wasn't doing any better.

A shrug. "As well as most."

Louis actually meant not as good as most, Morley thought. Leon Tindemans was a pinch-faced, middle-aged American of Belgian descent who naturally resented anyone who considered him incompetent. Which meant Tindemans resented him a lot. Louis asked him about Cailleau again and Morley helped himself to more coffee and entertained Louis with a brief description of Don Quixote and Henry VIII.

He had just finished his coffee and was about to push Louis for more gossip when Tindemans came into the kitchen. The interim Chief looked surprised at seeing him. Louis got up to leave but Tindemans waved him back. "It's not private, Louis." He was a thin, nervous man and looked as if he had been born with the harried frown that had edged onto his face. "It's too bad that Brussels is so disagreeable this time of year."

"It disagreed with me even more the last time," Morley said.

"I remember." Tindemans had too much to do and obviously resented having to spend five minutes being social. "We've got our share of problems this time around." He pulled a chair over to the table while Louis hastily poured him a cup of coffee. "Almost like old times, eh, Neal? The hospital bit go all right?" Tindemans stared blandly at him and Morley knew he was comparing him to the man he had known six months before.

"The stitches don't show," he said dryly. He changed the subject. "I'm sorry about Falk."

Tindemans coughed and Morley waited for him to pull out a handkerchief and dab at his lips. He was thin enough to be consumptive.

"Every war has its casualties, Neal." Then, stiffly: "His widow will be well taken care of."

"What happened to Jan?" Did anybody at all care about Falk?

"We're looking into it."

Tindemans drummed his fingers on the table top, anxious to get back to whatever he had been doing but too curious to make his excuses and leave. Morley knew Tindemans had been briefed on his assignment in Brussels but, like Simon, Tindemans probably suspected that he was up to something more. Tindemans's only real concern was just how much of a problem he might be.

"The newspapers, Leon. They're still a nuisance?"

Tindemans flinched. "We've been preempted by the European Union meeting. I can't say I'm sorry." Something was making a clacking sound in the background. Louis was playing with a small wooden acrobat that did somersaults when you squeezed the two slats from which it hung. Tindemans frowned and Louis looked guilty and slid the toy back on the counter.

Morley half-smiled. "United Europe in trouble again?"

Tindemans looked sour. "Don't laugh, Neal—the Common Market's going under almost as fast as the dollar. The only way the Community will agree on anything is for the United States to oppose it." He broke off. "But I forgot—politics isn't your strong point."

"Who's going to be the next Chief?"

"I can't say." There was a bitterness in Tindemans' voice, and Morley had a glimpse of a man who was dangerously tired of being number two. "It's still up in the air. For the moment, I'm running things."

Louis was playing with the squeeze acrobat again. It wouldn't be long before the big man broke it.

"They may not bring in anybody from outside this time," Tindemans said, his eyes hopeful. "It would make more sense to promote somebody on the scene. You might have to deal with me next time, Neal." At the last minute, he tried to make a joke out of it but the spite still showed.

"They'll know who to bring in," Morley murmured.

Tindemans colored and stood up, glancing at his watch. "I'm sorry I don't have more time. We're moving and there's a lot to do."

"I need to go through some records," Morley said. "Ones from six months ago."

"You need records," Tindemans repeated. There was a subtle change in his attitude. He could deal with somebody who wanted something. His voice suddenly became crisp, authoritarian. "You didn't choose the most convenient time. I told you we were moving."

"Just tell me where they are and I'll get out of your hair."

Tindemans pursed his lips, his voice frosty. "You're not in a position to demand anything, Neal." He paused, unable to control his resentment. "You should have come here the last time you were in Brussels, it might have saved you a good deal of grief. As I recall, you were under orders to check in, but you preferred to do your usual solo routine. It's too bad about the hospital, but frankly, you invited it."

Tindemans had come a long way from the obsequious paper shuffler of six months ago. "The records," Morley reminded him. "I want to see them." Louis looked nervously from one to the other, afraid he might be forced to take sides.

"I don't know if there are any records about you, we're not in the same business," Tindemans said coldly. "If we've anything at all, they're probably in the library. Louis can show you; you haven't been here often enough to know the way."

"I'm going to miss Falk," Morley said casually.

Tindemans stared, then turned on his heel and walked out.

"You should have scratched his back, Neal," Louis said. He looked worried.

"You scratch it," Morley said angrily. Tindemans wasn't the type to do anybody any favors. And he hadn't even asked about Cailleau, hadn't asked what Cailleau had wanted to talk about. If it had been anybody but Tindemans, that's the first thing they would have asked.

The refrigerator had stopped its humming and he was caught up in the sudden silence. It was too quiet; there should have been some noise from outside.

Children. From the kitchen he used to be able to hear children in the playground below. He walked over to the window, frightening away a pigeon that was pecking along the sill. Below, the raw earth where the slides and swings had sat a year ago had been scooped out for still another foundation. It was a poor trade; he missed hearing the kids.

There was a sharp snap and he spun around to see the acrobat collapsed in Louis' fist and a look of surprise on his face.

"When does the European Union meeting start?

Louis flipped the broken toy into a nearby garbage can.

"In a few days. You should have been nicer to Leon, Neal."

"You be nice. He's your boss, not mine." His leg was throbbing and he could feel the beginnings of a headache. He tried to keep the anger out of his voice. "Who's your third-rate expert in charge of the files?"

Louis looked sullen. Morley wasn't being very nice to him, either. "We've got a new man since you were here last. I'll show you."

Morley followed him out into the hall and down two doors, then turned a corner into a stuffy room choked with technical journals from a dozen different countries, a wall of file cabinets and a collection of dusty Belgian glass and Val Saint Lambert crystal owls.

Blinking at him from behind a desk full of computer print-outs, either coughing or laughing—he wasn't sure which—was *Docteur* Taca.

ten

LOUIS STARTED TO introduce them but Morley cut him short. "We've met."

He left the big man floundering and limped over to the antique desk. Taca ignored him, making a show of picking up a small china cup and handing it to Louis. "On your way to the kitchen," he said firmly. He was treating Louis like he was a busboy at Comme chez Soi, Morley thought. Louis started for the door, then hesitated, looking uncertainly from one to the other.

"If you'll drop my things off at the Metropole, I'd appreciate it, Louis." He watched Taca carefully but there was no hint of surprise.

Louis reddened, realizing he had lost face.

"Sure, Neal."

After Louis had left, it was Taca who broke the silence, his eyes blinking behind his thick lenses. Morley couldn't read his expression; Taca wore his glasses like a mask.

"I assume you've written up your notes for the *Enquirer?*"

Morley glanced around at the book-lined walls. "Théâtre de Vaudeville seems like an odd place for you to have spent the afternoon."

Annoyance flickered behind the lenses. "Need I remind you that yesterday this was not a very conducive place to work? But that's beside the point. I knew Serge well and I *did* have my assignment. Tindemans knew."

"I didn't need help," Morley said in a tight voice.

Taca looked amused. "A matter of opinion, since poor Serge Cailleau is now one with the worms. But as I've told you, I'm an analyst. My computer and I gather data. We're concerned with the ebb and flow of commerce, the conduct of statesmen and scientists. . . ." He paused to select a Godiva chocolate from a small ceramic cannister. "We have different skills, Monsieur."

They were still fencing, Morley thought. Maybe Taca even considered himself in the running for Chief; the fat man had to be smart enough to know that Tindemans was a long shot. He set his briefcase against the foot of the desk and sat down, favoring his left leg.

Taca waved at the cannister. "Help yourself. Making chocolates is one of the things we Belgians do best."

Next to the cannister were a dozen small stacks of coins, neatly arranged in order of denomination. Morley guessed that was probably the first thing Taca did every morning, empty his pockets and count his small change. If he took one of Taca's expensive chocolates, the fat man would probably resent him the rest of the day.

"Since you seem to be the resident expert, why is this European Union meeting so important? Haggling over a common currency again?"

"You'd have to be European to understand—" Taca began.

Morley interrupted. "We're not talking about marionettes."

Taca looked offended. "I'm a European, Mr. Morley. I'm proud of the countries on this continent, I'm proud of their diversity. Having finally settled on a common currency, the next logical push will be for a common language, and after that we'll be just like you—a United States of Europe with all of your problems, only magnified a dozen fold. I hardly think that would be a utopia."

He sounded surprisingly bitter.

"Then that's it?"

Taca shook his head. He suddenly became pedantic, the professor tutoring the slightly dense pupil.

"It's much more involved than that. The former Soviets owe more than a hundred billion dollars, most of it to the West—and they need a great deal more in credits, trade and technology. Their eventual economic prosperity depends on securing a permanent trading relationship with the rest of the industrialized world. They've proposed another agreement with the European Community."

"And?"

Taca paused and took off his glasses to rub the pinch marks on his nose. "Their proposal will not be accepted. Nobody believes they have sufficient control to deal on a market-to-market basis. In time the commissioners would prefer bilateral agreements between the Common Market as a unit and individual countries of the former Soviet empire." He polished his glasses on a tissue, then slipped them back on. "Do you understand?"

"The Community is in the driver's seat."

Something glinted behind the spectacles. "Not really. The hearse, to build on your analogy, is a runaway, no one has a firm grip on the wheel. Despite all the talk, in reality Europe is still fragmented, more divided than ever. And in more trouble. Europe is overrun with inflation, unemployment, unable to deal with the influx of refugees or even legitimate immigration. Each country is barely hanging on, waiting for somebody else's recovery."

"Then it's a watershed conference, everybody will be there."

Taca nodded. "Every financial minister in the Market and quite a few from the non-member countries." He squinted at Morley through his thick lenses. "Your interest in European politics fascinates me, Monsieur. I had no idea the *Enquirer* was expanding its coverage. I'll be glad to help you, of course, though I'm afraid it will have to be another time." He fumbled for the chocolates without taking his eyes off him. "As you can see, we're quite busy."

"I'd like to look at a file," Morley said casually. "The one on Chimie Française, an import-export firm. The Bureau was involved in an operation with it six months ago."

Taca made a steeple of his fingers. "*You* were involved. The Bureau was not."

The *docteur* was going to make it difficult for him. "I want the file," he repeated coldly. "I wouldn't recommend you try and stop me from looking at it."

Taca shrugged. "Why should I stop you? Unfortunately I don't know whether there is such a file or not. That computer is down, and you saw the girls in the corridors filling the cartons. Almost all of our files are packed away for moving; some are even now in transit. There is no way in heaven or hell that we can take the time to unpack those boxes and search for six-month-old records. You can try again later, in a week or so, we should be in new quarters by then." He waved at the cabinets against the wall. "You can look if you wish, but they're all empty."

They were bundling off his past right before his eyes, and there wasn't a damned thing Morley could do about it.

"You didn't stay at the Hilton," Taca said suddenly. He let the statement float in midair.

"That's right. I didn't know you, why should I have told you where I was staying?" It was an effort for Morley to take his mind off the files and concentrate on what the fat man was saying.

"The clubs I mentioned," Taca said. "You might have enjoyed them." He stared at Morley, trying to gauge his reaction. "You left your bags with Louis. Perhaps you stayed with the girl?" His large eyes blinked in nearsighted scrutiny.

"Perhaps."

"I envy you your expense account."

Morley stood up, furious with himself for grunting with sudden pain when he put his weight on his left leg. "I've forgotten where the toilet is, *Docteur*. Could you show me?"

Taca looked annoyed. He took off his glasses again, polished them and dropped the tissue in the waste basket. He stepped out from behind the safety of his desk and led the way down the hall, sidling past the stacks of cartons.

"As I told you, we'll be moving soon. Over to Parc de Cinquantenaire, a still useful but less exposed address."

Taca took out a ring of keys and opened the washroom door. A moment later he stumbled across the tiles as the flat of Morley's hand caught him in the back. Morley kicked the door shut, his free hand slamming the lock home. His other hand was at Taca's neck, pinning him against the white-enameled wall.

"You hedged your bets and sent the kid to follow me, didn't you, you bastard!" In his mind's eye, he could still see Leather Jacket crumpled in the alley, blood pooling beneath his head.

Taca's glasses were askew, little bits of tissue still sticking to the hinges. His eyes were angry and frightened and his voice came out in short bursts of fury. "You knew there'd be a contact, yet you deliberately lied—"

Morley's voice was stone. "How the hell was I to know who you were? But *you* knew that I had a meeting with Cailleau—you know everything that happens here. What Tindemans doesn't tell you, Louis probably does. You knew who I was, fat man, but you never let on!"

For a second, a look of contempt brushed aside the fear on Taca's face. "Of course I knew—you were transparent, absurd. I had heard you were better."

Morley could feel his hand start to shake. "How is he?"

"The boy? He may be able to go back to the theater. Eventually. With luck he'll be able to manage as a prop man or a projectionist in a sex-film house. Your signature is indelible." He struggled once more, and Morley realized that the fat man's flab was partly muscle and remembered his surprise when he had first pumped Taca's hand. Taca was coughing again and Morley thought he was tiring, then realized it was laughter. "I trust you treated the girl better?"

Morley let him go and leaned against the sink. "I didn't need help," he repeated.

"Obviously. Not to handle poor Hans, at any rate. But you should have assumed you were covered. You were just out of the hospital, everyone knew that." Taca brushed the front of his suit and made a production of straightening his tie. "You were supposed to report here first. Did you fear ridicule after your last fiasco in Brussels?"

"I don't need a backup, least of all you."

"You need somebody. Otherwise this trip to Brussels will end more unfortunately than your last."

So London hadn't told them about Hannie. Thank God for small favors. He turned back to the sink. "Get the hell off my back, fat man."

His response encouraged Taca. "You're a relic from the seventies," he sneered. "Excess clogging the system."

"I'm sorry about your boy," Morley said sarcastically. "Given time, he might have made an interesting Sister." He regretted Leather Jacket, but he couldn't resist the barb.

He heard a shuffle and caught a glimpse of Taca's furious face in the mirror. He whirled, ducking the blow, and grabbed Taca by the necktie, yanking him forward and down until his face was an inch from the porcelain sink. In the same move, his other hand flipped on the hot water. The open faucet spurted steam, clouding the fat man's glasses so he was blind.

"Don't be an asshole, Doctor. You interfered once, don't try it again. Your boy has you to blame, not me."

He let go and Taca straightened up, swearing in French. The front of his shirt was soaked, his glasses dripping, the eyes behind them looking like pale, imprisoned goldfish. He took out his handkerchief and swabbed at his beet-red face. *"Cachon!"*

Morley bellied him up against the wall, his face close enough to Taca's so he could smell the fat man's sweat. "You knew about Cailleau, you knew about me. Tell me what else you know, fat man. What are the rumors?"

Taca's voice was thready, his words bubbling out. There were some rumors about a death squad, but there were always rumors about death squads—they had checked with G.I.S. . . .

Despite his anger, Morley grinned. Taca was a bureaucrat and loved acronyms. But to Morley *Gis Intervention Speciale*, the gendarmeries's counterterrorist squadron, would always be *Diane*—the old name the men in the squadron now avoided. Tired of jokes, they were sissies and not as macho as the legendary huntress. . . .

They had checked, Taca sputtered, and couldn't get a confirmation. Aside from that, he knew nothing. . . .

Morley backed off, leaving Taca huddled against the wall, shaking. *"Merde, cachon!"*

"So tell Tindemans." He turned to the mirror to smooth back his hair, watching Taca in the still-steamy glass.

"You have only one skill," Taca blurted, almost strangling on his anger. "It won't go very far, Monsieur!"

"It'll go far enough."

"I know all about you," Taca hissed. "The last time you were in Brussels, three men died. Two consular officials plus the head of an import-export firm."

"*He* went out too easily. And the consular officials were hit men, everybody knew that." The Bureau knew a lot more about it than he did, but apparently nobody was going to fill him in. And the Bureau records were out of his reach, at least temporarily.

Taca was regaining his composure. "You played both judge and jury, Monsieur. You delight in playing those roles."

Morley watched his own face in the mirror turn white. "If I hadn't, they would have asked for diplomatic immunity. And somebody would have granted it—for enough money."

"You think you can legislate morality?"

"The shit they were dealing wasn't heroin, it was poison. Nobody got high, they died."

He didn't tell Taca that stopping the flow of heroin had been a sideshow, that what they had really been trying to do was to stop the flow of money.

"You won't get any cooperation from us this time," Taca said, wiping his glasses with his handkerchief.

"Can you guarantee that?"

A sneer slipped over Taca's face. "Just what do you think you can do without us?"

Morley stepped over to the toilet, glancing up at the graffiti still faintly visible on the recently scrubbed enamel. The

States, Vietnam, Europe, Pompeii—the graffiti were identical no matter where you went. All of it could have been drawn by Louis.

"Piss," he said, pulling the worn wooden knob on the chain that hung from the water closet. "Piss and waste time with the Bureau and Diane."

A faint, sardonic bow. "Good luck, Monsieur."

"Don't forget to tell Tindemans," Morley said.

He stayed in the john after Taca had gone, soaking up the semidarkness and the quiet. He looked in the mirror once more. He had put on a lot of years in six months. Then he thought of Taca and reflected grimly that it wasn't Tindemans he had to go through to get at the files. It was really the computer analysts who were running the world.

He wiped his hands and straightened his tie. It wasn't until he reached the door that he realized he had made another mistake. He should've guessed it by the look of contempt Taca had given him as he left. It had been too easy to get the better of the fat man; there had been too much muscle under that bulk for him to have put Taca through the routine with so little effort.

Taca had been testing him, and now knew for sure what Louis and Tindemans had only suspected.

eleven

YESTERDAY, THE GLOSSIES in front of the
Théâtre de Vaudeville hadn't meant much to Morley. Today,
he recognized François' handsome, carefully painted features,
tailored silk suit and patent-leather riding crop from as far away
as the bookseller's. He noticed Leather Jacket in some of the
photographs, too, but it was François who held his attention.
The eyes that stared back at him were wide and inviting with a
promise of . . . what? He wondered what she was really like beneath the costume and the greasepaint. And what, if anything,
she could tell him about Cailleau and his fantasies. If they were
fantasies.

The rain had almost stopped, the only sound in the almost
deserted gallery the slow but steady dripping on the slick flagstones. He glanced at the book dealer thumbing through his
stock and the newsgirl staring off across the empty plaza. Nobody else was in sight. He tried the theater's doors until he
found one unlocked, then stepped inside.

"Bonjour?"
Nothing.
He could hear a high-pitched whine somewhere inside,

and walked into the lobby. At the far end, the elderly concierge was pushing a vacuum cleaner over the worn carpeting. He shouted again. The old man looked up and motioned for him to go outside, it was too early for the matinee. Morley frowned and didn't move, impatient with the old man and resenting the time he was going to have to spend with him.

The concierge tugged nervously at the yellow-white tufts on either side of his shiny scalp. The little ribbon Cailleau had mentioned was pinned high on the lapel of his smock; it had shriveled and darkened with age like a wilted flower. The old man didn't understand what he was saying.

He shouted again, motioning for the concierge to turn off the machine. The old man finally nodded, kicked the switch with his sandal and waved at the closed pay box and bar. He looked indignant. Morley guessed he only spoke Marollien, an archaic bastardization of French, Spanish, German and Flemish, incomprehensible to everyone but the commune's oldest residents.

"Cailleau . . ." He spoke slowly, hunching over and moving his fingers up and down as if he were working a puppet's strings. " . . . outside . . ." He pointed at the puzzled old man, then toward the front doors, making a gun with his thumb and forefinger. *"You . . ."*

The concierge smiled, showing teeth like yellow popcorn. He was excited now, the words spilling out in a torrent. The thugs were giants . . . pygmies . . . They spoke Arabic . . . Hebrew . . . Japanese. . . . They were dressed as Gypsies. . . . No, no, as Nazi SS . . . Morley didn't understand any of it.

He clapped the old man on the shoulder, nodded in deference to the greasy ribbon and walked backstage. A small, naked bulb gave off just enough light to show him the top of the stairs. Out front, he could hear some of the cast rehearsing. He'd get to them later.

The sound of the vacuum cleaner started again and he turned to watch the concierge try to manhandle the machine across the carpet. There was no way the old man could have scared off any terrorists. If they had wanted to kill Cailleau that day, they would have.

If there had been any terrorists to begin with. The truth probably was that the concierge and Cailleau had shared more than one bottle of wine that night. It must have been years since the old man had been able to distinguish between fantasy and reality.

He juggled the pieces in his mind, found no pattern and felt vaguely uneasy. He flicked the wall switch and walked slowly down the narrow steps, resting every fourth step. The muscles in his thigh were threatening to spasm again as they had that morning in the bathroom.

The dressing room was cold and dark, the day's grayness dulled even more by the film of cigarette smoke that coated the grimy window. He pulled on the light cord and studied the tiny cubicle bathed in the yellow glow. When he had first seen them yesterday, the marionettes had overwhelmed him with their *joie de vivre*. Now all he saw were painted bits of wood and odd remnants of cloth and metal—inanimate caricatures lifted from the theater and fables. What was it Taca had said about George Sand? That she imagined the souls of her puppets stirred when she slid her hands under their skirts? He had laughed at the image then, but today he couldn't shake the feeling that Cailleau's creations had died along with Cailleau.

He glanced around the room, his eyes locking on the table. Something was missing. He pulled open the drawer to check. The Luger was gone. The empty glass and the wine bottle were still there, along with yesterday's paper, but the only traces of the automatic were a few drops of oil that had soaked into the table top. There were a few more drops in the bottom of the drawer, bare except for three boxes of aspirin and cough drops and sleeping pills laid out as precisely as the marionettes perched atop the trunk.

He turned to the window, muscled it open and inhaled the chill air. The sash cord had frayed apart long ago, and he propped the window open with a stick he found on the sill. The crumpled pack of Caporals was gone, too. That and the Luger were the only things that seemed to be missing.

Whoever had taken them hadn't been from the police. And then: Hannie had said the girl who played François smoked too much.

Cailleau's loden coat still hung beside the door. He took it down and emptied the pockets, spreading the contents out on the table. Fingernail clippers, a pair of worn leather gloves, a folded sketch of a puppet's head inked on a bar napkin, a beer chit and a five-franc coin that rolled off the edge of the table before he could catch it.

That left only the trunk.

He picked up Don Quixote gently, remembering the over-protective look in Cailleau's eyes, and set him on the table. Then he raised the trunk lid, leaning it back against the wall. There were more puppets inside, along with thick balls of twine, wire, scraps of fabric, needles, thread, worn woodworking tools and a collection of yellowing sketches similar to the one he'd found in the loden coat. Under the sketches, the bottom of the trunk was filled with bundles of letters, some of them written on browning paper where the ink had faded almost to invisibility. He picked up one bundle and felt the edges crumble as he pulled it out. He touched the string that held the bundle together and it broke at the knot, leaving a faint stain beneath.

The letters were Cailleau's family history and went back three generations. He took out what looked like the most recent bundle, one held together by rubber bands. Hannie had written the first when she was seven years old. Her handwriting had grown more confident, more graceful with the years, but the letters had been written more hastily and less often. She had sent the last one a year ago—an almost formal note on Christmas.

At the other end of the trunk's bottom was a bulging pasteboard box stuffed with photographs. Most were old and faded, including a few daguerreotypes. But the picture that caught his eye was a three-shot dating from the war, taken when Brussels was an occupied city. Cailleau, another husky, dapper man and a third with bright, expressive eyes and a hesitant smile. They were leaning against a bar, their backs to several other young men in uniform—German uniforms. The trio's arms were locked around one another and they were clutching steins and mugging at the camera. Cailleau's hair was dark and unruly; a walrus moustache topped a schoolboy grin. The dapper man had wavy hair and showed a hint of arrogance in the way he stood. He was the serious one of the group.

It took Morley another moment before he recognized the third man, the one with the somewhat wan smile. Brussels and the Resistance were a long way from London. Moses had changed a lot since the war years.

Comrades in arms. The classic shot from every war.

He slipped the photograph into the bundle of Hannie's letters and pocketed them, then started to close the trunk. A letter shoved next to the side of the trunk kept the lid from closing. The paper was new, the ink was fresh; it had been written recently but not mailed. He opened it. A love letter, and a graphic one at that. Written to Cailleau by someone named Bernadette. He shrugged and pocketed it as well.

He closed the trunk and started for the door, brushing past a rack holding a dozen marionettes. He automatically felt the texture of the costumes, then tugged at the strings of one of them. The puppet waved a palsied hand and jerked a wooden foot.

It was no use. There was no vitality, no real animation when he plucked the strings. No one else would ever make Cailleau's creations come alive.

He paused in the doorway for a last look. Cailleau's world, strangely old-fashioned and nostalgic, preserved in the bottom of a trunk and staring out at him from the painted faces of the puppets. What was it Taca had called Cailleau?

One of the last great Europeans.

He sniffed the air and glanced again at the table where the Luger had been. Somebody had been there, chain-smoking. Somebody close enough to Cailleau to be frightened. Somebody who had grabbed the gun and run.

The girl?

Probably.

One final look, and the sense of unease he had been fighting flooded in. Maybe the concierge was a crazy old man, but Cailleau hadn't been. Cailleau had been able to bestow life on bits of cloth and wood and dabs of paint. And the letters and photographs had proved he had compassion and courage and a gritty sense of reality. And Cailleau had certainly been able to see through him. *"The situation is too dangerous for anyone who is not . . . well."*

What had Cailleau known that he hadn't told anyone, not even his old friend in London? And why did it have to be told in person?

Somebody had put a worn tape of "It's Three O'Clock in the Morning" on a player. Morley could hear it as he climbed the sagging steps. He rested a minute at the top, listening to the shuffling sounds onstage. There were more lights on now, the glow spilling into the wings. He walked to where he could get a clearer view. A couple were rehearsing: The man and woman and their trained dogs. The poodles saw him first, arching their backs in curiosity as they pranced about on their hind legs.

The woman saw him, too. Her face remained cautiously blank but she ground her hips more provocatively as she danced with one of the dogs. Her partner, thin and bony with slicked-down black hair, had his back to the stairs. Morley couldn't hear what he said, but it was obvious that the woman didn't like it. He suspected her grinds were as much because of boredom with her partner as a desire to taunt him.

The man suddenly sensed that someone was there and turned, scowling. His white shoes and trousers were dusty and stained, his pink, wide-collared shirt and navy blue ascot wrinkled. Closer up, Morley could tell his hair had been dyed. He was puffing.

"*Oui, oui, Monsieur.*" The man grabbed the collar of a terrier trying to hump the bitch alongside him and petted him fondly. His eyes were bloodshot and Morley guessed from the way he squinted that he wore contact lenses. He managed a smile—Morley didn't look official—and yelled: "You like the family, yes?"

Morley stepped out of the shadows. "How did you know I spoke English?"

A touch of smugness softened the wrinkles around the tired smile "Your shoes. Americans always have big feet. Also, I heard you yesterday—with the girl in the lobby." He winked. "You left together, yes?"

"Edo, let someone else talk." The woman was miffed at being left out. "You were a friend of Serge's?" Her voice was nasal with a harsh Dutch accent.

"We understood each other."

The man sighed. "There will never be another Serge. He had a touch, a magic. . . ."

The woman threw a biscuit to one of the dogs, which caught it in midair. "Many have tried, Monsieur, none ever came close." She made a valiant attempt to sound sultry. "In everything, he was *special.*"

She was ten, fifteen years younger than Edo, though the flesh on her arms had started to sag and she had the beginnings of a double chin. She struck Morley as a little desperate, as tired of her partner as she was of the dogs.

Edo shot her a veiled glance, his smile forced. Edo didn't like the way she was playing up to him. "Tomorrow afternoon the troupe presents a tribute, a memorial to Serge—perhaps you'll come?"

"Perhaps." He hesitated. "The girl who worked with Cailleau . . ." He let the sentence dangle.

"Bernadette." The woman supplied the name in a sharp, bitter voice. Edo looked uncomfortable.

"You don't like her either," Morley said to Edo.

"We would never say anything when Serge was alive. . . ."

"But you don't."

Edo looked down at the boards. "No."

The woman this time, scornful: "Without Serge, what can she do?" She had lost interest in him, misinterpreting his questions about Bernadette. She turned back to the dogs.

"Where's she working now?"

Edo glanced at the woman's back, then shrugged again. "I don't know, some sex show, probably."

"Were you here the first time someone tried to kill Cailleau?"

The muscles in Ego's face twitched with the memory. "No, no, but we heard about it from the concierge." He shook his head, puzzled. "In this business, there is sometimes jealousy, sometimes passion—but nobody was jealous of Serge." He glanced at the woman, who had moved out of earshot. "As for passion, Monsieur, the years take care of that. The eyes are bigger than the stomach, no?"

"Perhaps his politics . . ."

A flutter of something that vanished quickly. Flatly: "*None of us is political.*"

"He'd just come back from Bulgaria, Romania. . . ."

The woman started up the tape player, then walked back to them. She had decided that something about him was definitely fishy. "So?"

"He was a *fluchthelfer* during the Second World War. Perhaps he still was."

"The police asked us about that," she said easily. "And a gendarme. We told them we knew nothing." She wanted to get back to rehearsal and caught Edo's eye, nodding toward the dogs. Her voice was a dismissal. "Come to the tribute, Monsieur. Perhaps you'll understand Cailleau better then." She clapped her hands for the poodles to start walking around the ring again.

"Have it easy," Edo smiled weakly. He whistled to the terrier.

"Sure," Morley said to the air. "Take a good time."

twelve

CAPTAIN WILLY VAN DEN HAUTE tapped his fingers on the desk and stared at Morley for a long moment. Finally: "Death was instantaneous. There were no fingerprints on the pick, as you undoubtedly guessed. He had no enemies, at least none of whom we're aware. No strangers were seen backstage, but then, nobody was looking for any. The police interviewed the entire cast as well as everybody who worked at the Théâtre de Vaudeville. Nobody saw anything, nobody heard anything. Obviously somebody was lying."

Even in the warmth of the Captain's office, with the hiss of the radiator in the background, Morley could feel the dampness of another Brussels winter. Already his muscles were aching.

"Obviously."

He glanced away from van den Haute to study a curling black-and-white photograph of a boy about eight or nine years old—it could have been van den Haute himself at that age. Next to it was a model 1924 Lancia Lambda in a small plastic display case. Among the memorabilia was a framed letter from President Ronald Reagan to *"Willy van den Haute, Capitaine du Gen-*

darmerie, Bruxelles" thanking him for his cooperation during the writer's recent visit to his great city. The letter was discolored around the edges.

Van den Haute pushed back his chair and stood up to peer out the window. Outside, the streetlamps were already on, small halos in the mist.

"Monsieur Cailleau was your only assignment?"

"It was minor." He was finding it difficult to look at van den Haute. Six months ago the head of Diane had struck him as middle aged, his growing paunch hidden by a loose wool sports coat and baggy flannel slacks. He had seemed soft and out of focus, old before his time. Today, his bushy moustache was carefully trimmed, his thinning brown hair recently barbered; he had shed some weight and his pants were neatly creased. He seemed almost excessively healthy. Well fed. Young.

It was all relative, Morley reminded himself.

"None of your assignments are minor, Monsieur. I find it hard to believe that London would use a hammer to swat a fly. Besides, we have our own dossier. Monsieur Cailleau had been inactive for years." Van den Haute looked expectantly at Morley, who said nothing.

The Captain sighed and put on a pair of reading glasses to examine a folder on his desk. "Which leaves the case of one Hans Eberle, age twenty-six, who was found badly beaten in an impasse not far from from rue des Chandeliers. He was one of Théâtre de Vaudeville's regular troupe; next week he was to become an assistant stage manager. He weighs approximately sixty-six kilos—not exactly an impressive victory for whoever beat him." He looked thoughtfully at Morley. "He gave us a description of his assailant."

His status in Brussels had changed, Morley realized; the last time they hadn't asked him for explanations. "He was tailing me and got too close. I didn't know why or what he was carrying."

Van den Haute pushed back in his swivel chair. "Following you was not the wisest thing to do. Neither was what transpired next. No weapon was found on his person, nor were there any indications that he even carried one—no shoulder harness, no shells, no telltale wear on his clothing where he might have carried a pistol. We found a pocket knife in the street but, of course, he denies that it was his. Your prints were on it." The silence in the room was heavy. "Hans Eberle is a Belgian citizen, Monsieur."

"A *good* citizen, no doubt." The Captain hesitated and Morley added: "Diane pulled his records?"

A sour smile. "G.I.S., please. Not the best of citizens. Not the worst. Minor burglaries, some confusion over who had signed a check. A renter, I believe the English call them. Older men befriended him."

"And he paid them visits when they weren't home?"

Van den Haute slid the sheet of paper on his desk back into its folder. The Captain wouldn't declare him persona non grata without being able to give London good reason, Morley thought. And Leather Jacket wasn't good enough.

Van den Haute stole a glance at his desk clock, then placed his fingers behind his head and leaned back in his chair. Belgian gendarmes liked to imagine themselves as more democratic than the French, stricter than the Germans. But Morley had the feeling that the Captain had more on his mind than deciding which role to play, that his casual air was forced.

"Belgium is a small country, Monsieur, little larger than your province of Vermont. All the great nations of the world guaranteed our neutrality a century-and-a-half ago with the result that we were the only nation in Western Europe to have been occupied in both wars." He stared at Morley, his fleshy face

117

creased and grim. "We're still occupied. The Russians are here, the English are here, the French are here, you Americans are here. And now, the floodgates are opening. . . . It's very crowded here. Why do *you* remain in Brussels, Monsieur? The puppeteer is dead, he can tell you nothing more."

"I want to know who killed him. And why."

"Really?" Van den Haute was amused. "God forgive us our petite white lies." There was a discreet knock on the door and a lanky cadet came in with a silver coffee service. He set it on the edge of the desk. "You enjoy our coffee, I remember." The Captain was suddenly cordial. He offered the cream and sugar, protesting when Morley waved them aside. "Only the condemned drink it black." He unwrapped several cubes of sugar and dropped them into his cup. "That's all, Jules, you may leave."

After the door clicked shut, van den Haute sighed once again and started leafing through another folder on his desk.

"Neal Morley, attached to an intersquad unit of various nationalities assigned to Brussels seven months ago. As I recall, your status was that of an action agent. The object of the squad was to interdict the monies flowing to a network of terrorist organizations from a drug ring—seize bank accounts, investigate contributions by wealthy businessmen, look into so-called 'laundering' schemes, that sort of thing."

He took a sip of the coffee.

"Simple enough. A team of accountants and lawyers along with—to use an American expression—some 'muscle.' We offered our complete cooperation. Within a month, three men were dead. You were responsible for that." He put down the cup and lightly tapped his desk blotter with a pencil. "Why?"

"They were smuggling heroin, the money went to the network. It was important to stop it."

"I'm aware of that. We would have been glad to stop it—

did stop it once and for all after you had left. But you did not first come to us with your information. You executed those involved." Another six taps of his pencil. "Again, I'm curious why, Monsieur. I would have asked you then, but you were in no condition to provide an answer."

"I recognized them," Morley said tightly. "From the border camps in Pakistan. They were recruiting there."

Van den Haute's eyebrows arched. "And?"

"And I knew them from 'Nam—a lot of men died because of them."

"They were an obsession of yours, I understand." He paused, thoughtful. "Monsieur Morley, six months ago you had some business in Brussels and you all but died. More to the point, you were an embarrassment, one that G.I.S. does not intend to suffer again." His voice was silky. "I would be distressed if I thought you were in Brussels to pick up where you left off."

"That would be foolish, wouldn't it?" Morley murmured.

"More than you might think. Your people investigated and decided the incident was closed. We investigated as well and the incident *is* closed."

Morley didn't say anything.

Van den Haute read resistance in his silence. "You disagree, Monsieur?" He looked severe again. "Let us go over it again—briefly, there is still much for me to do today. Six months ago you were responsible for the deaths of two junior officials at the French Embassy as well as the head of a small import-export firm, Chimie Francaise. They were trafficking in a rather poor grade of heroin." He paused. "I appreciate that there are times you can do things others cannot, but there were diplomatic repercussions. You should have told us."

"The truth is I shouldn't have told the gendarmerie a goddamned thing," Morley said bitterly. "I spent six months in the hospital because of it."

Van den Haute went back to tapping on the table. "You assume an informer here. Not so, Monsieur—we checked our duty roster very closely after your unfortunate incident. But that was yesterday. For today, remember that we will not tolerate such actions again." He took a sip of his coffee, frowning when he realized it had cooled off. "I called London after you were sent to the hospital. They told me about your tour in Vietnam and that you had been operating in the border camps."

There was a sudden gentleness in van den Haute's voice.

"The war in Indochina is best forgotten, Monsieur, let it rest in peace. Forget your personal vendettas. In any event, there is nobody left for you to talk to."

Which wasn't quite true. There was Tindemans at the Bureau and van den Haute here at Diane—but neither one was willing to tell him anything.

"There were more involved than just the three," Morley said tightly. "They had friends. And they're still here."

Van den Haute shrugged. "Even the lowest among us has friends. That doesn't mean they were in the same profession."

"You intend to expel me?" It didn't matter whether London called him back or van den Haute sent him; in either case he would be going back.

The Captain considered it for a moment. "No, I don't think so. But I have more to do than watch you, there is the Conference to worry about. The overall security, the personages who must be assigned bodyguards . . ." He lowered his voice to a confidential level. "To be frank, the case of Monsieur Cailleau has us worried. I do not agree that his was a minor assignment."

Morley shrugged. "Cailleau was an old man who drank too much."

"You think so? He was neither too old nor too drunk to smuggle in a team of six terrorists, Monsieur."

Morley could feel the sweat suddenly pop out on his forehead. "You're sure of that?"

"Of course," van den Haute said, his voice smug. "One of them is in the annex."

He had made another mistake, Morley thought. He hadn't wanted to believe Cailleau's story, not even when he had plunged to the stage with an ice pick sticking out the back of his neck. If he had believed it, he would have had to tell London and they would have sent in somebody else. Now his luck had run out and his brief tour of duty was over. The only person who would feel as badly about it as he did would be Hannie.

Then he realized van den Haute wasn't sure of himself, that the Captain was fishing. He was the last person to have talked to Cailleau, which meant that he was too valuable to be sent back. At least, not yet.

Van den Haute was staring at him.

"You look startled, Monsieur."

Morley cleared his throat.

"He was an old man, I didn't think he was capable of it."

"So you misjudged him. That surprises me."

The old Morley wouldn't have misjudged Cailleau. But then, London would have let the old Morley stay in Brussels once he'd informed them of new developments.

The Captain leaned closer to Morley, his face all angles.

"You did not contradict me a moment ago when I said that Monsieur Cailleau had been inactive. I was hoping you would volunteer vital information. I am disappointed that you didn't. But I am not fencing now, Monsieur. It's important that I know what Cailleau told you. Most particularly, who were they?"

"Cailleau said he had brought in seven—a Japanese woman and a Slav, the rest were Egyptians and Sudanese, several Iraqis."

Van den Haute relaxed back into his chair. "And what would that mean to you, Monsieur?"

Morley reddened. Van den Haute was leading him through it like a teacher would lead a pupil.

"That he had brought in a hit squad of broad-based radicals." He'd considered it before and dismissed it because he'd dismissed Cailleau himself.

Van den Haute suddenly looked haunted.

"You recall the bombing of your government's building in Oklahoma, Monsieur? I have nightmares about half of Brussels being treated the same. There are too many tempting targets here—the European Union meeting is only one. And I'm responsible for the safety of the city."

"Cailleau mentioned no explosives—"

Van den Haute turned impatient. "It's a question of will, not technology. You know that, Monsieur. Any imbecilic farm boy could blow Brussels sky high with a load of fertilizer and motor oil. No secret is involved."

"There's the matter of money," Morley said slowly. "The Russians aren't sponsors anymore and the Saudis have clamped down on private citizens contributing to the cause. And the other Arab governments have frozen any obvious assets. They need money and their usual sources have dried up." Van den Haute nodded slightly and Morley pressed his advantage. "They need to live, they need supplies—even fertilizer and motor oil cost money, and they need contacts." He paused. "And to corrupt security is expensive."

Van den Haute looked grim. "So you think there may be a paymaster right here in Brussels. You would like that, wouldn't you, Monsieur? A link between the old and the new. We will consider it, but I'm afraid it has all the earmarks of an obsessive mind."

Morley actually hadn't given it that much thought until now. He made a mental note to give it a good deal more.

Van den Haute went back to his coffee cup.

"What else did the puppeteer have to say?"

"Nothing—" And then Morley backtracked, picking up on an earlier comment by van den Haute. He was anxious to co-operate now; his stay in Brussels depended on it.

"Cailleau said there were seven. He was definite about that."

Van den Haute shrugged. "Our sources are quite reliable."

"What sources?"

"Monsieur Morley . . ." The Captain had a way of pre-tending that his patience had been stretched to the breaking point. He did it quite well and Morley assumed the ploy must be effective since he used it so often.

He waited until van den Haute started to fidget in the silence, then said: "A mutual exchange of information. That's part of the agreement."

"There is that information which is *confidentiel*, vital to the state."

If the Captain wasn't willing to deal on equal terms, then there was no point in trying to deal at all. But if he walked out now, he'd be on a plane to London before evening. Morley was still debating it when van den Haute changed his mind and said, "The Russians. They say six."

Morley hid his surprise. "What else do they say?"

"That they're not sure these are Islamic extremists. They think the team may be a successor to the old Baader-Meinhof gang, with links to most of the other groups—the Popular Front for the Liberation of Palestine General Command, the Japanese Red Army, even the Red Army Faction. You remember, they blew up the limousine of Alfred Herrhausen, chief executive of the Deutsche Bank and right hand man to Chancellor

Kohl. Very sophisticated, that one—a bomb attached to a bicycle parked along Herrhausen's route and detonated when his Mercedes broke a laser beam trigger."

"Do you believe them?"

Van den Haute shrugged. "Who knows? Their intelligence sources aren't what they used to be."

"When did they tell you?"

"Yesterday. Various apartments in Paris have already been searched. Also in Tel Aviv and Zurich. Nothing was found, though just an hour ago, Paris expelled three members of the Iraqi embassy staff."

Van den Haute was sweating it, Morley thought. Which meant that he could stay in Brussels as long as he was helpful.

"You have a prisoner." It was a statement, not a question.

Van den Haute's eyes lidded. "I've told you quite enough, Monsieur."

"When did you pick him up?"

Van den Haute looked like he regretted having mentioned the terrorists at all. "Four days ago. A boutique on boulevard Anspach. We should have them all soon."

Morley's mind raced. The Captain couldn't be all that confident. For years London had poured sophisticated equipment, training and money—especially money—across this desk to shore up the antiterrorist unit. But Diane didn't have the experience of the squads in France or Israel or for that matter, Italy.

"Can I see him?"

"You won't discover anything we don't already have in transcript. He's like a squeezed orange."

"How long's your transcript?"

Sarcastically: "I appreciate your offer of help, Monsieur." Van den Haute studied a memorandum for a moment, then glanced up. "The prisoner talks very little, though yesterday he slipped and identified Cailleau. He calls himself Karim Arif. An Iraqi. Very young. Interpol has some information on him. Not much." He handed the sheet of paper to Morley. "One of the idealistic rich, a catspaw. One more day and he'll lead us to his friends."

Morley doubted that the Iraqi would lead Diane anywhere. Arif's was the most exclusive of clubs. New members were old, proven friends. None of them talked easily.

He glanced again at the letter from Reagan that hung on the wall and wondered if van den Haute missed the good old days of escorting politicians around town. Once, he remembered, the Captain had reminisced about the years he had been in charge of the city's traffic department. He had liked the job— he could see the results, count the day's traffic accidents and compare them to the year before. This time, keeping score might not be so easy or so pleasant.

"What happened to Falk?" Morley asked. "The most I got out of Tindemans was that he was checking into it."

Van den Haute shrugged. "For Monsieur Tindemans, 'checking into it' means that he called me. Falk was a friend?"

"He could have been. Maybe he was."

"He had his enemies. Personal as well as professional; I think this was the former—the bomb was amateurish. Monsieur Falk had a taste for other men's wives."

Morley didn't remember him as the type, but then, he'd hardly known him that well.

Van den Haute buzzed for an escort. "Fifteen minutes," he said, then hesitated. "You understand, the interrogation unit is separate from us. My jurisdiction is limited." He almost sounded embarrassed.

It hadn't turned out so badly after all, Morley thought. As long as he was valuable van den Haute would intercede with

London to keep him there. His talk with Karim Arif might even make him more valuable.

And then the sense of uneasiness returned.

Arif and his friends had failed too easily the first time they had tried to kill Cailleau.

thirteen

THE MAXIMUM-SECURITY CELLS were in the basement of the annex, a cobblestoned vault with large rooms feeding off a central corridor. The air was chilly and damp and Morley guessed it was always the same, summer or winter, that no amount of central heating would ever dry the damp stone walls or warm the chill air. Bare stringers with banks of fluorescent lights lined the ceiling. The glare hurt his eyes.

"Is it always this bright?"

The turnkey glanced at the fluorescents. "The tubes burn out occasionally, Monsieur. But we never turn them off. We work twenty-four hours a day down here."

The turnkey was maybe five-seven, with a drooping moustache and expressionless eyes that Morley had seen many times before. They were eyes that seldom blinked, that had seen it all and were still incapable of registering outrage.

Morley put the turnkey's age at anywhere between forty-five and sixty-five, and knew without asking that the man had been a watchdog all his life. The meek would never inherit the earth, he thought cynically; it already belonged to the jailers.

He reached the last of the iron stairs and stepped onto the

chilly concrete floor. All jails had their points of similarity, but for a moment the stone walls surprised him. Then he remembered that the holding cell was housed in a reconverted cellar left over from the days of Napoleon.

"This way, Monsieur."

Morley followed him around a corner, almost slipping on the slick floor. The turnkey reached out to steady him and Morley noticed that he was wearing a poorly fitting brown suit instead of a uniform. Morley wondered if he'd once been with the Sûreté, the Belgian political police.

"Remember, Monsieur, a quarter of an hour—no more." He stopped at a locked steel door and fumbled with a ring of keys.

"Have you learned anything about the others?"

The turnkey glanced back at him. His eyes had a reddish cast that seemed almost purple in the pale face. "They would like to think so upstairs, Monsieur. If a prisoner tells his real name in the morning, they think he will spill his insides by noon. Not this one. His kind play hero until they cannot talk even if they want to."

A twist of the key, a push and the steel outer door clanged shut behind them.

To the turnkey, Morley knew, there was very little difference between those whom his key locked in and those whom they locked out. Everybody was guilty of something.

The room on the other side of the door was large, with whitewashed walls and white-enameled floor. There was a double bank of fluorescents overhead so the light shimmered and bounced from the moisture-slick stones and concrete. In the far corner, two uniformed guards played piquet.

In the center of the room, a good eight feet from the nearest wall, was a steel cage, the bars at the sides and top dazzling in the glare.

128

"Remember—fifteen minutes, no more."

Morley started to step forward. "Monsieur." A light touch on his shoulder and a motion to the other two guards who dropped their cards and walked over. "Your attaché case. It will be upstairs where I left your guns."

He handed his briefcase to the turnkey. The guards frisked him once again, then without a word went back to their card table. The turnkey trailed after to kibitz.

All three had lost interest in him.

Up close, it was the smell that he noticed first. The slop bucket hadn't been emptied and the food hadn't been taken away. It was suppertime but the tray held a thin layer of yellowish oatmeal; the milk on top was curdled and the dish was sour-smelling. How many times had Karim tried to piece together what time it was? Breakfast in the evening, lunch in the middle of the night. Two days would seem like a week.

He spent a moment studying the slender young man sprawled face down on the dirty mat. A slight film of perspiration coated Morley's face and dampened his collar. Interrogation, it was what he did best. What he *used* to do best. It would be a contest of wills and emotions and he didn't know if he was up to it.

His moves were simple. To play the good cop, to convince the prisoner you were on his side even if he knew to the core you weren't. He had been beaten, broken, and you acknowledged his existence, offered a cigarette and waited, not striking a match until, maybe, he spilled his guts. Some did. But the prisoner worked you, too. His job was to convince you that he was human just like you, that he had been badly used, that his only fault was in believing his own faith could move mountains—or justify the slaughter of a dozen or a hundred innocents. He did it for time. He did it because it was all he had left to do. Eventually, the interrogator won, but the end was always messy, like gutting a fish while it was still alive.

Interrogation was delicate, precise surgery, as delicate and precise as any that ever occurred in an operating room. But if you underplayed your hand, you lost the game. Overplayed and you could lose your self. You could never afford to forget who your enemy was.

Morley took a deep breath. Time to go to work. He had a lot of questions to ask, and all he had to do was to get the Iraqi to answer them. Willingly.

"Karim." The man on the mat didn't move. "Can you hear me?"

A weak, muffled voice that sounded as if it were being thrown by a ventriloquist. "I can still hear."

"Has a doctor seen you?"

Still muffled: "Are you my lawyer? Or perhaps you have come to fix the toilet." He groped out with his left arm and slapped the side of the slop bucket. "My apologies for all the blood."

Morley didn't say anything. Time was ticking away, but he had to give curiosity a chance to work. After a minute, the man on the floor stirred and rolled over, propping himself up on his elbows so he could see him.

Like Leather Jacket, Karim Arif was small and dark-skinned, with a heavy head of jet-black hair, partly matted with blood. His shirt was in shreds, his pants stained and dirty with the seat torn out, and no belt to hold them up and no buttons to keep the fly closed. The overhead light was bright enough so Morley could see the bruises on the dark skin. When Karim moved, a thin line of red spots that trailed down his arms and below his waist rippled like a snake.

Electrode tracks. Someone had been trained well.

The Iraqi cracked his eyelids open. His dark Mediterranean features were untouched. Clothes would hide the bruises on his body, but a television camera would pick up any cuts and bruises on his face.

Morley guessed that Karim was in his early twenties, even though his face looked like a grunt's after six months on the line. It was haunted, the face of a man who in his mind's eye had died a hundred times. . . . And then Morley caught himself. It was the face that he was supposed to see, the face of a young man who was willing to give his life for what he believed. He was not supposed to see the face of a man who would kill without hesitation, who was willing to blow up buildings and school buses without a second thought.

The enemy was young, pathetic and idealistic, but he was still the enemy.

Karim licked dried lips and cocked his head, frowning. "You're not a Belgian." The words came out slowly, as if he didn't trust his voice. "And you're not a Brit." A thin smile. "I learned from the IRA. I know you're not a Brit."

Karim was talking too much.

"And you're not Israeli," the fragile voice whispered on. "Though with Mossad and Shibbeth, who can tell?" The sly smile again. "I know—you're the Policeman of the World!"

He suddenly scrambled to his feet and lunged for the bars, screaming: *"Khong danh cho co! Khong danh cho co!"* His voice died to a whisper once again. "That's it, isn't it? *'If they're not guilty, beat them until they are!'* "

The guards glanced over, then went back to their cards. "Ten minutes," the turnkey called out.

He should have known better than to think he could leave the gendarmerie without scars of his own. For a moment Vietnam and the border camps and their neverending chain of betrayals were vivid in his mind. Morley had been responsible for setting up the community-relations program in 'Nam, the "turn-in-your-neighbor" campaign. It had been weeks before he'd learned its real purpose. And then the country had crumbled and the bureaucrats had made no provision for evacuating the network of Vietnamese that he and other string men had set up. They were on *his* conscience, not on that of his superiors fighting for a seat on the last chopper off the embassy roof.

He'd watched the old people, women and children being thrown from the helicopters by the bureaucrats and senior officials trying to climb aboard and then it had been his turn. He couldn't remember whether he'd fought his way onto the chopper or not. He hadn't wanted to remember. Until this moment he had blanked his mind of the escape from the capital, of the shouted motto of the Saigon police and the sounds of the wooden sticks they had used to beat their suspects.

For another invaluable minute, he stood by the bars of the cage in silence, the old memories turning over inside him. And then he steeled himself: both the innocent and the guilty died— and the guilty didn't always go first.

Karim was staring at him, his large brown eyes leaking tears. He held up an arm to show an ugly scar running under the armpit. His hoarse whisper echoed in the room but Morley doubted the guards even heard it. "See? See what they do?" A finger without a nail jabbed at the reddish spots on his arm. "The electricity, the tiny little jolts. You do not sleep, you get so tired you cannot eat."

The tears vanished now, and the look in Karim's eyes became almost sultry. "You dare not eat, not if you want to keep your pride, Monsieur. They break you by stealing your pride." A sly look and a glance at the flourescents overhead. "There is no darkness here, you piss in the bright lights, you relieve yourself before the world. You get hungry and you eat and that makes you thirsty so you drink and and eventually you must piss again. And then you discover they have put the blister beetle in your food and there is not even the dark in which to abuse yourself."

He suddenly let his trousers slide to his feet and grabbed at his crotch. "Watch, Monsieur! Why don't you watch? *They* do!"

He was screaming now, and one of the guards walked over with a bucket. He motioned Morley away, then threw the dirty water between the bars. "My apologies, Monsieur—he likes to show himself, no?" The guard returned to the table. Karim stood there for a moment, the water streaming down his face and chest, then pulled his pants back up around his waist, holding them closed with one hand.

"They remind you that you're an animal," he whispered. "It does not take much."

The guard was only doing his job. Making the good cop's job easier.

Morley stepped closer to the cage and said softly: "If I had to kill an innocent man to save a city, I would. And so would you. If I had to torture one to save ten, I would. And so would you."

The sense of trust was as fleeting and fragile as a soap bubble. "You give me back my pride, Monsieur." Karim's tears were suddenly real.

Morley waited a moment, then: "Why Cailleau?"

The lemur-like eyes looked through him at something in the distance. "He could identify us. We tried one night but too many people came." His eyes slowly swam into focus. "No more, Monsieur. My pride is my own."

The recognition, his of Karim and Karim's of him, hung in the air like mist. The Iraqi had taken the bait, even though he must have played the game before. The cellar was cool, almost cold, but Morley found himself sweating even more. He, too, was caught, identifying more than he wanted. It was a mistake. He was slipping. He gestured at the cellar behind him.

"You could stop all this." He cursed himself the moment he said it.

Karim stepped back as if he had been slapped. His laugh was short, bitter, his voice stronger. "No, all this will go on. Only terror can trigger change. And there will be terror until victory comes." He closed his eyes and threw back his head, striking a pose. "I do not deceive myself—I will not be alive, but the day *will* come!"

Karim was delivering the punch line of a speech, one he must have given hundreds of times before at student demonstrations, surrounded by a thousand cheering young men desperately willing to trade their bodies for a slogan. And how hollow it sounded in the steel cell, screamed by this shell of a prisoner who could be made to debase himself at will.

Morley swore to himself. The Iraqi knew the game too well. The touch of pathos, the instinctive appeal for sympathy . . . He had read Morley immediately, recognized the psychological profile, had gauged the weakness. Nobody ever held all the cards. Sometimes the prisoner had the winning hand.

Karim opened his eyes. "I fight for the liberation of humanity," he whispered. "I fight for my faith."

Morley felt like he had just walked out of a fog. It was bullshit, and the Iraqi must know that he knew it. Or maybe not. How naive had he seemed so far? Morley only knew one thing. They were never going to break a man more interested in preserving his image than his life.

But *he* was blowing it, too. The minutes were skipping by, and he hadn't found out anything about the others or their mission. His mere presence provided Karim with an audience, and that was all the Iraqi needed to hang on, to convince himself it was all worthwhile.

Karim started to shiver again and Morley turned to the guards. "He needs a blanket."

The turnkey said: "He knows how to get one."

Six minutes.

"Your civilization no longer works," Karim whispered. "The slaughter of a hundred million people in little more than fifty years proves that. Things will change. Something else is possible—it has to be."

Another few minutes and the Iraqi would hate the sound of his own voice as much as he did, Morley thought. But *he* didn't have that long. And he couldn't leave Karim to play the hero for whoever walked in. If they let him, Karim would twist the interrogation into his own personal struggle against the System. He would die with that belief before he broke.

"You took your chances." He watched the Iraqi closely. "All seven of you. You knew the rules."

Karim didn't correct him, and Morley realized with a sudden spurt of confidence that he had made a minor score. Karim's brown eyes opened wide in a wan smile. "Whose rules?" His teeth began to chatter and he wrapped his shirt tightly around himself. Then he caught Morley's expression and forced his arms away from his body, opening his shirt to the air. "You see—it is all a matter of will." Another pose. "Your journalists denounce us, but they say nothing while you prop up all those who slaughter freedom." He shook his head, his expression benevolent and forgiving. "We're not lunatics. I would like to change everything without spilling a single drop of blood. I don't believe in revenge, not even for *this.*"

In the corner of the room, one of the guards laughed and swept some coins off the card table into his hand. The turnkey glanced over at Morley and said, "Three minutes, Monsieur."

Morley tapped a cigarette out of his pack, lit it, then offered it to Karim, who puffed on it greedily. Morley was calmer now, more aware of his own role as well as that of the Iraqi. "We're running out of time, Karim," he said in a quiet voice. Then, confiding: "There's terror in here and there's terror out in the streets. It's like original sin, everybody's guilty of it."

Again, the feeling of identification was almost palpable. Karim's eyes were lidded, the expression in them shifting, pleading. He was very good. Very convincing. He had been through the mill before.

Another five minutes and he could do it, Morley thought. But there was no more time for subtlety, for compassion. "Before he died, Cailleau told me everything."

He knew it was the wrong thing to say as soon as he said it. He was watching the clock and that was always a mistake. Karim's eyes jerked open briefly and he realized that Karim hadn't known Cailleau had been killed. He had been picked up four days before, and nobody had told him.

The expression on Karim's face turned to one of contempt. "The marionette man told you nothing. Why else would you be here?"

Two minutes.

Morley managed to sound friendly but distant. He alone stood between the Iraqi and whatever hell his interrogators had waiting. He had leverage. Any favors granted would come from him. "There won't be any heroics, Karim. No demands for a plane, no South Yemen. Only another unidentified corpse in the morgue." He lowered his voice so the Iraqi had to strain to hear. "Nobody knows you're here. According to the papers, the suspect picked up on boulevard Anspach was let go yesterday. They can do anything they want with you." He ground out his cigarette on the damp concrete. "Nobody gives a shit about you, Karim."

The Iraqi began to tremble. "What do you want to know?"

136

It was a trap but he had to use it. "Who you came in with and why."

Karim grinned, triumphant. "Then I know what not to tell you!" He turned his shivering into a shrug and once again his eyes were large and liquid. "I have brothers now that I can be proud of, people who understand revolution and know in their hearts what human liberation is. I never knew humanity was so large." He thumped his thin chest. "Many people are in here with me." He said it simply, without bravado.

The turnkey walked over and tapped Morley lightly on his shoulder. "Time, Monsieur."

Morley studied Karim a moment longer, then instinctively reached out to touch him lightly on the shoulder. He knew it was a con and that the guards would despise him for it, but it was his last chance to make contact—and making contact was the major part of the job. It could go either way.

The moment he did it, he realized the Iraqi had won, that he had lost the game. Karim batted his hand away, his eyes blazing. "Never shake hands with the capitalistic insect!"

"The young," the guard said, quietly steering Morley away. "It is easy to identify with them, to think of your children. You can even forget those they murdered." He didn't try to hide his contempt for Morley.

Morley didn't either. "Nobody's young anymore. I've met monsters who were five, six years old."

The sense of failure was overwhelming. Karim had recognized him immediately as a fellow victim, and forged an identification with him before he had even realized it. Cailleau had been right, his own scars hadn't healed yet. Like the others—Simon, Taca, even Louis—the Iraqi had sensed the depths of his injuries.

Morley had held up a mirror so Karim could see himself.

137

The Iraqi had grabbed it and twisted it around and Morley hated him for it.

Just before the outer door swung shut, Karim shouted: "They know my mother! Tell her I was larger than my fears!"

Morley looked back. Karim was standing in his cell, clutching at his trousers, staring up at him. He looked small and weak and desperate. The guard was a good cop. Annoying, but a wise one. Unless you were careful, you could feel more pity for the Karims than you did for the innocents who had died in the rubble in Oklahoma or the elderly Jews lying in bloody tatters beside a crumpled Tel Aviv tourist bus. Or the innocent villagers lying in mass graves in 'Nam, the natural prey of both sides.

Morley felt wrung out.

"I'll tell her," he grunted. He wasn't sure if Karim heard it, but he knew van den Haute would as he listened to the tapes.

At least he was good for another few days in Brussels.

fourteen

"HE'LL NEVER TALK," Morley said.

Van den Haute sipped another cup of coffee and stared at him with faint disapproval. "There is no such thing as a man who will not talk, Monsieur. You, of all people, should know that."

"He'll overestimate his physical resources—men his age often do. If you break his spirit, it will only be after he's exceeded his own strength. He'll die quickly then."

The Captain looked annoyed. "Those handling him have had the same lessons as you, Monsieur. They know what they are doing."

"They're butchers. The job requires a surgeon."

"I run a gendarmerie, not an inquisition. But prisoners seldom leave you a choice, you know that. And by comparison, both of us are amateurs. You remember the massacre of the Jewish athletes at Munich?"

"I would suggest other methods," Morley said stubbornly.

"Subtlety, perhaps? I have seen the effects of your subtlety on the boy from the theater." The Captain gave him a dark look. "You're an easy man to resent, Monsieur."

His leg hurt, and he was tired of being lectured to by van den Haute, especially after the basement. He'd had enough of interrogation rooms. "You resent our generosity, too?"

Van den Haute pushed the coffee service away. "I can hardly believe you bleed for the Iraqi, Monsieur, so you must be pursued by your own devils. But a moment of truth, please. At one time in the past, I was responsible for the curtain shops—what you Americans call the 'red light' district. I know how difficult it is for the girls to leave the houses. If they retire from the business, they cannot go to the hairdresser's every day, they cannot take a taxi for two streets. It is a hardship to have to go back to an ordinary life." His eyes lidded. "But that does not mean they find working in the curtain shops pleasant. So please do not mention anyone's generosity again. We might all be whores, but not all of us love the profession."

Morley didn't like van den Haute, and he was having difficulty not showing it. The Captain was too smug. He was also too healthy, and Morley resented him because of it.

"You won't persuade him to tell you what he knows by stealing his dignity."

"With criminals like the Iraqi, Monsieur, it isn't theft, it's petty larceny. But perhaps they should break the bones of his face or rupture his spleen. You think he would tell us more then?"

Be nice to the man, Louis had said about Tindemans. It applied to van den Haute as well. The Captain could ask London to call him back or have him put on a plane himself. Morley changed the subject. "The Russians told you Cailleau had smuggled in the death squad?"

"You can tell the size of a man by the ease with which he apologizes," van den Haute said dryly. "You misunderstood me, the embassy did not mention Cailleau. Only that six terrorists had been smuggled in. Our guest provided the information about the puppeteer." He smiled without humor. "Somebody failed to serve him a six-course supper and kept him up for twenty-four hours. He broke under the strain."

Morley ignored the sarcasm, suddenly curious. "Which Russian told you?"

"They have a free agent, here, too." Van den Haute made the word sound distasteful. "I'm sure that doesn't surprise you. They've reduced their numbers, but if both your countries put all their agents on the street, they would outnumber my own men. Add the other nations and Brussels could become the greatest free-fire zone in the West." He flipped through a small card file. "He's with Department V. From the Karlshorst Residency. He came across twenty-four hours before you did."

The Russians were still in business, if only on a reduced basis. It took Morley a moment to run through the agents Moscow Central might have detached from other areas.

" 'He wears a tweed jacket' "—van den Haute was reading from an index card, obviously enjoying telling him something he didn't already know—" 'bought at the English Shop in Copenhagen.' " He marked his place on the card with his index finger and looked up. "About your height and build, only now . . . a little heavier. Well tanned, a professional athlete twenty years ago. His English and American are quite good, almost native." The Captain looked disapproving once again. "His operation's similar to yours."

Vasiliev. In Hanoi, they said he wore camouflage coveralls as if they were black tie and tails. The description fit perfectly. It had been more difficult to recognize him when he had surfaced briefly in the Pakistan border camps. He had passed himself off as an American then, wearing dirty khakis and a three-day stubble of beard.

Van den Haute closed the card file. "Do not forget what I told you in this office half an hour ago. There are no White

141

Mice in Belgium. Things are done differently here." He was the professional police officer again, and Morley knew better than to interrupt. "You are as welcome here as you would be in Paris or the Hague or Rome. We do not wish to make difficulties, but neither will we be embarrassed."

He leaned back in his swivel chair and folded his hands in his lap. Morley guessed that van den Haute had been saving something special for him.

"I do not think there is much left for you to do here, Monsieur." A faint smile. "I understand that your Bureau will have a new Chief within days. They assure me that so long as you're here, you'll be under his jurisdiction. They also assure me that your duty is temporary."

The first act of the new Chief would be to send him back. Van den Haute caught the expression on his face and softened slightly.

"Perhaps not to your liking, but much more so to mine. The very qualities that make you a good agent in one sense make you a bad agent in another. You are impulsive, quick to anger, and violent—which means, Monsieur, that your own service considers you self-destructive. Free agents belong to another time, another world. I assure you, their numbers diminish. This time in Brussels, perhaps you can play the role of tourist. You've probably never ridden our new subways, met our good people. It can be an enjoyable city, Monsieur. You should look at it with that in mind."

Morley stared at him coldly. Van den Haute and Tindemans were boxing him in. He could stay in Brussels, but only on their terms. The past was to be buried forever and nobody would object too much if he were buried with it.

"The seven terrorists—"

"Six," van den Haute corrected. "They may be well trained, but I think for them to visit Brussels at this time was an error in judgment. Would you like to hear our plans?" He didn't wait for an affirmative but flipped through another stack of memos on his desk, elaborating on the security for the Palais de Congrès, the large convention hall that was to be home for the European Union meeting. He talked in detail about the agenda, the seating, the menus. If Morley were to believe it all, everything down to the after-dinner mints had been checked out. "So you see, Monsieur, we are quite prepared."

Van den Haute's reputation would rise or fall depending on what happened or didn't happen over the next few days. And despite his air of confidence, he was badly rattled.

"You have some comment, Monsieur?"

There was unfinished business in Brussels, and it was just as unfinished for van den Haute and London as it was for him. Everybody had a hand to play, but nobody was dealing him in, nobody was really talking to him and neither was anybody listening. Morley could feel his anger start to rise.

"The extremists—"

"—are not above making mistakes," van den Haute interrupted. His face betrayed his smug words.

Morley suddenly got to his feet and reached for the coffee pot to refill van den Haute's cup. "I remember an old Vietnamese I once went to see. I wanted some information from him but he only served me tea." He kept pouring even after the cup was full. The coffee ran over the brim and filled the saucer, then splashed out on the desk, running in little rivulets toward the edge facing the Captain.

Van den Haute, red-faced, jerked back in his chair, blotting furiously at the puddle with a handkerchief. "*Merde!* What are you doing?"

Morley put the pot down, his hand shaking with reaction. "The old man let the tea run over and ruin my best pair of suntans. When I asked him why he had done it, he said I was too full of my own opinions and speculations, that he couldn't tell me anything until I first emptied my cup."

"I never knew you were a philosopher," van den Haute sneered. He jabbed angrily at a button on his intercom and almost immediately the cadet who had brought them coffee came in. "Jules, get some paper towels. Then show our guest out of the building." His voice turned icy as he faced Morley. "For your sake, I hope we do not meet again."

It had been a dumb thing to do, Morley thought on his way downstairs. But he had learned something. Van den Haute had had the chance to throw him out but hadn't. The Captain wanted him to stay in Brussels.

Jules got his guns from the custodian and Morley studied the cadet while he filled out the form. Jules was about the same size as Karim, though his coloring was fairer. They were of the same age; probably both had the same sort of idealism. Karim would kill for it, and Jules probably would, too.

It had been a long time since Morley had felt such idealism.

Outside he paused on the top step, pulling up the collar of his mac. It was raining again, the drizzle darkening the cadet's blond hair and spotting his wire-framed glasses. Jules nodded at him politely, holding open the heavy door and waiting for him to start down the steps.

Morley looked at the cadet's youthful features and clear eyes and tried to recognize himself in them. Jules was still holding onto his hand and had started to open his mouth to say goodbye when a motorcycle with two riders roared around the corner. Morley turned just in time to glimpse the Plexiglas-masked driver almost standing on the pedals, the rider behind him holding a rifle at eye level with both hands.

Jules stood there gaping, hypnotized. Morley reached for

his Beretta. He fell back, kicking the cadet toward the safety of the building.

There was the whisper of a silencer and the small *poofs* of bullets chipping at the stone steps and cleaving cloth and flesh. Jules' blue-gray uniform was suddenly sopping with blood.

Morley, now free, spun around, his gun in both hands. But the hit squad had already vanished into the evening traffic.

Somebody on the street started to scream and he heard running footsteps outside the gendarmerie. Jules rolled beside him, moaning, blood streaming from his mouth and arm.

Morley crouched, ready for any follow-up rider. People were boiling out of the building now, seemingly in slow motion. Then somebody turned Jules over and shouted to the others behind him that he felt a pulse.

There was a crowd on the steps and shouted commands and the usual air of panic and confusion and anger. Morley struggled to his feet, aware of the pounding of his heart and several small cuts on his face where flying chips of concrete had slashed his skin.

The hit men hadn't wanted Jules. And Morley suddenly wasn't convinced that their prospective victims were limited to finance ministers or businessmen.

Add one more. Himself.

fifteen

THE CONCIERGE REACHED for the key, then hesitated. She inspected Morley, his damp grocery bag, his briefcase and bouquet of flowers. Her scowl faded. "Your wife is upstairs, Monsieur. Room eleven."

"*Bien!*" The bouquet had done it, he thought. The old woman in the Metro needed the francs and the cut roses would hardly make Hannie feel worse. But more important, they had satisfied the concierge. He smiled at the suspicious, ruddy face peering at him from behind the bifocals. "A friend"—he hesitated—"Serge Cailleau, stayed here."

"You knew Serge?" She shook her head. "A shame! Such a fine man."

"In the prime of his life," Morley agreed. He was struck by another thought. "He had a lady friend, Bernadette—"

The angry eyes filmed with frost. "I would not know, Monsieur."

"A reddish-blonde, she—"

Firmly: "Not *here*, Monsieur. Not at *my* pensione."

The lift was just stopping on the ground floor but Morley deliberately took the time to climb the stairs that boxed in the open elevator shaft. The exercise would do him good. Besides, he could think of only one other lift that was as slow—and that had been in the building on *Duong Thong Nhat*, a street of barbed wire, sandbags and MP's.

Somebody was in the communal john—he could hear the toilet flush just before he knocked on number eleven's door.

"It's not locked."

But it should have been. . . .

He had expected the light to be on, but the room was dark and he hung back until his eyes adjusted. She had pulled the drapes to keep out the drafts and they let precious little daylight in. The room itself was small and plain to the point of being bare, but it would do for the night. He set his briefcase and the groceries on the small table by the window, then found the light pull hanging over the bed and yanked on it.

She was dressed in a bulky knit cardigan and gray wool slacks and looked as fresh as she had that morning. It was chilly in the room and she'd pulled the blanket up over her knees. She'd been napping. She winced at the sudden light, then saw the roses and smiled. "It's a nice thought, but I'm allergic."

Morley was disappointed. "You can throw them out. They were really for the concierge downstairs." But they weren't. They'd been for Hannie right from the start. How long had it been since he'd brought a woman flowers?

Her smile turned sour. "My husband bringing home flowers. How sweet."

"Knock it off, Hannie, I'm beat." He hung his raincoat on the back of the door, then sat down to work his feet out of shoes so wet the leather had started to crack. "I wouldn't have objected if you'd liked them."

"Sorry." Her tone was apologetic. "It's just that sometimes I don't know how to take you."

"I should warn you—I'm capable of being charming." His socks were soaked, too, and he squished across the floor to his suitcase and dug through it for another pair. "How did it go?"

"All the arrangements are made. There's to be a tribute tomorrow at the theater. There's a stepsister still living in Paris and a cousin living here." Hannie made a face. "She's not a very pleasant person."

He only half heard. He was running through the schedule of flights to London, wondering how much they had changed in six months. He was also wondering how he was going to break it to her that it was now too dangerous for her to stay in Brussels with him, that he was going to have to send her back to London.

As usual, his socks were on the bottom of the suitcase. He sat down again and lifted a foot, annoyed at how heavy and stiff his leg felt.

"When will he be cremated?"

"I didn't ask, I didn't want to know."

His feet began to warm up in the heavy wool socks and life was suddenly more bearable. He looked around the room again and thought that one of the differences between a young girl and an older woman was that an older woman would have demanded a different room. There wasn't much light, the furniture was heavy and brooding and the peasants populating the faded wallpaper were right out of a poor copy of Brueghel's *Wedding Dance*, complete with codpieces. He wondered whether the concierge had approved.

He picked up the bag of groceries and walked to the sink in the corner. Half the crumbling linoleum was green, half red. Like leftover Christmas wrappings. Another month and it would be appropriate.

"I bought some *beignettes*, Gouda, apples . . . some beaujolais." Their only glass was the one on the wash basin, but they could share it. He splashed some cold water on his face and rubbed it hard with a towel.

"Are you going?"

He dropped the towel on the edge of the sink. "Am I going where?"

"To the tribute."

He shook his head; he hadn't even thought of it. The drapes were blowing open and he shivered and walked over to close the window. Outside, flickering kerosene lanterns lit the pilings and the blue and yellow work wagons surrounding the boulevard. In their glow, the disemboweled boulevard with its tarpaulin-covered construction forms looked like a tent show that had been half-struck and was waiting to be trucked away into the night.

Hannie started washing the apples in the sink. "When do you want to eat?"

"It doesn't matter, I'm too tired to be hungry."

He sat in the chair by the table, stretching his legs out in front of him. Ever since he had walked into the room, he'd been aware of her scent. He closed his eyes and reminded himself that it was only something she poured from a bottle. A moment later, he heard her moving between the sink and the table. Real luxury was wool socks, warm feet, the muttering of the radiator and somebody asking when you wanted dinner. They were both playing house, but then, who knew what discomforts tomorrow might bring. . . .

He had just started to doze off when she touched him on the shoulder and said everything was ready. Dinner was bread and cheese and apples and several glasses of wine. To his surprise, he discovered he was hungry after all.

"Sorry about tomorrow, Hannie, but I'm not big on either tributes or funerals."

"I may not go myself."

He nibbled at a piece of cheese. She would go, he was sure of it. "What did you find out at the ECC?"

"It's built on a site once occupied by a girls' school. Does that help?"

"I'm serious."

"Everybody's talking and nobody's listening." She cocked her head. "Do you want the pros or the cons? Should I spell out a dozen reasons to go full speed ahead? Or give you another dozen why they better not? Do you want to hear how much everyone is in hock to each other? Or should I stress how much we *need* each other if everyone is going to survive?"

"I can read that in the papers." Something was eating at her, but he didn't know what.

"Then maybe you're interested in the story about the staff member who took some Commission doors off their hinges and used them to complete his home in the country. Or do you prefer the one about the employee who regularly set off the fire alarm, timing it so that his cousin, who owned an ice cream truck, was on hand when everybody poured into the street—"

He put down his glass of wine. "What about the security?" His voice was savage. "Did you have to show any identification at the door? Any metal detectors? If there were, how many guards were manning them? Were they alert? Any preparations for setting up roadblocks on the surrounding streets? If there was any security at the building, did you watch long enough to notice if the tradesmen were exempt? Was a photo ID needed to get into the building?"

The flush of anger faded from her face. "I thought you wanted to surround me with people so nobody could shanghai me."

"Or push you out a window or run you over or knife you while you're standing at a busy intersection. That one's very popular, Hannie—quick and simple and everyone around you is too stunned to help." He fought a moment for control. She had a knack for pressing his buttons. "Yes, I wanted to surround you with people. I also wanted to know about the security. *Especially* about the security."

"You walk through a metal detection device at the door," she said in a small voice. "There are two guards. They were very thorough, they went through my purse. There were complaints from the line in back of me, but that didn't seem to bother them. Everyone had to go through the detectors. I didn't see any photo badges. Men in military uniforms were directing traffic around the building and at two intersections, I saw buses with more men in uniform sitting in them. They weren't regular gendarmes, it was some other kind of uniform."

Van den Haute was more efficient than he thought.

"And the parking garage underneath? Easy access, or is it patrolled?"

She thought for a moment. "It's patrolled; you have to show identification."

Not enough, he thought. There should at least be spot inspections.

"You were being sarcastic before, Hannie. Why?"

"I didn't think you were taking me seriously." She suddenly sounded cool. "I was on my own in London, I have no intention of playing housewife over here."

"You're doing a professional's job, Hannie. I'm treating you like one."

She looked contrite.

"Something happened today, didn't it?"

He nodded. "A cadet named Jules was gunned down on the steps of the gendarmerie this afternoon. He was holding the door open for me."

"You could have told me."

"I am."

She toyed with a piece of cheese. "Why did you go there?"

He didn't want to play the game this time, to spend the night trading tiny bits of information. "To find out what happened to me six months ago. What I found out is that they're holding a prisoner, an Iraqi named Karim Arif. One of the seven Cailleau smuggled in. They gave me a chance to talk to him."

She had started to cut small slices from an apple, eating them off the end of the knife. "So Serge really did smuggle in terrorists," she murmured.

He nodded. "Diane confirmed it. A broad-based group—not just Muslim extremists. The Belgians are worried they'll try and blow up the Palais de Congrès; the casualties would be enormous." He had a momentary flash of sympathy for van den Haute. By comparison, his own problems were minor.

"What's he like?"

"Karim?" The image of the whitewashed basement and the small, dark-haired man in a steel cage flashed into his mind. "Small, handsome. Your age. An ex-student with upper-class parents. A lot of courage and a cause. An Islamic fundamentalist. For what he is, a professional."

She looked up from the cheese, curious.

"Tell me about him." When he had finished, she said: "I suppose in his own way, you'd call him admirable."

"You're bleeding for him," he accused. He couldn't believe he was jealous of her reaction to Karim.

Stiffly: "You sounded sympathetic yourself, you know."

"Not really."

She stood up. "So if he's not on your side, he's—"

"—a terrorist," he finished.

"Don't give me that shit!" she flared. "So was half the government of Israel—they blew up British soldiers by the hundreds in Palestine!" She stalked to the window and threw back the drapes, standing in the cold draft and looking out at the night.

"You're backlighted," he warned, pouring himself more wine. "They couldn't miss you."

"Right now, I don't give a bloody damn!"

"I do," he muttered. He strode over to her and yanked the drapes shut, then stood behind her so she was trapped between him and the window. She was close enough that he could feel the heat of her body.

"You're part of his peer group, I expect you to identify with him." He couldn't disguise the contempt in his voice. "A part of you would like to think you share his idealism. But there's a difference. Karim realized he wasn't going to change the world by holding campus rallies, so he settled for a more direct approach. You're not the type."

"I'm hardly pure in heart," she said sarcastically.

"Based on what? Some hot little love affair in a two-room London flat? Not enough sin in that, Hannie, you'll have to try for something better." He suddenly wished they were throwing dishes rather than slashing each other verbally. He didn't want to prove they were just two strangers who didn't really know each other and didn't really trust each other.

She whirled. "He believes in defending his cause—is that so difficult to understand? I know what *he* believes in, but you've never told me what the bloody hell *you* believe in!"

Morley gripped her by the shoulders, squeezing so tight he could see a glint of fear in her eyes.

"Winners and losers, Hannie," he said bitterly. "That's what I believe in, because that's all there is."

She started to struggle, and he realized he couldn't stand the pressure of her body against his. Six months in bed with only his emotions and desires, and now they were flooding in and he couldn't handle them.

"Let go of me!"

Her voice was shaking; she was close to panic. He let her go and stepped back, then fumbled in his wallet for a couple of photographs, plucked another from his coat pocket and flipped them at her. They fluttered to the floor.

"Winners and losers, Hannie. Those are some of the losers."

She didn't look at them. "Atrocity photographs. My God—you see them every day in the papers, each side has its collection. It doesn't matter who kills you, Mister Morley, you're dead just the same!"

He hit the wall with his fist. "What the hell do you think we're talking about, a mugging in Soho? It matters *why* you die!" He was fighting for control again. "The purpose of terror isn't to change society, Hannie, it's to shatter it. And once that becomes your policy, then everybody's a target, there are no innocent bystanders. And that makes a goddamn big difference."

She glared at him, then bent down and picked up the photographs.

"The black-and-white was shot in Jerusalem," he said, his voice shaking. "The girl was three years old—they also got her mother. I was ten feet away, and there wasn't a damn thing I could do. The next one's a morgue shot of the victims from the World Trade Center bombing; the papers didn't dare publish it, every innocent Arab in New York would have been in danger from the mobs. The Polaroid was taken on the steps of the gendarmerie this afternoon." He remembered the young cadet's grip on his hand. "Jules . . . deserves sympathy, too, Hannie."

She sat down at the table and picked up her glass of wine. Her hand was trembling.

"Given the same—"

"Don't say it, Hannie. Don't tell me there's no real difference between Jules and Karim. I know better and so do you."

She concentrated on the wine. "You talked some more in your sleep last night. You should see someone about your nightmares."

He started to ask what he'd said, then changed his mind. There was very little more he could now tell her about himself. He limped over to the table and sat next to her.

"I'm not a clerk, Hannie—I'm an action agent. I don't shuffle papers, I don't make policy. I'm strictly on my own, and if something goes wrong in my head I have to heal myself because I don't dare let anybody else see what's in there, not even our own shrinks."

He said it matter-of-factly, trying for the first time in years to explain himself to somebody else.

"I'm sorry," she said after a moment. "I'm not sure what about, but my God, I'm sorry."

But he hadn't wanted her to feel sorry, he thought uncomfortably. He had wanted her to understand.

Morley sipped his wine in silence, then remembered the snapshots and letters he had picked up in Cailleau's dressing room. He dug the bundle out of his briefcase, slipped the top photo out from under the rubber band, then shoved the package across to her. "I found these in Cailleau's trunk. I thought you might want them."

She picked up the bundle and slowly went through the letters, going from tinted sheets to hotel stationery to yellow school paper with wide lines.

"I didn't know he'd saved them." Then she broke completely, turning away so he wouldn't see her tears.

"Hannie—"

"No, please . . ."

He waited until she was ready to face him, then handed the photograph to her. "Who are they?"

She studied it. "That's Serge in the middle. . . ." This time, she didn't bother to hide her tears.

"And the one on the left?"

"Monsieur Schlöndorff."

"Who's he?"

"Serge's agent. They were old friends."

"He helped with the escapes?"

She shook her head. "I don't know. He has an office across from a Congolese disco, the Mambo. That's all I know."

He'd have to look up Schlöndorff, find out who'd arranged Cailleau's tour to Hungary and Romania. He took the photograph and slipped it into his pocket. "I'll return it later."

She wasn't listening; she was smiling at a drawing in one of the letters showing a horse-drawn van in red crayon, with blue and yellow puppets trying to push it out of a drift.

"I told you how Serge and his brothers and sisters played the puppets? One night some boys found the family wagon stuck in the snow. Serge and the others were at the wheels, trying to free them from the ice. Fantastic stories about the puppets that could come alive spread everywhere they played." She laughed. "It was good for business."

"You really loved him," he said quietly.

"He was—" She floundered for a moment, searching for words, then gave up, dissolving in tears once again. "—my father."

Morley spent the next half-hour sitting at the window and watching the street below while Hannie read through the letters. It was a rainy, gusty night and few people were out. He watched as two men in a panel truck stole some timbers from one of the construction sites, and then the boulevard was deserted even of cars.

He felt a brief moment of panic when he heard Hannie slip

down the hall toward the bathroom; he should've checked out the hallway first. He turned away from the window when she came back and watched while she got ready for bed. Another tantalizing view of her tan lines and smooth bottom before she disappeared between the sheets. She seemed unaware of his interest but then, he reflected, women often hid their awareness.

He realized once again he liked her too well.

"You're not through with the Iraqi, are you?" she said.

"No. I have to find the others."

"He's not going to help you."

Morley poured the last of the wine into his glass. "He's already helped a great deal." He had to talk to her about sending her back, and wasn't sure how to start.

"That's not what you told me half an hour ago."

He pulled his chair around to face her. She was young, with taut skin and firm muscles that made him acutely aware of how thin he was, and how pale.

"He said he'd learned a lot from the IRA. By now Interpol has his photograph. We'll see what description come back. And he knew a lot about 'Nam. It's almost certain he's an exstudent who attended university in some western country, probably England. Finally, he mentioned his mother, not his father."

"Meaning what?"

"His father's probably dead. Which eliminates one line of follow-up." He shook a cigarette out of the pack on the table. "He asked me to tell his mother that he was brave."

"So she'll know that he's alive."

He shook his head. "Not necessarily. Not by the time she's heard." He tried to shake the image of Karim, the large, liquid eyes that were both sensual and hostile at the same time. "He didn't deny it when I said there were seven of them."

"Should he have?"

"Van den Haute claims the Russians said six. Cailleau said seven and he should have known."

"You're right," she said, sounding irritated. "The Iraqi told you more than he thought." She pulled the covers up around her chin, reminding Morley that the heat had gone off an hour ago and it was cold in the room. "He also tried to work you."

He shrugged. "Of course. He showed me a year-old scar and said he had gotten it at the gendarmerie. You lose credibility quickly that way."

"I suppose he also lied about the electrodes and the Spanish fly."

"No, they were real."

She leaned up on one elbow, her breasts clearing the edge of the blanket. "And you work with those people!"

"*We* work with those people, Hannie." He wanted to make sure she didn't work with them any longer, and one way of doing it was to make her feel responsible as well.

"What did you feel about him? I know what you think about him, but what did you *feel*?"

"What he wanted me to. Compassion, sympathy. I liked him. I identified with him."

"Professionally."

"That's right. Professionally." He felt uncomfortable. "It's an occupational hazard, Hannie. It's easy when you start out and everything is black and white. Then you begin to meet your opposite numbers and discover that they're not that much different from yourself. They have feelings, they have families, they worry about the kid's teeth, about the cost of groceries. . . . After a while, it's not so black-and-white any more, everything is gray. It isn't, but you *think* it is. And once you start thinking that, things become a lot more difficult."

"I don't see where Karim fits in," she said. "With you. With Vietnam."

158

"There were a lot of Karims in 'Nam. On both sides. At least there were in the beginning." He was silent for a moment, his eyes closed while the images played on the inside of his lids.

"Vietnam was pretty bad, wasn't it?"

"Yes," he said softly. "It was pretty bad."

"They say everybody has a war," she said. "That was yours."

He'd thought the same thing about Cailleau. Now both van den Haute and Hannie had picked up on it with regard to him. They were right. 'Nam *had* been his war. And it was as real to him today as it had been twenty years ago, as real as World War II had been to Cailleau.

"I think you're probably very good at it, but I don't admire you for what you do," Hannie said after a moment.

He was about to correct her and say "What *we* do." Instead he said, "You're going back in the morning. I have to call London; I'll tell them you're on your way."

He could sense her stiffen clear across the room.

"I didn't realize I was so much of a hindrance to your private plans."

"It's not that," he said gently. "They weren't after Jules this morning. They were after me. Stay close to me and you'll be in the line of fire."

She sat up on the side of the bed, naked. "Nobody gives a damn about Serge!"

"I do," he said. "I have to. The same people who killed Cailleau are after me. Maybe they think he told me enough so I could identify them or figure out where they are. But I don't think so. He could've talked to everybody at Théâtre de Vaudeville and they've yet to bomb it or set fire to it. It has to be some other connection."

"Simon will decide what to do with me," she said in a low voice. "You don't have the authority."

"I don't want you to work for them," he said, and felt helpless when he said it. There was no commitment between them, no real relationship. He was lonely and she was pretty, there was nothing more to it than that.

"You like me," she said sarcastically. "How touching. And what a nice way of showing it. But you're not related to me, you're not my lover. Whatever happens between me and London doesn't concern you. I'm flattered by your interest, but that doesn't give you any power over me." She slipped under the blankets again. "Throw me the cigarettes, will you?"

He lit one for her and she puffed a moment in silence. "I'm sorry, Neal. I'm staying. If I can be of help to you in regard to Serge, fine. If not, then I'll do what I can on my own."

If she stayed with him, it might be dangerous, but at least he would have some control over what happened to her. On her own, it would be even more dangerous and he would have no control. And then he wondered if he thought that because he wanted to think that.

He fought briefly with himself and lost the battle. "After the tribute, go to the Euro Technical Consortium—that's our cover, ETC, 'et cetera' to the insiders. I'll give you a name there and the address. See what they have on Karim Arif. Get everything you can on his friends and family, ask them to contact Interpol if they have to. Then meet me at Roi d'Espagne in Grand'Place for dinner."

"You're not manipulating me?"

He got his coat out of the closet and made himself comfortable on the chair. "I honestly don't know, Hannie. I don't think so." He could sense her satisfaction.

"I know how you'll use the information," she said.

"I told you it was a dirty business."

She was quiet for a moment, then said casually: "The Iraqi. You said I was sympathetic toward him." She hesitated. "Perhaps I am. But you also said you identified with him."

He bridled. "Professionally, Hannie."

She kept her voice calm, but there was a hard edge to it.

"I don't think it's just professionally. I think it's personally as well. Both of you have something in common."

His voice turned cold. "Like what?"

"Like feeling sorry for yourself."

He caught her look then and recognized it immediately. It was the same look that Karim must have seen on his face when he was interrogating him, the look that had told Karim everything he needed to know. He turned away.

"Fuck you, Hannie."

Her voice was suddenly brittle. "There're only a few people you think about, aren't there, Mister Morley! You think about the Iraqi and you think about the people who almost killed you the last time you were in Brussels and you think about yourself. What about the people at Palais Berlaymont? If your terrorists set off a bomb there, how many do you think might be killed? A dozen? A hundred? Do you care about them?"

Like Karim, she had held up a mirror and he hated what he saw. He had been wallowing in self-pity ever since he had arrived in Brussels. He had wanted a real job, needed one, and now he had it and was afraid of it. Goddamnit, he was an action agent. It was the one thing left in life that he was proud of. One thing he knew for sure, he was better at being an action agent than Diane was at being Diane.

"You're right," he said after a long moment. It hurt to say it. He wasn't just picking at a scab, he was tearing it off. He made himself look at her. She was half-smiling. "What's so funny?"

"Nothing," she said. "But if you *were* a broken-down Hollywood cowboy, I think I might be cheering."

He had almost fallen asleep sitting up when she said, "You're being silly."

"How?"

"Trying to sleep in the chair."

He stripped quietly in the darkness. The sheets were cool, the mattress remarkably comfortable, and Hannie was a smooth patch of warmth beside him. It was a long way from the hospital and the night nurse who had tried to help him and failed. She wouldn't have failed now.

Hannie slipped into the crook of his arm and said, "I want to know what happened the last time you were in Brussels."

Somewhere along the line he was going to have to trust her, he thought. He started talking and, surprisingly, it all came up. The agony and the hurt and the feeling of betrayal. She soothed him and only after she thought he was asleep did her own breathing become deep and regular.

He'd call London in the morning, report in. Then he'd find Bernadette and look up the booking agent, Schlöndorff.

He yawned and decided that the bed was the most comfortable he'd ever slept in. Next to him, Hannie stirred in her sleep and he thought of waking her and making love. He touched her lightly on the breast, then hesitated.

He was still wondering whether he should wake her when his body rebelled and he drifted off to sleep.

sixteen

THE TELEPHONE-TELEGRAPH COMPANY was crowded. Morley had to strain to understand the operators shouting out the names and the booth numbers over the confusion.

"*Señor Ibarra, numero nueve . . . Señor Ibarra . . .* "

He found himself searching for number nine among the booths along the wall and waiting for someone to walk toward it. Nobody did, and people began to eye each other questioningly.

"*Madame Rajagopal, number twelve . . . Senor Ibarra, numero nueve . . .* "

An old man and a young woman sorted themselves out from the crowd milling around the vinyl chairs. Morley watched the woman move toward the row of paneled doors, wondering how she could glide so easily in a sari. The old man hesitated, cupped his ear and looked uncertainly at the operator punching buttons on the console behind the counter.

The operator glanced up and poked his thumb toward door number nine. "*Numero nueve, señor—Torremolinos en numero nueve!*"

Morley stepped aside to let the old Spaniard pass and continued his pacing, ignoring the empty chairs. London knew Cailleau was dead, they could still recall him. He was actually depending on van den Haute to keep him there, at least for the moment. But the doctors could overrule the Captain on the grounds that Brussels under any circumstances might be too strenuous for him. His choice might lie between a disability pension or a desk job which would gradually turn him into one of the aging cold warriors who filled their days reminiscing about their various wars and how they had all been won by Intelligence.

He retraced his steps past the rack of directories, idly running his index finger along their spines. *Genève . . . Luxembourg . . . Bari . . . Lucca . . . Mannheim . . . Stuttgart . . . Dijon . . . Bruxelles . . .*

He slipped the book from the rack and flipped through the pages. *Schlöndorff, Hans. Agent Théâtral, rue Fosse-aux-Loups. 19 . . . 18.93.57.* He dug in his pocket for the ticket from Théâtre de Vaudeville and copied the address on the back. Schlöndorff's office was nearby; it wouldn't take long to walk there once his call to London went through.

"*Signore Peruchetti, numero sei . . . Mister Morley, number seven . . .*"

Booth seven was on the other side of the room. A young Asian woman carrying a plastic shopping bag from Sarma was already slipping into the booth next to it. Morley was half a dozen steps away when a laughing young man in a pullover and scarf walked up to the booth with his girlfriend. He kissed her lightly, then they both squeezed into the booth before Morley could stop them. The young man and his girl had been so engrossed with each other they hadn't checked the booth number. Then the uneasiness Morley had been fighting since coming to the telephone center suddenly surfaced.

The two kids should be in booth six; the Asian woman in booth eight hadn't been announced at all. And then he remembered. One of the team that Cailleau had smuggled in had been a Japanese woman.

He stepped over and grabbed the doorknob to booth seven, spun it and froze. A dark red puddle was already spreading under the door. He cracked the door slightly and could feel the dead weight pushing against it from the other side. He opened it a few inches further, blocking it with his body. It had happened as soon as they had stepped inside—the receiver was still on the hook. Even during his brief glimpse, there was a sharp splintering sound and the bodies on the seat jerked upright.

Morley abruptly leaned into the door to force it shut and lunged for the handle on number eight. The Japanese woman was just stepping out, closing her bag, when she saw him.

She paled, then screamed hysterically, pointing at Morley and the soaked carpet.

"Assassin! Assassin!"

Nobody moved toward Morley but several people stepped back, giving the Japanese woman enough room to slip past and dash through the double doors. Morley raced after her, the Beretta in his hand, pushing through the doors just in time to see her running down the escalator.

He plunged after her, shouldering aside the people on the stairs, then ran through the gallery of boutiques and out into the crowded intersection. He barely managed to keep up with her, his heart pounding. Once he nearly slipped on the cobblestones; another time he lost ground in the traffic as she dodged across the boulevard. Then he sensed someone close behind him and swore; the gendarmes would stop him before they'd stop her.

In the next block, she darted into an alley and he smiled

slightly. She'd been damned good, but now she'd blown it. There'd been too many people around, she must have realized that. They'd provided cover for her, prevented him from taking a clean shot. Now she had abandoned the crowd.

The first shot came from *behind* him and was much too close—he could hear the whine. He dove for a doorway, tried to sight her behind a Volvo, then found himself trapped in a cross fire. *Jesus!* He flattened himself in a doorway, turning slightly to search the street behind him. He could feel the seconds squeezing themselves into minutes in his mind. He felt as if he had suddenly gone deaf—the whole damned city seemed silent.

"Morley!"

So they knew where the fuck he was—what were they waiting for? He had let himself be suckered again, and in a few minutes he'd have the goddamned cops to worry about, too.

"Move in—you're covered!"

He didn't recognize the voice, debated whether to trust it, then gulped the damp air, slipped out of the doorway and ran toward the sedan, his back to the gun behind him.

She was already dead, sprawled on the wet cobblestones, her eyes staring up at the gray sky. Morley memorized her face. She was pretty, in her mid-twenties. Vasiliev—it *had* to be him, he fit van den Haute's description—sprinted up just as a crowd started to gather at the far ends of the alley. Both of them worked quickly, silently.

Morley ran his hands through the dead woman's pockets, then felt for anything hidden in her bra or waistband. Nothing.

He watched as Vasiliev dug out the plastic shopping bag from beneath her. The Russian tumbled the body roughly to one side and upended the bag, dumping out her purse along with a handful of cartridges and a pistol with a silencer still screwed onto the barrel. The squawk of a police car sounded in the distance. Vasiliev grabbed the purse and ran toward one end of the alley. Morley raced for the other.

At the corner, he slowed to a fast walk, breathing deep but steady. The boulevard was crowded with pedestrians, the air filled with the sound of horns and the squeal of brakes. He caught a glimpse of himself in a department store window, ran a hand through wild hair to brush it back. He yanked open his mac.

Christ!

He was hot. Sweaty. Pumped full of adrenalin. His heart was beating too fast, skipping beats.

But it could have been worse—a lot worse.

He let a laugh slip out along with his raspy breath. He'd forgotten all about the pain. It was still there and coming back strong, but he had forgotten it during the chase. He was out of shape and that had slowed him down; the pain hadn't.

He forced himself to fall in with the crowd around him. He'd managed to stay with her, to stay with Vasiliev.

Vasiliev.

He remembered the dossier, could conjure up each of the glossies tucked into the folder's pocket, knew by heart all the facts spewed out on the printouts, could recall at will all the stories he'd heard about the Russian—even the more preposterous ones that had circulated in Saigon and the border camps.

In their own way, the stories had served as a forecast of what might happen when they actually met. Now they *had* met, and were running on what passed for the same side. But he didn't know Vasiliev's interest in the Japanese woman. Or him. Which one of them had the Russian been tailing?

He elbowed his way to the curb. There'd be time to call London later; he wasn't going back to the telephone-telegraph office now—not so some clerk could become a hero. Tindemans and van den Haute would love that; he'd rot behind bars before they would help him. And London would hardly rush to bail him out. Their instructions hadn't covered his getting into trouble on his own.

He looked around the crowded boulevard. Vasiliev was here somewhere, waiting for him. He knew it because that's the way *he* would think, *was* thinking.

They spotted each other at the same time.

The Russian was standing under a machine that blew bubbles past the entrance of a smart boutique. A trace of recognition flickered in his eyes, then he turned to move with the crowd. Morley sidestepped a tram racing toward avenue du Silence and caught up with him at the corner.

Vasiliev was staring into the street. "Magnificent, isn't she?"

The girl directing traffic was young, trim, with brunette hair teasing the small of her neck. She caught a glimpse of Vasiliev staring and flashed a quick smile.

"Tell me," Morley asked. "Which of us were you tailing?"

A mocking grin. "I always follow the girls."

Vasiliev was about his own height. Not as trim as he had expected, a man who in middle age was tending toward a typical Slavic chunkiness. Not much younger, but maybe a bit less worried-looking. The blue eyes were still bright, the hair a dark blond, his sharp features just beginning to soften. A Russian Aryan—Vasiliev would have made a great triple agent in World War II. Morley ran through van den Haute's description, double-checking it out of the corner of his eye. He was still a natty dresser. The overcoat was camel's hair, custom cut so it hung close under the shoulders. English tassel loafers—Church's. He wondered about the gun, then remembered that in the alley Vasiliev had slipped his M61 Scorpion into a holster low on his back.

Vasiliev nodded toward a swirl of red neon. "We can talk there."

Morley dug his fists deeper into the pockets of his mac and squeezed lint. Vasiliev was casual, relaxed. The son-of-a-bitch sounded like he'd been born in Hartford or Boston. He followed the Russian through the door of the McDonald's. Vasiliev slipped into a corner booth, hugging the wall so he could watch everybody.

"How are you, Neal?"

Morley was sure Vasiliev owed a lot of his accent to old crooners and ancient movies.

"As good or as bad as you've been told."

"*Bonjour*, M'sieurs!"

The waitress couldn't have been much more than fourteen, the baby fat giving the lie to her efforts to look like a cover girl for *Vogue*. Her lips and nails were glossy, the stockings under her short skirt chalk white. They reminded Morley of the night nurse's.

Both Vasiliev and the young waitress were staring at him. "Well," Vasiliev repeated, "what will it be?"

"Coffee. Black."

"Of course. And no sugar."

Morley nodded. He wondered just how complete his dossier was. Vasiliev continued to study him, obviously gauging the extent of his recovery and filing any conclusions for future reference. Morley realized his dossier probably contained photographs of himself before he had gone to the hospital, that Vasiliev had expected to meet a different man—a man perhaps twenty pounds heavier with fewer lines in his face and less gray in his hair. Cailleau's slurred appraisal surfaced in his mind.

"That's all?" Vasiliev sounded like Taca at Comme chez Soi.

"That's all."

He didn't hide his own assessing of Vasiliev, noting the strength in his shoulders and neck, the thickness of his fingers and hands. He had lost the trim look of the athlete; now he came across as more of a bull. Vasiliev was the type who would keep all of his hair and probably retain its color as well, as many Russians did. But neither of them was likely to die of old age in any event.

Vasiliev shrugged, smiling at the girl good-naturedly. "Put everything on one check—accounting won't mind. I'll have a hamburger, rare, with cheese. *Frites.* And tea with plenty of ice."

She eyed them both over her little pad, shooting Vasiliev an extra smile as she turned away.

"You have a fan," Morley said.

"Let's hope she isn't fickle, like some of our former comrades these days." Vasiliev smiled easily, revealing a slightly crooked set of teeth, the one flaw that all truly handsome men had to have.

Morley made a production of digging through his pockets for matches.

"Here." Vasiliev produced the Japanese woman's worn leather purse and dumped the contents on the table. Morley picked out a cheap plastic lighter, lit his cigarette, and studied the forlorn pile between them. A room key with a brass tag numbered 4. A punched ticket from the Metro. A hairbrush with a bone handle. A small hand mirror and cracked contact lens case. A tiny metal tin, a pack of cigarette papers, a small wooden case with a hinged lid, an almost empty card of birth control pills, a scattering of French and Belgian francs and a box of 7.65 mm cartridges.

And finally a worry stone shaped like a kidney and worn smooth and dark from rubbing. It hadn't helped much.

Without a word, Vasiliev picked up the key and pocketed

it, then sat back waiting to see what Morley would choose.

The small teak case flipped open easily. The five joints inside were fat and tightly rolled. The tin was more difficult, but even before he twisted it open, he could smell the Tiger Balm. The contact lens case was large, for soft lenses, and empty; she must have been wearing them. The worry stone felt as cool as it did smooth. Vasiliev looked at him curiously when he palmed it. Neither of them said anything.

Vasiliev began to roll two of the Thai sticks toward him, then stopped, bemused. "I almost forgot," he said, pocketing all of them. "You don't indulge." Then: "I thought she was going after you."

"She was. She got somebody else by mistake."

He must have been pointed out to her—perhaps she had been briefed with photographs—but she had slipped into the booth first, she hadn't waited to make sure. She had heard the door to number seven open and close and then squeezed the trigger.

"I didn't know you were on anybody's list, Neal. I'm assuming this wasn't anything personal."

So the Russians didn't know of any connection between him and Cailleau either. He shrugged. "How long have you been on her?"

"Since early in the morning."

He watched, curious, as Vasiliev scooped everything but the lighter and the francs back into the purse. The restaurant had grown quiet and he picked up one of the coins, dropped it into the record selector on the wall and punched several buttons without bothering to look. Across the room, Simon and Garfunkel started singing "Bridge Over Troubled Waters." It was old home week in the DMZ. . . .

"She was watching outside your pensione this morning."

Vasiliev made disapproving sounds. "You kept the sweet young thing waiting. She was there at daybreak."

Morley smiled. Two could fish in the same waters. "If she had gotten there any earlier, she could have kept you company."

There was little except his tone of voice to indicate Vasiliev was now all business. "It was strictly routine, Neal. A tip that an aide from the Syrian embassy was to make contact with someone from the death squad—we don't even know if the Syrians themselves are involved. So I followed him and he obligingly led me to her."

Morley listened intently, neither believing nor disbelieving, concentrating on catching it all over the blare of the jukebox, on culling out any possible lies from the carefully dealt-out truth.

"When did you pick her up?"

"Just after midnight on rue des Veterinaires, near gare du Midi. Sympathizers hang out there."

"And then?" He'd been right not to order anything besides coffee. The hamburger patty looked paper thin. And even in Belgium, McDonald's succeeded in making *frites* that looked uniformly skinny and under-fried.

"They talked for five minutes and then she left." Vasiliev's voice was now flat, factual and faintly Slavic in accent; he could have been reading a report. "She went to a late-night cafe not far from petite rue des Bouchers. She may have expected a meet. Maybe she couldn't sleep. Who knows? Nobody showed, and three hours later she left to see you."

Morley felt a grudging admiration for Vasiliev. They were mirror images in some respects, two 'Nammies. It was a shock to realize how similar they both were.

"You told van den Haute there were six," he said. "You were wrong."

"I'm no mathematician. Besides, I wasn't there to keep count."

"The man who brought them across said there were seven."

Vasiliev concentrated on scraping the mayonnaise off his french fries. "Six, seven. Both of us want to find the rest of them, right?"

His first slip, Morley thought with a small feeling of satisfaction. Vasiliev knew perfectly well there were seven. "How did you get onto them?"

"I get instructions just like you, Neal. And I don't get any more background than you do."

"What's your interest?"

"Not my interest—Russian interest." Vasiliev blotted at his mouth with a paper napkin. "Off the record, under ordinary circumstances I don't think the government would be too upset about a group of terrorists running loose in Brussels. But what's ordinary anymore? We're . . . concerned."

He sipped at his coffee, frowning. "You must know as much about it as I do, Neal, you were the last one to talk with the *fluchthelfer*. You interrogated the Iraqi." Vasiliev had enough respect for him that he was willing to admit he had his own contacts inside the gendarmerie. "And you admit it was you the Asian was after."

"Would you believe me if I said I didn't know why?"

Vasiliev looked at him skeptically. "Maybe."

"The Iraqi didn't tell me much," Morley said. On the other hand, Vasiliev had already told him a great deal. The Russians wanted to cooperate. "Cailleau never had a chance to tell me much, either. We were supposed to meet again after his performance."

Vasiliev changed the subject. The horse was dead, it would do no good to beat it.

"Do you like Brussels, Neal? I find it oppressive and boring—it almost makes me homesick." Vasiliev had been waiting for Morley's glance. He smiled. "I mean, of course, the constant gray—and here often without even any snow to go with it."

"You should be thankful it's not as hot as Saigon."

"I was back there last year."

Morley felt a sudden stir of interest. "How was it?"

"You'd hardly recognize Saigon—only the tourists call it Ho Chi Minh City anymore. The girls who used to work the joints along Tu Do are gone. Most of them went to the schools for 'returning the dignity of women.' Presumably they learned a useful trade. Myself, I thought they already knew one." He laughed. "Now they're weaving baskets and doormats, but I don't think the demand will be as great." He had found a toothpick in one of his pockets and began picking his teeth. "The black market's still busy, only the prices have changed. A stereo set costs as much as it does in Paris, but you still can't make them work—you remember, the heat and the humidity spoil everything."

He chewed on the pick, then pointed with it at the crumpled cigarette wrapper in the ashtray. "Know how many dongs a pack like that costs now?"

"Not as much as Kents used to be in Romania."

"Yeah," Vasiliev laughed. "But in 'Nam they still smoke them."

They both laughed this time. Both knew first hand how in Bucharest a pack had gotten a table, and even more impressive, service in any restaurant, or a cab or an hour's massage. With two cartons you could buy a lawyer or a surgeon.

"Some government officials still insist that in thirty more

years they'll turn Saigon into a model of virtue and austerity." He said it deadpan and Morley started to protest. Vasiliev suddenly roared with laughter. "They know it's bullshit. Refrigerators are as much a status symbol in the North as they were in the South. Nobody wears black pajamas anymore. You Americans won the war after all, Neal. They're all struggling to become capitalists as soon as possible."

It was hard not to like Vasiliev. "In Saigon, the rumors were that you had a pipeline to the British Embassy, that somehow you managed to outflank Security and lift a whole set of battle plans we had given them."

Vasiliev looked bemused. "I never set foot in the Embassy. But they should have checked out their personnel. You know how Brits have a thing for natives. Their cooks, especially, were charming—perhaps they could even cook. I made love to one and she was kind enough to repay me with the plans." There was sudden laughter in his eyes. "Caucasians have a reputation, you must have discovered that."

He fished out another toothpick to chew on. "I heard stories about you, too, Neal." There was honest admiration in his voice. "You were very good, you were ruthless."

"I did my job," Morley said in a flat voice.

Vasiliev shook his head. "No, no, Neal, it was far more than that. We're both reliable, we both do our jobs, we're both professionals. But you always had an edge. You're a patriot."

His eyes strayed to watch the young waitress three tables away. "In our job, it's patriotism that keeps you from dropping. But you have to let go sometimes. Otherwise you burn out." Morley wasn't sure whether Vasiliev was giving him advice or not. "We're patriotic in Russia, though it's more what you might call love of the land. 'Mother Russia' and all that." He sighed. "Vietnam was a long time ago, Neal. You remember it far better than I do."

Morley couldn't decide whether he meant it as a reproof or merely a comment.

"It's a stinking job, Andrei. Why do you do it?"

Vasiliev shrugged. "The salary is good and my family's taken care of—it has its fringe benefits, you might say. And I don't know anything else." He scribbled a number on a card and gave it to Morley. "That's an answering service. Perhaps we can be helpful to each other. If you remember anything about Cailleau that would be useful, let me know." He stood up, pushed the francs into a pile on the table. "The Japanese woman can pay."

On the way toward the door, Vasiliev said, "I heard you might be going back to London, Neal."

"Didn't van den Haute tell you?" Morley glanced at his watch. It was about time to pay Schlöndorff a visit. "I'm not going back. I'm staying."

seventeen

"You have to wait your turn!" The woman's voice was shrill, agitated. "We all do!"

Morley stared at the four of them packed into the booking agent's small foyer. A thin-faced woman with a voice like a razor, an eight-year-old girl with a head full of curls, and two middle-aged men. Give the room an aquarium and some ancient magazines and it could have passed for a dentist's waiting room.

"Heidede's next." The woman smiled at the little girl and nodded at the man sitting next to her. "You're after him," she said to Morley.

He recognized the magician from the Théâtre de Vaudeville. Without his greatcoat and with his mussed hair exposing his bald spot, Electro looked seedier and older but just as disdainful as he had before. He ignored them all, contemplating the cracks in the ceiling as if he were getting ready to wave a wand and make everyone disappear. Morley was suddenly alert; long ago he'd stopped believing in coincidences.

There was room for one more on the couch—the woman and the magician sat as far away from each other as possible—and he eased in between them. The other man, a gaunt cello player, glanced up from his paperback, then down again. The little girl stared at Morley. She sat perfectly straight, one leg crossed over a dimpled knee. She waited patiently until Morley automatically smiled at her, then crossed her eyes and stuck out her tongue.

"Heidede!"

She scowled at her mother.

"Remember—hand at your waist, little chest out. And your hips, dearest—remember your hips when you sing."

Morley tried again. "What are you going to sing, Heidede?"

She continued to stare, her lower lip outthrust, then decided to answer him. " 'See What the Boys in the Back Room Will Have'."

"Marlene Dietrich sang it," her mother murmured, motioning Heidede to sit straighter.

The room sank into silence for five minutes, broken finally by the crackling of paper. The magician was eating a cheese sandwich, smoothing out the paper bag in his lap. There was a drop of mustard on his chin and Morley, still wondering why the magician was there, watched to see if he would catch it. "I saw you at the Théâtre de Vaudeville. You were very good."

The magician nodded, swallowing the last of the sandwich.

"So was the puppeteer," Morley continued. He let his voice trail off. "It's too bad . . ."

The magician drew an egg from the flattened bag. He shelled it as he twirled it, as if he were peeling an orange. "Apparently they cared even less for him than for me."

"Monsieur Schlöndorff is your agent?"

A shake of the head. "Not yet—we *all* audition, Monsieur. But he comes well recommended." He popped the egg in his mouth. As he chewed, the room filled with muffled, chirping cries. Oblivious, the magician—a damned good ventriloquist as well, Morley thought—palmed another hard-boiled egg from the empty bag. While the four of them stared, mesmerized, he cracked it open on the heel of his shoe and shelled it. Still chewing, he popped the egg in his mouth and then produced a third as the chirping swelled in volume and frenzy.

There was something calculated about the magician's tricks and Morley was convinced he had launched into the egg routine to squelch conversation about Cailleau. The magician wasn't the sort to give a free show. Then he realized it wasn't the tricks that repelled people, it was the man himself.

He stood up. He was wasting time. He hadn't phoned London and knew he wasn't going to. He'd cut all of his strings to get another day, maybe two. Van den Haute's reluctance to send him back was an ace in the hole, but he couldn't count on it.

He ignored the shrill protests from Heidede's mother, opened the door and walked in.

"The balls, Nina—watch the balls!"

Something ricocheted off the piano, followed by a flashing blur between the startled children tap-dancing. Morley stooped and picked up a hard rubber ball. The audition room was larger than he'd anticipated—and stifling; a high plaster ceiling kept in the heat and the noise. There was a balancing bar along one mirrored wall, a grand piano in the corner and between them, a bare wooden floor wide enough for a dance studio or stage. The other walls, like those in the basement of the annex, were whitewashed and soundproofed.

The chaos inside was overwhelming.

A dozen performers were in the room. A barrel-chested man, his wrinkled dress shirt open down the front, was bent over the piano belting out an aria. Half-a-dozen children were in a miniature chorus line, tapping to an intricate number blaring from a portable cassette player. Morley stared at them, his gaze coming up to rest on a man with a close-trimmed graying goatee trying to teach a frail, haunted woman how to juggle.

The wavy hair was nearly as thick and dark as in Cailleau's snapshot from the war. The shoulders had begun to settle, bowing slightly to the years, but for a Belgian of Monsieur Schlöndorff's generation, his belly was really *insignificant*; the booking agent had kept himself in decent shape. Morley ducked around the others and held out the balls. Without looking at him, Schlöndorff snatched them up and began juggling.

"The *balls*, Nina. Watch the balls. Forget your hands—you'll never drop them."

His eyes were already on the far side of the room and he shouted in Italian at the baritone. Morley followed him as he moved among the acts, finally cornering him against the piano. Schlöndorff started to brush past. "Wait with the others, your turn will come."

"This won't wait, Monsieur."

"Everything waits."

He ignored the photo Morley held out and ordered the acrobats to begin their routine again. Morley shoved the print into his hand. "I don't handle publicity shots until I've accepted the client," Schlöndorff snapped.

"It's yours and Serge's."

Schlöndorff stared at the crumpled picture, then looked up, for the first time realizing he wasn't another performer. Morley knew the others in the room were watching surreptitiously, going through the motions of their acts and at the same time straining to see and hear all they could. *Nobody* interrupted the booking agent. Except for the suddenly muted tap dancers, the room was quiet.

Schlöndorff nodded toward the unmarked door that led to his office. "It will be more private there."

There were autographed glossies on the office walls, an orange filing cabinet next to the desk and a huge Rolodex by the telephone. The two chairs looked comfortable enough but Schlöndorff didn't sit, nor did he offer one to Morley.

"Years ago, two East Germans came here, just like you." Like a border guard studying a passport, Schlöndorff was studying Morley's wristwatch and shoes. "They were Vopos, policemen from Magdeburg. They told me what I already knew. They said there was a price on my head and they made me an offer. They guaranteed safe exits for my clients—*most* of my clients. I could pocket everybody's money, turn their names over to the *Schartze* and not be too upset when they kept a few." He glared at Morley, his face flushed. "I told them what they could do with their offer. I don't know what you're offering, I don't care. Nothing has changed."

Morley leaned against a chair to take the weight off his leg. "That was a long time ago. I didn't come here with any offer. But Serge would have been proud of you."

Schlöndorff's eyes looked watery. He fished in his pocket for a handkerchief to blow his nose.

"He had brought in a load from the East," Morley said quietly. "They killed him."

"I knew he had been murdered," Schlöndorff said in a pained voice. "I did not know why." He stared at the photograph for a moment, then put it down on his desk and sank into a chair. "You haven't told me who sent you."

Morley pocketed the snapshot. Hannie would never forgive him if he lost it. "Serge sent for me through a mutual friend from the war, *his* war." Only a flicker of an eyelid betrayed that Schlöndorff knew the friend. "We talked about the good old days and about his last load of seven. We were in his dressing room, the third door on the right, bottom of the stairs. There was a life-sized puppet in a tutu and a trunk with the photograph in it and his Luger. . . . You remember the gun he never turned in? It was on the table. He told me that you were both duped, that your clients had sworn they needed your help."

Schlöndorff glanced at his watch, suddenly bored. "Serge told you nothing, Monsieur. I haven't helped in years. I don't know what Serge was involved in, but there's no need for *fluchthelfers* anymore."

Morley wasn't sure whether to believe him or not. He glanced at the glossies of nightclub and music hall acts. "There's more money in other bookings, is that it?"

"There's more gratitude, more honesty."

"And all you wanted was gratitude?"

Schlöndorff gripped the edge of his desk, his knuckles white. "Monsieur, I offered everyone the plans and the tools so they could take the risks if they wanted to. Nobody ever did."

Morley was quiet for a moment, weighing Schlöndorff's comments. "When did you book Serge into Théâtre de Vaudeville?"

"I didn't."

It was Morley's turn to look surprised. "I thought you were his agent?"

Proudly: "Always." Then, with an angry shrug: "Arrangements were made this time before I knew anything about them."

"Who made them?"

"The manager of Théâtre de Vaudeville says Serge himself."

"You don't believe that."

"No." Schlöndorff took a deep breath. "I thought, 'In forty years, Serge has always been satisfied with our arrangement.' I thought, 'I am furious.' Then I thought, 'Serge is Serge—we'll discuss it over cognac.' "

"And?"

"He didn't want to talk about it, he was preoccupied. Then it no longer mattered."

"Would Serge book himself?"

"Serge would do whatever he pleased." He stood up. "You must excuse me, the acts are waiting."

"The woman," Morley said slowly. "She's never juggled."

A tired smile rippled across Schlöndorff's face. "She scrubs floors—it's not work that will take her children and her back to Firenze. There is a circus traveling there. . . ." He looked cynical. "I had not heard it was against the law to help a widow go home." He reached for the doorknob, turned it. "As I told you, I am no longer involved, I haven't been for years. The borders are open. For most of us. Most of the time. I don't know who Serge was helping but they could have helped themselves. If they couldn't, then something was badly wrong."

He held the door open, the blast of noise almost drowning out his next few words. "I wish I had known the bastards Serge thought he was saving. He would still be alive."

"Where would he have taken them?"

"If I knew, Monsieur, I would not be here. I would be there, with my own Luger."

Morley followed him back into the audition room, raising his voice. "Bernadette was with him in the East?"

Schlöndorff stopped. "Yes. Of course."

"I understand she's playing some club—"

"Le Couvent." He looked pained. "Any taxi driver can take you there."

"You handle her, too?"

Schlöndorff was staring at the acts working out in the

room and seeing none of them. "I did once. Long ago. She was a chanteuse."

Morley was surprised at the tremor in his voice. "You loved her?"

"Of course, Monsieur," Schlöndorff said softly. "Everybody did."

eighteen

MORLEY PEELED OFF his raincoat, shivered from the chill that rippled down his damp back, and studied the marionettes hanging from the rough-hewn beams. Roi d'Espagne had been his favorite cafe in Brussels, and he'd passed under the dusty puppets often. They weren't as cleverly crafted as Cailleau's. Their leather boots were cracked, their copper shields dented and their scraggly beards less lifelike—they were props to give the bar atmosphere. But to really appreciate Cailleau's handiwork, you had to see the others.

He hung his mac on a hook near the stuffed horse and stepped around the crowded tables, looking for Hannie and Louis. He found them huddled at a window table on the upper floor, away from the heat of the blazing fireplace. He had phoned Louis from Schlöndorff's and asked him to meet Hannie at the bar and wait for him. The big man would be protection, if not a witty conversationalist.

From Louis's laughter, apparently Hannie was witty enough for both of them. When Morley got closer, he saw that Louis had bought another toy, a tumble ladder, and the two of them were setting the small wooden figures on the top rung and racing them against each other. He glanced around for a familiar face among the waiters but didn't recognize any of them. He flagged one down, ordered a Trappist beer for himself and refills for Louis and Hannie, then eased into the remaining chair.

Hannie handed the toy to him. "Here, try this." He set the racer on the top perch, nudged it with his knuckle and it fell to the table. She took it back. "Not like that, like *this.*"

He tried it again, with no better luck. "You've got a head start, you've been practicing." He felt relaxed. Louis had his faults, but more than once they had shared what passed for a good time in Brussels. And when the chips were down, Louis had saved his life. Hannie he was getting to know—and trust.

"Louis has been telling me all about you."

"Not everything, I hope." What worried him more was how much Hannie might have told Louis about herself. He put the toy to one side and turned to Louis. "What's Tindemans been doing?"

"You should have been nicer to Leon, Neal—"

"Nobody's going to report back, Louis."

The big man looked relieved. "Leon says Diane has one of the men the puppet master smuggled in. He'll talk soon, if he lives. Leon is sure of it."

He said it as if it had just happened. Morley was surprised. So van den Haute had confided in him about the Iraqi before he had told anybody else. A peculiar vote of confidence. Louis finished his beer, waved at the bartender for refills all around, and headed downstairs to the john. After he had left, Morley turned to Hannie. "What did you find out about Karim?"

Hannie took it for granted that he didn't want to talk about the Iraqi in front of Louis. She ticked off the information on her fingers. "His father is dead, he died before Karim was a year old. He has three brothers and a sister. All younger, all still in school."

186

"And his mother?"

"She lives on a small pension. She has high blood pressure, but they say she'll live for years." Hannie finished off her glass of wine. "You were right about the speeches. He had a reputation for being a rabble-rouser in college. And he had a following."

It wasn't much. The waiter put down their drinks and Morley asked, "Does Philippe still work here?" One familiar face, that was all he wanted.

"Philippe, Monsieur?" The waiter looked blank. "I could inquire if you wish, but I've been here four months and I know of no Philippe."

"It's not important." Hannie was staring at him and he said, "I used to drink here. Philippe and I had a rapport. He always wanted his own pub—I hope he has it."

"You must have been lonely."

Oddly, he didn't want her sympathy. "I've never been here long enough to be anything but a tourist. That's been true of almost everywhere but 'Nam."

She looked surprised. "You considered Vietnam home?"

"For a while." Then Louis was back and he said, "Do they still have food here?"

Louis waved for the waiter to come back. "Sure, Neal, a *croque monsieur* or just some cheese?"

He shrugged. "Order whatever you want—we won't be staying here long. I think it's time for a night on the town." Louis's face lit up and Morley remembered other nights on the town with the big man. He had a feeling Le Couvent wouldn't disappoint him. He didn't tell Louis that he wasn't interested in watching a skin show so much as seeing the woman who had done such a superb job of fooling him before she had fallen on top of Cailleau's body. She had traveled with the puppet master, she had worked with him, she had probably slept with him.

She had to know something about the terrorists Cailleau had brought back across the border.

Halfway through his slab of cheese, Louis said, "Hannie told me about the puppets when she was young." He squeezed her hand, his eyes alert for any encouraging response. Morley had to remind himself that it was unlikely Hannie would see much in Louis. "The life-sized puppets that come alive." Louis grinned. "I believed her."

Morley shot Hannie a glance. She hadn't been able to resist putting Louis on, probably because he had been pumping her and she had tried to avoid direct questions by flirting with him. She didn't realize she was encouraging something in Louis that might be difficult to turn off.

When they had finished eating, they piled into Louis's cab and drove through the rain to Le Couvent. Louis didn't ask for directions, but then he was a devotee of the skin shows; he knew by heart where they were.

"The Convent" flourished in an impasse on the fringes of the Ilot Sacre, the maze of crooked little streets near Grand' Place, spattered with nightclubs, bars and discos that operated behind closed shutters and catered to specialized clienteles.

The cab lurched. Louis was explaining the intricacies of Sizzling Sue, the latest electronic arcade game, to Hannie and keeping only one eye on the street. He suddenly braked, jammed the cab into second and gunned it over the curb, jarring the three of them but avoiding a man who had stepped in front of their car.

The pedestrian, a middle-aged Moroccan dressed as a Boy Scout, ducked nimbly to one side, swore at them in a high falsetto, then vanished into a shadowy doorway. Louis drove another block, jockeyed the cab into a parking spot and they spilled out. Hannie slipped on the cobblestones and Morley grabbed her arm, shielding her as they bent against the wind.

Le Couvent was a black, padded cave with music, specializing in skin shows for drunken Eurocrats—Morley knew that much without even climbing the stairs. The club was situated over a shop that had, Louis cheerfully insisted, recently belonged to an undertaker.

"*Mon poupée!*" Hannie's heel had caught in the loose carpeting on one of the steps and it was Louis' turn to clutch her arm and help her up the remaining steps. Morley felt another flash of jealousy which he quickly smothered. For God's sake, he didn't own her. Then he stumbled over a threshold two inches higher than it should have been. He wondered if it were deliberate, if the management used it to help gauge how drunk new arrivals were.

"*Cheri, M'sieurs. . . .*"

Louis took over. "Table for three." He flashed a roll of bills with one hand and gave Hannie another squeeze with the other. She slipped away, ostensibly to see the stage, and Morley stepped between them. Both Louis and Hannie were playing a dangerous game.

The dimly lit stairs had been dazzlingly bright compared to the smoky darkness just beyond the landing. It took Morley a moment before he could make out the score of tiny tables squeezed into the blackness. These were crowded with wide-eyed revelers, expense-account spenders hypnotized by the exotic beauties around them—the Swedish, French, Chinese and African hostesses who glided between the tables and the more intimate booths. The customers were drinking Belgian beer or French champagne and trying to decide between watching the hostesses or the raunchy Little Bo-Peep on the small stage who spread her legs for them under the yawning lavender spotlight.

It wasn't difficult to see all of her. Violet lips pouted under rouged cheeks and a lopsided tangerine-colored bow clashed with a yellow wig. But Morley knew it was her swelling, dark-nippled breasts swinging free as she bent to caress her slightly bruised thighs that fascinated the audience.

He turned to the manager who was busily exchanging Louis' francs for their memberships. "When does Bernadette go on?"

" 'Bernadette'! That's good, that's really good." The manager chuckled. "It's been awhile since we had ourselves another nun!"

Morley pressed some francs into his hand. "Bernadette, Monsieur. She works here?"

The manager winked. "Here she goes by the name of Belinda. You're in time—she's next, after the scag."

"When do you go on?" Hannie asked sarcastically.

He glanced at her without a change of expression. "I haven't worked the stage in years, Mademoiselle, but it was nice of you to remember."

The manager led them into the darkness, his flashlight picking a path among the tables. The one he gave them was down front, by the stage, bathed now in a bluish-white light. He held a chair stiffly for Hannie, pocketed the Reserved card and motioned for a waiter who lit Louis' cigar and promptly suggested champagne. Hannie ordered a Cinzano, Morley a double Scotch. But a grinning Louis sent the waiter scurrying for a bottle of champagne and three glasses. Louis was trying his best to impress Hannie. Morley wondered where he got the money; the Bureau didn't have a reputation for generosity.

On stage, Little Bo-Peep vanished and an odd couple took her place. The statuesque blonde was wearing a very red, very tight gown. Her friend wore a ruffled dress shirt, black patent-leather dancing shoes, powder-blue tie and tails. He was dressed rather smartly for a dummy. A pink spot found them, their arms thrown around each other. The music quickened. Belinda and

190

Edouardo, her mannequin friend, began an intimate dance.

Morley had seen it all before. It was one of the Continent's classic striptease routines. Still, he was impressed. In the first few minutes of her charade, Belinda exhibited an inspired, exotic animalism, a feverish imagination. Whatever her faults might be, nobody would ever call her ordinary.

Her dumb friend was about average height but in her stiletto heels, Belinda stood taller—much taller. Edouardo's empty head nestled between her petite breasts. It rested there, nodding with each deep breath. A gloved hand pulled Belinda's own head down, a painted face brushed against her chin.

"Recognize her?" Morley asked in a low voice.

Hannie shook her head, frowning.

On stage, Edouardo coaxed his partner and Belinda laughed a deep, throaty laugh. She was holding the dummy closer with its coat hanging open. Morley could see how her slender hands could easily dip down into Edouardo's empty sleeves and then into the large white gloves sewn to their cuffs.

She looked directly at him and winked.

Belinda and Edouardo spun around. Her gown hung open in back, showing off a sheer red bra and equally sheer panties. A white glove tugged at the zipper and Morley could hear the dummy murmur in her ear. Moaning softly, Belinda nudged the gown off both shoulders.

Louis had been watching, entranced, and now whispered, "She isn't really talking, Neal, that's a tape. Look, she isn't even moving her lips."

Trust Louis to know the truth about the moans and the laughter. On stage, Edouardo shook Belinda and her gown fell to the floor. She stepped out of it and Edouardo and his Lady in Red clung to each other in a golden spotlight.

"I only saw her for a minute," Hannie said in a low voice. "She was wearing sandals and jeans and she didn't have a wig."

On the tiny stage, Edouardo slipped a white glove beneath Belinda's panties. The couple turned. No one in the quiet, smoke-filled room could miss the bright streak of lipstick smeared across Edouardo's cool, expressionless mouth.

The waiter materialized with another bottle of champagne and left as silently as he had come. Morley watched him go and then heard a cough and glimpsed a flash of gold-rimmed glasses three tables over. He nudged Louis's foot, all the time keeping his eyes on Taca. The platinum blonde coyly teasing the near-sighted librarian was made up like a schoolgirl, complete with braids and a tired face.

Louis grinned. "He writes reviews so he can lick the candy."

The man sitting with Taca was middle aged and almost as portly. He was staring intently at the stage, ignoring the show at his side.

"Who's his friend?"

"One of the finance ministers—money is Taca's other hobby."

At the table, the blonde had taken off Taca's glasses and was toying with his ear. The librarian was too preoccupied to notice the three of them. Morley had to give the fat man credit—it was the perfect meeting place. Everybody would be watching the stage, nobody would be watching anybody else.

His attention drifted. They had gotten a good table. Hannie was reason enough for the manager to steer them toward the stage-side table, but Morley was uncomfortable. He would have much preferred the shadows to the spotlight.

On stage, Belinda was moaning with ecstasy. Under Edouardo's persuasive coaxing, her heavy sighs were breathless, demanding. Louis's forehead was sweaty, his eyes bright. Belinda and Edouardo were obviously one of his skin-magazine fantasies come to life. Hannie was staring, publicly interested but privately bored. Morley found himself fascinated for reasons of his own.

In the spotlight, the foxy lady with the red velvet collar, small moon breasts and glistening pubic hair writhed as Edouardo's gloved hand slid her sheer panties down. Her cheeks bobbed into view as she trembled in the dummy's arms, naked except for her stiletto heels and simple neckband.

"Like her?" Hannie asked. "She's interested in you, you know."

She was trying to sound casual but there was an edge to her voice. And then Morley realized she was right. The pink-and-white blonde had grabbed one of the dummy's gloved hands between her teeth; the other was clamped between her thighs. Now she straddled Edouardo. She was less than an arm's reach away from their table; they could have touched her easily. Her bare, long-fingered hand tugged at Edouardo's fly. Her body humped slowly up and down. Her gray-green eyes fixed on Morley, definitely taunting.

He stared back at her, interested. But not in the way she imagined.

After Belinda had left the stage, Morley touched Hannie lightly on the shoulder. "I have to see her," he said. "I'll meet you later, at the pensione." And then to Louis: "She's mine, Louis—don't get any ideas." He wanted it to sound sophisticated and funny, but it didn't come out that way. He bit off his apology. To hell with it, subtlety would have been wasted on Louis anyway.

He ignored Hannie's angry protest and pushed aside the curtains. He owed Louis a lot, but Taca wasn't the only one with a taste for candy. And Hannie had made a tactical error two hours before when she had let Louis know she found him amusing. Now he would think a "no" was just her acting coy.

His last glimpse of Hannie was of her angrily pouring the rest of his champagne into her glass.

Behind the stage, a narrow wooden staircase led to the top floor. The stairs were bowed, steep. Morley grabbed the iron pipe that served as a handrail and found it less steady than the steps themselves. The cubicle at the top was large, lined with mirrors and filled with three tiny dressing tables. Costumes and street clothes hung on hooks between them. The room had been doused with the same heady perfume as the *artistes* below. The fumes were smothering, but the girl sitting in the chair seemed oblivious to them.

She had close-cropped, ebony hair and smooth, honey-colored skin. She was studiously painting her toenails two shades of green. The eager smile she gave him was the one she reserved for paying customers. It faded when he mentioned Belinda.

"*Les amoureux,*" she snapped, concentrating once again on her toes. "They are in the *privé* dressing room."

He knocked on the door, heard nothing, turned the knob and stepped inside. It was a cubbyhole of a room, with drab apple-green walls. The heavy fragrance that clung to the rest of Le Couvent was refreshingly absent. He took a deep breath, felt the muscles of his stomach relax, and turned to look at the woman sitting at the dressing table. The face watching him in the oval mirror looked blank and curiously aloof. She didn't move. The only trace of motion was the curling wisp of cigarette smoke.

Edouardo sat in a chair next to her, one slender arm swung over the back, his head tilted to one side, an ashtray balanced on his knee. The smoke came from a cigarette in the tray. For a moment, the tableau was one of shocking reality, the dummy as much alive as the woman.

Belinda picked up the cigarette, inhaled deeply, then returned the butt to the ashtray. She leaned forward, her breasts pushing against the dummy's chest, and flicked loose strands of long blonde hair off his shoulders. Her red velvet gown was tossed over the rim of the mirror. Her red bra and panties lay among the crumpled packs of Gauloises, Caporals, Chesterfield Kings and imported Pall Malls, along with small metal tins of cosmetics, neckbands, scarves and letters from admirers that cluttered the dressing table. There were a lot of letters.

She was still wearing the red velvet choker around her neck. That, and a sheer robe that had fallen open.

"*Pardon*, Bernadette."

She sat there smoking and watching him in the mirror but said nothing. It was a moment before he noticed her hand resting inside the dressing table drawer.

"You don't need Serge's Luger. I tried to save him, not kill him."

Somewhere on the crowded table, a clock ticked. It was sitting next to an open bottle of Chaudfontaine water, a folding clock in pebbled red leather with a square face and luminous numbers.

Bernadette watched the flick of his eyes. She still didn't move except to stub out her cigarette and light another.

"It's not what you think," he said, feeling uneasy. "I'm here because of Serge—"

He spun around when he heard the door creak open behind him. The bushy-browed manager. Who else would reek more of cheap cologne than the girls? He strolled over to Bernadette and began to lightly massage the back of her neck and shoulders. She had nothing to say to him, either, though Morley could see her body tense.

"She is magnificent," the manager murmured, his eyes

wary. Morley wondered if he was her pimp. "You are an admirer, yes? One of many, I assure you." He sounded apologetic. "Her performances are demanding, exhausting. You understand, please—she must rest."

The look in Bernadette's eyes was one of mild curiosity. She slipped her hand from the drawer and held it out to Morley, ceremoniously. He bowed slightly and took it.

"*Adieu*, Mademoiselle, Monsieur."

As he turned to close the door after him, he could see Edouardo still staring at him. The cheap mirror had twisted the little dummy's grin into a sneer.

"Too bad she didn't make you happy." Satisfied with her nails, Greentoes was now absorbed in applying a beauty mark to the shady side of her right breast. "Raymond likes her," she mused, tossing her head toward the back room. "She's very good with the dummy." She paused a moment to appraise him again and made a show of liking what she saw. "But with a *real* man, I'm much better." Her voice turned coaxing. "Perhaps after the show?"

"Perhaps." He started down the stairs which somehow seemed steeper and shakier than before. This was a world he understood. The people and the games were the same as at Ramuntcho, Givral or La Pogode, the houses in Saigon where anything could be had for a price. For a thousand francs, Greentoes would blow him right on the stairs.

Bernadette was something else, a courtesan held captive in a two-bit house. She had probably known Cailleau better than anybody else. She had lived with him, she sure as hell must have known about his smuggling. He guessed she'd also fulfilled Cailleau's physical needs, that she was an expert at fulfilling men's needs.

He glanced at the address on the small, tightly crumpled envelope she'd pressed into his palm when he'd left. She might be an expert at fulfilling his, too.

At least when it came to information about Cailleau.

nineteen

SNOW. HE HAD known all along that it was coming, had sensed it in his game leg, but it still surprised him. The cold flakes swirled around his face, caught in his hair and melted under the mackintosh's upturned collar.

Only two cars had passed in all the time he'd stood watching, and already their tire tracks were disappearing under a thin sheet of white. A taxi had double parked for several minutes down the street and a woman wearing a fur coat had finally gotten out, waving to the driver who pulled away as she let herself into one of the houses. A minute later, Morley saw a soft glow behind the curtains of a window under the eaves.

He almost hadn't recognized Bernadette. In street clothes, she looked as different from Belinda as she did from François.

The other car, a small Fiat, had twice tried to nudge into a parking spot too short even for it, then sped around the corner. He could hear it for some time in the cold air. It slowed twice but never stopped. Aside from the cars, there was little sound: the rustle of branches, a few anonymous ripples of noise far away in the night. He shifted his weight and revived a wet foot gone numb. His legs were heavy, his hands cold. He took his eyes off the street only long enough to glance at his watch.

Ten minutes since she'd gone in.

He'd never thought the invitation was a setup, but he'd gotten there early and stood watching for nearly an hour. He still felt anxious and wondered if he'd missed anything. Finally, he slipped from the shadows and walked silently toward the houses.

Hers was like all the others, distinguished only by the scarlet letter box that hung on the stucco wall beneath a statue of the Madonna. Four brass name plates lined the door frame. He stepped to one side so he could read them in the yellowish glow from the streetlamp. Three of the plates had turned green long ago. The fourth was still shiny, with raised script bearing the same name that was on the crumpled envelope in his pocket.

Schiaffino.

He didn't have to ring; she had been waiting for him just inside. She heard him approach, opened the door and squeezed against the wall so he could pass by. She'd taken off her shoes, but even in her nylons she was almost as tall as he was. She was still wrapped in her fur. For a moment it seemed as if it were crawling, then he realized she was cradling a cat under the coat.

He closed the door, locked it.

"Go on up," he whispered. "You'll both catch pneumonia."

The greenish-gray eyes studied him for a moment. Then Bernadette tapped a wall switch that turned on the dim bulb at the top of the landing. He could hear the timer ticking. Before they reached her door, the landlady's *minuterie* switched off, leaving them in darkness. The glow Morley had seen from the outside showed through Bernadette's open door. It came from a brass oil lamp with a delicate, handblown chimney and a round, etched shade. Her flat was small but much larger than her dressing room, and furnished with leather and chrome and thick wool carpets.

His shoes were soaked, covered with snow. He took them off and left them on a newspaper in the hall. Bernadette shut the door, then set the long-haired marmalade Tom down on the shag rug. The cat promptly lost itself in the thick orange and brown pile. She held out her hand for Morley's wet raincoat and hung it on a hook in the nearby kitchen. She hesitated, then slowly reached behind her neck, undid the silk scarf and tossed it on the couch.

"What do you want from me?"

It wasn't a hiss or a whisper. Her voice was a hoarse, ripping sound forced from the tube that marred an otherwise smooth neck. The surgeon who had implanted the tiny piece of plastic had had considerably more training than some of the "specialists" who had cut into him. But Morley doubted that any man would consider her throat a work of beauty. He found himself listening to her tense, raspy breathing, remembering what Schlöndorff had said and thinking that once this woman had a voice people paid to listen to.

"You did not know." She was proud that he hadn't suspected the all-too-pragmatic reason for her ascots and scarves and silence. "Cancer." She spit out the word defiantly, lit a Lucky Strike and blew the smoke at the ceiling.

"The doctors were so sure I'd lose everything." She paused as if to emphasize that *this* was not her real voice, to deny that the sound she was making had anything to do with her. "I proved them wrong." A rattling intake of breath. "What I lost was more than enough."

She slipped out of the fur, studied him again.

"What do you want?"

He sat down in the armchair. His hands were wet, sweaty. He slid forward and locked them around his knee.

"Tell me what happened at Théâtre de Vaudeville."

"Why should I tell you anything?"

He could feel the wool pile beneath his wet socks and wanted to take them off, too.

"I'm curious about the people who killed Cailleau." He didn't add that they had tried twice and almost succeeded in killing him as well, nor did he mention that they had far bigger game in mind than either he or the puppeteer. She looked at him uncertainly, and he guessed she would stall for time while she debated telling him anything.

As if she'd read his mind, she crossed to the window and raised the lid on the mahogany bar just beneath it. "You're not from the police."

"No. I'm in Brussels because Serge sent for me. We had a mutual friend in London." She had been close to Cailleau; Serge had probably told her all about *the* war, bragged about his "connections." She turned, holding a glass and a bottle, waiting for him to say more. "He was going to tell me about the refugees he brought in, about their mission." She opened the small refrigerator to get some ice. The tinkling of the cubes in the glass bothered him; it brought back memories of the sweets girl and the ice pick and Cailleau.

She turned around and thrust the glass at him, splashing some of his drink on the carpet. *"Voilà!"* He took the glass and gulped down half the contents, rewarded a second later by a flush spreading out from his stomach.

He held up his glass. "To Serge." He felt faintly foolish, but he needed some gesture to inspire her to talk.

"I spent the morning with friends. I was late to the theater," she said, folding into one of the other chairs. She paused to sip her drink. "Serge was above, waiting. I went on stage. A few minutes later, he fell. There was confusion . . . they pulled the curtain and I left. I was frightened." She shrugged. "That's all there is."

"How did you get the refugees across the border?"

She didn't answer but turned to look at a white pagoda-shaped cage by the window. "See the little birds? *Moineaux de Japon.* Pretty, yes? But they do not sing. Only chirp. Like so."

She paused and they both listened to the chatter. She was right; nobody would call that singing.

"Once, we had canaries. They sang beautifully. But their songs drove Noenoesch mad." She bent down to pet the cat, who had curled up around her feet. "So one day, Noenoesch killed them. They had driven him to it. Now we have the *Moineaux.* No one gets angry. No one gets hurt."

She looked up. "I'm like the *Moineaux.* I do not sing. Certainly not to you, Monsieur."

Morley wasn't willing to give up so easily. "I found a letter in Serge's trunk. I read enough to know you loved him."

"We were good for each other. That does not mean I loved him."

She was protecting herself, Morley thought. Everybody had wanted Bernadette's body, but few people had wanted Bernadette. She hadn't been bedding Cailleau for money—money would be no problem for her. She had wanted something else from the puppet master.

"Karim Arif is an Iraqi. Twenty years old. A few centimeters shorter than I am." He felt like a tutor preparing a student for an examination. "He weighs maybe sixty kilos and speaks fluent English. He could be a medical student or a philosophy major. An old scar cuts across his chest and under his left arm."

He found his attention wandering. She had beautiful eyes and a lovely face, but all he could see in his mind was that piece of plastic tubing.

She lit another cigarette from the butt of the one she had been smoking and nodded for him to go on.

"The Japanese woman was younger than you," Morley

202

said. "Maybe twenty-five." Bernadette was older than he'd thought after seeing her at Le Couvent. "She was short, no taller than that mantel." He pointed at the fireplace. "Pretty. Perhaps fifty kilos. She wore soft contact lenses and took the pill." He couldn't tell whether she'd decided to cooperate or not. She was an old hand at defiance. "I need to know about the others."

"There was another Iraqi." She tried to clear her throat and the sound almost made him cringe. "Older than the first. Maybe two, three centimeters taller. Brown eyes."

Her voice faded. She splashed Pernod in a glass, took a sip and retreated for a moment into memory. Like an older woman, she was already beginning to live in the past.

"And the others?" he prompted.

"Two of the other men were Egyptians. In their mid-twenties. Both had light-colored eyes—blue or gray. One was taller than either of the Arabs. Thin, shy; he worried a lot. The other was shorter. He had a belly. There was a Sudanese man. Older. He stammered when he talked. He weighed maybe seventy kilos."

She fell silent again and Morley said, "That's only six."

"Yes."

He watched the cat rolling on the carpet, batting at a wad of string. "Serge told me there were seven."

"There were six of *them*," she amended. "And the Slav."

"How old?"

"Thirty-five. Maybe more."

"A big man?"

"Small. Black hair. Glasses. I don't remember his eyes. A gray suit under the other clothes. It didn't fit him well."

"You said he was Slav?"

She nodded. "Maybe Polish, maybe Russian. He didn't talk

much. He was sick. Or frightened. He was very uncomfortable with the others."

"How did Cailleau get them out?"

She smiled for the first time. "As puppets." On stage her smile had been part of her act. Now, it made her look younger, less hard. "A gendarme. Baker. Pirate. Ballerina. . . ." She counted them off on her fingers. "They wore wigs and thick makeup, like François. Underneath their costumes, they wore shoulder harnesses. Just before we reached the frontier, Serge hung them up with the marionettes in the back of the van."

Morley stared at her, disbelieving. There was no way it would have worked. The infra-red detectors—were they on the scrap heap now as well? He didn't think so. Nobody threw expensive toys away. But allowances got cut, expensive toys left to rust. So maybe . . .

"Where did you cross?"

"The autobahn at Sopron."

Not as busy as Bratislava, some thirty kilometers north, but just as close to Vienna. And even more relaxed, Morley thought, given the times. Getting to Austria through Hungary wouldn't have been difficult. But not the way Cailleau had done it.

"Where did you cross out of Romania?"

"Gyula. It was early morning and I was scared. But the guards were ready for a smoke; they had just turned back a truck loaded with mourners and a casket and there was nobody else around." She was matter-of-fact about it. "I gave them cigarettes, kept them amused."

"Serge was paid?"

She hesitated. He wasn't sure why but he had stepped into a sensitive area. "I don't know."

He was certain Cailleau had collected a fee, but she obviously didn't want to talk about it. Maybe she was disappointed that Serge had had a price after all.

"And you never asked?"

A cold smile. "It was his business, not mine."

He waited a moment, watching the cat. "When did he tell you about it?"

"During our last night in Berlin. In the dressing room after the show."

"What did he say?"

"That they were refugees and needed help."

"And you believed him?" He didn't believe *her*.

She shrugged.

"I've seen the Iraqi and the Japanese woman. They hardly looked like refugees to me," Morley said.

"There are all kinds of refugees."

"Do you know who approached him, who he saw who might have set up the deal?"

A hesitation once again. "He saw many people." She was losing interest in the questioning. "I really cannot say."

"Did Hans Schlöndorff book you into Théâtre de Vaude-ville?"

"No—ask him."

"Who did?"

She lit another cigarette, and for a moment her face was hidden in the smoke. "Serge phoned Hans. He said we were going to play there. He said it was all arranged. He didn't say who had arranged it."

"Why call Schlöndorff at all?"

"They were friends. Hans would have found out. Then there would have been bad feelings."

She was lying and Morley knew it. He sank back into the leather chair, his thoughts slipping back to Le Couvent. He kept seeing a pair of thick, gold-framed glasses and the overage St. Trinian's schoolgirl playing with them.

Bernadette yawned and stood up, her wrap falling off one shoulder. The transformation was startling. One moment she had been a tired, slightly bored hausfrau, relaxing with her shoes off and her nylons rolled partway down. The next moment, she was—Belinda. The expression on her face was the same one she had worn at Le Couvent, the way she moved a reprise of her role on stage.

"Something else I can do for you?" She had read him as Cailleau had, although she had read a different set of symptoms.

He stood up to go. She had said as much as she was going to. He would go back to Karim with the information she had given him and see how much of it he would confirm.

She ignored him when he got his coat and picked up his shoes, studiously indifferent whether he left or not. He hesitated at the door, watching her in the mirror that hung on the back.

She dropped the wrap and toyed briefly with the red panties, her movements just as enticing as they had been at the club. Morley remembered how her body had glistened on stage, recalled the throbbing of the music and the moans that had been recorded on tape along with Edouardo's heavy breathing.

"There's a draft," she said. "If you're going to stay, close the door."

He closed and locked it, then followed her into the bedroom with its thick goose-down mattress and huge pillows. She lay on her back, one knee drawn up, and watched him as he undressed. He was already hard. She reached for the lamp.

"Do you want it on or off?" she husked.

"Off." The curtains were thin and he and Bernadette would make a fine target on the bed. As it was, the streetlamp shown through the cloth, its reflection multiplied in the windows across the way. Still, he regretted asking her to turn off the light. She would think he didn't want to look at her, at the piece of plastic. And she'd be right.

206

He slid onto the bed, lightly touching the outlines of her body and feeling the softness of her skin. He ran his fingers slowly through her hair, doing his best to associate the fantasy of the pink and golden body on the stage with the reality beneath him.

She helped him, touching him lightly on the chest and fingering the inside of his thighs. She was careful with the left one, feeling the pucker of the scar tissue and knowing that it hurt him. He turned into her, the coupling frenzied and violent for him, professional for her. He had been away from women too long and climaxed much too soon. He felt like a schoolboy who had been bred for the first time by the village whore. When it was over, he lay back on the damp sheets, the automatic endearments dying in his throat as he listened to her raspy breathing in the darkness.

He lay silent, exhausted, his hands pressed against the warmth of her body, stealing a glance at his Smith & Wesson on the nightstand the same way another man might look for his watch. He wondered why Bernadette hadn't asked about Hannie, then realized that, like the girls who worked the houses on Tu Do, she accepted the wife-who-didn't-understand. She would have been amused or bored if he had told her that he wasn't married to Hannie, that he had slept with her but never touched her.

Then Bernadette's hands were touching him again. The thought that she, like Cailleau, had guessed at his stay in the hospital and was merely being kind, vanished. She hadn't stripped for his sake, she had gone through the routine for her own. She had wanted him the moment she had seen him at the club. And she hadn't compared him to whatever he had been before. She had never known the other Morley.

He smiled and moved toward her again, suddenly confident. Only once did he think of Hannie waiting for him at the pensione. When he returned, he'd have to give her an explanation. But, like going back to the gendarmerie to see Karim, he'd worry about that in the morning. . . .

An hour later, he awoke, drenched with sweat, for a moment not knowing where he was. The cries of the little girl, sounding oddly like Bernadette's raspy voice, filled his ears. In his mind, the thatched doorway of the village hut gaped wide.

He lay there for a moment, weak from exhaustion, trembling from the nightmare. Bernadette hadn't stirred. He slid away from her in the bed, not wanting to be close.

The rest of the night he dozed fitfully, afraid to close his eyes.

twenty

IF HE HADN'T known Brussels so well, Morley might have thought the downpour was over. The drizzle had stopped since he'd left Bernadette's, and now the concrete steps looked almost bleached, the sky a paler, more buoyant gray. Rijkswacht. Gendarmerie. Every official sign in this schizoid country had to appear in both Flemish and French. He focused on the twin plaques as he climbed toward the double doors, ignoring the throbbing in his leg. Surprisingly, it was a little less than he had anticipated it would be.

He shifted his briefcase into his other hand, pulled open one of the heavy doors and then gave in to an impulse to glance back in the direction the motorcyclist had come. It was ten o'clock in the morning, but the street was almost deserted. Saturday, he remembered. He slipped between the doors, his mind starting to plan what he would say to Karim.

The desk sergeant was hostile, obviously holding him to blame for what had happened to Jules two days before. *Capitaine* van den Haute was in conference, he was not to be disturbed. Morley leaned over the desk.

"Tell him it's about Arif."

The sergeant, still stony-faced, reached for the phone. A moment later, he said, "A cadet will take you up." And under his breath: *"Cachon."*

Van den Haute was as grim as the sergeant. "You save me the trouble of looking for you, Monsieur."

"If I had known you wanted to see me, I would have come sooner," Morley murmured. This time around in Brussels, he was going to have to play politics with the Captain.

"You told me Cailleau had smuggled in seven and I didn't believe you. I would have if you had told me who the seventh man was."

"I couldn't, I didn't know. Besides, I thought the Russians told you everything."

Van den Haute looked bitter. "You're not in a position to tell jokes, Monsieur. A good Russian never tells anybody everything. They tell you only as much as they have to and never soon enough. This last drop of information came from their embassy just half an hour ago."

The Captain was deliberately keeping from him who the man was. He'd have to wheedle it out of him later.

"You first, Monsieur," van den Haute continued. "What do you want?" He looked bitter again. "Then it will be my turn."

"I want to see Arif."

"You already have. You wasted everyone's time."

"I can break him."

"You assumed you could do that last time. You were wrong." The Captain's hand hovered over the buzzer. "Yesterday I had a report that a Japanese woman was shot in the street after running from an assailant in a phone exchange. A witness described you at the scene but I discounted it." He grimaced. "If it was you, Monsieur, you have a flair. Perhaps you also have an explanation."

He settled back in his chair, his fingers tapping nervously on the desk top.

"I didn't shoot her," Morley said. "You can have my guns, go ahead and run a ballistics test. Did your informant say I was the only suspect on the scene?"

"There was one other," van den Haute admitted ungraciously. "But I'm not asking about his involvement. I'm asking about yours."

"Apparently she was part of the committee welcoming me back to Brussels. She tried to kill me."

Van den Haute looked impatient. "She must have had a reason. A lady friend whom you jilted, perhaps?"

"She was one of Cailleau's seven," Morley said dryly.

The Captain pulled his hand back from the buzzer. "It is true her identification did not prove out. And the other party on the scene?"

"You've already guessed. The Russian."

"The real assailant, I take it." Van den Haute's mood changed. "Coffee, Monsieur Morley? It's a cold morning out."

He shook his head. "I'm wasting time."

The Captain settled back in his chair. "I don't suppose she lived long enough to say anything?"

Morley studied his fingernails, riding out the silence.

"Arif first?" Van den Haute sounded annoyed.

"Not first—at the same time. Listen to the microphones."

This time the cadet took him through the back corridors where the floors and the cracked plaster were painted a locker-room green. Here the gendarmerie smelled like a gymnasium. Morley's mind flitted back and forth between Karim and van den Haute. The Captain was giving him far more rope than he had anticipated. And London hadn't contacted Diane notifying them of his recall. Both Simon and van den Haute were leaving him out in the open. He welcomed it, but he hadn't expected it.

Below, in the annex, the same turnkey met him, relieved him of his briefcase and escorted him down more stairs. He still wore the same baggy suit, even more wrinkled now and stained with sweat. Morley guessed the turnkey hadn't been home since his last visit and doubted he'd slept much. His shoulders drooped and his slow walk had become a shuffle.

They were turning the screws and Karim wasn't the only one suffering from the pressure. Morley remembered it all too well. He recalled, too, that the screws were given another twist every time a new shift came on. He might already be too late.

"He can still talk?"

The turnkey paused beside the steel outer door, resting his hands on the latch bar. "He talks. About learning to tell time and how to tie his shoelaces. He has become very young, Monsieur."

"He's conscious?"

"*Le médecin* . . ." The turnkey left the sentence dangling and made a large circle in the air with his empty hand. "He comes, he goes. And everyone waits to catch him."

They were injecting Karim with stimulants to keep him alive. He probably hadn't eaten, hadn't slept. But his internal resources shouldn't have run out this quickly.

"I need more than fifteen minutes." Despite what he had told van den Haute, an eternity might not be long enough with Karim.

The turnkey hung the key back on his belt. "We cannot allow you more time, Monsieur. Fifteen minutes, like before. That is all we gave his last visitor, that is all we give you."

"What last visitor?" Van den Haute should have told him, he thought, irritated. Why the hell hadn't he?

A shrug from the turnkey and then they were in the cell

area and there was no more time for questions. The guards slid their cards face down on the table and stood up as the steel door clanged shut. The one who frisked him didn't like him any better than he did the Iraqi. Unfortunately, the guard's attitude was wasted on Karim, curled up in a fetal position on his thin mat. If Karim had known the guard hated him as well, it might have given Morley an edge.

Morley stood there for a long moment, waiting for any sign of recognition. Karim lay with one arm twisted beneath him, his eyes barely open, oblivious to the stench or the lights. The torn trousers and shirt looked several sizes too large and Morley guessed he'd dropped a few more kilos in the two days since he had seen him. He stared, counting. He took three breaths before he saw Karim's chest even tremble. He glanced across the stained mattress at the food tray. The tin cup was dry, the contents of the plastic bowl unrecognizable under the cloudy film.

Somebody had gone too far. The Iraqi wasn't going to make it.

"Karim."

He whispered it but there was no response. He raised his voice a little.

"Karim."

He called out half a dozen times before the body on the mattress finally stirred.

"Karim—remember me?"

". . . I remember." Karim's voice was faint and garbled through a throat clogged with phlegm. Morley had to press his head against the bars to understand what he was mumbling.

". . . fight your terror . . . only then can you do anything for liberation . . ."

Morley strained to hear more but the surge of rhetoric faded as abruptly as it had begun. He waited to see whether ex-

213

haustion or drugs or something more permanent had silenced Karim. Again, he had to struggle to remain clinically detached, to maintain control. Half a cigarette later, Karim moved. He grabbed hold of the bars to pull himself upright, groping between them to clutch at the cigarette. He took a deep drag, coughing as he swallowed the smoke. He was having trouble with his eyes. They kept slipping out of focus and he had to fight to keep them open. There was some strength in his hands and then Morley could sense that Karim's mind was clearing. It was the drugs. They must have given Karim an injection and it was starting to have effect. The shots were probably the only thing keeping him alive.

Morley fished in his coat pocket and held out his cupped hand. "I have something for you."

Karim stood in watchful silence, his arms wrapped around his waist, holding his shirt closed against the faint dampness of the basement.

"Throw it on the floor. You never know what the capitalistic insect has in his hands."

Morley dropped the Japanese woman's worry stone between the bars so it landed on the edge of the mat. Karim picked it up and stared at it, then rubbed it slowly with his thumb. When he spoke again, his voice was clear and matter-of-fact. Morley knew instinctively that something basic had just changed, that there would be no more rhetoric. Karim had accepted the fact that he wouldn't leave the basement alive.

"Tell me about it. I want to know."

Morley held out another cigarette. Karim didn't move to take it, didn't take his eyes off Morley's.

"There was a shoot-out. Two days ago in an alley off boulevard Anspach."

"Who killed her?"

Vasiliev's pissed-off expression flashed across his mind.

For a brief moment they had exchanged accusing glances when they realized she wouldn't be able to tell them anything.

"I'm not sure."

Karim rolled the stone between thin fingers. It was difficult to think of him as a seasoned terrorist; he looked very young, very vulnerable. Morley glanced away; he didn't want to fall into that trap again.

"Teiko's father is a banker. He's an an ultrarightest who talks a lot about 'justice.' He doesn't know much about it. Her mother killed herself when Teiko was three." Karim was silent for a moment. "Teiko said society had destroyed most of the women who could have been her role models."

Karim wasn't seeing him anymore. Morley sensed that he wasn't really talking to him, either.

"Like all of us, Teiko was terrified. Her hair used to be long. When she was frightened she would pull it down in front of her face and hide."

Morley glanced at his watch, then back at Karim. "I saw her cramming a gun in her bag just after she had killed a young man and his girlfriend. They didn't have time to be terrified."

"Teiko and I aren't the only martyrs to oppression."

In his mind's eye, Morley could see the reels of tape turning and van den Haute fidgeting at his desk. He let the silence build, then said, "Your mother's health is good. The doctors say she should live many years." He paused. It would do no good just to say it; he had to make Karim believe that he would actually do it. "It's up to you just how long she lives." Morley felt cold when he said it. There was too much riding on Karim's answers, the lives of too many innocents who might be working inside the Palais Berlaymont or just walking past it.

The hands clutching the bars tightened and the knuckles went white. Karim trembled but said nothing.

"There are no innocents, Karim. We both know that.

Only murderers and their victims and those who look the other way and pretend there are neither."

There was nothing left to say. They had played a vicious game, a brutal one, and Karim had finally lost. To believe the end justified any means in the pursuit of terror was to make yourself vulnerable. You forced the other side to find the means that would destroy you.

Silence. The ticking of his wristwatch, his own breathing and Karim's, the soft snap of cards being dealt at the table behind him.

"You're very good, I should take lessons from you," Karim whispered sardonically. "What do you want from me?"

The turnkey was walking toward them.

"How many of you did Cailleau bring across?"

"Seven, you knew that. The Slav ran away."

"Who was—"

A tap on his shoulder. "Time, Monsieur. No more questions."

A few minutes, he thought. He would have to ask van den Haute for a few more minutes. The Captain had been listening to the microphones, there'd be no problem getting it. Karim was now willing to tell all he knew.

He left with the turnkey, feeling oddly naked the moment he turned his back to the Iraqi. He paused at the door when he heard Karim call to the guards for water, that his heart was going crazy. It was probably a ploy but even if it wasn't, he couldn't help.

The guards would do everything possible to keep Karim alive. At least they would now.

Tricking Karim into talking had been the most he could do for him.

Morley had reached the landing just behind the turnkey when the first shot exploded in his ears. He dropped to his knees. The turnkey turned as if in slow motion, his dough-colored face registering disbelief and anger.

Another shot ricocheted up the steel and concrete stairwell. Morley cursed the guards, his hands clutching at his empty holster. Karim's visitor, why the hell hadn't they found the gun? And why had they taken Karim so much for granted? Why had he? It was like assuming a tiger was helpless because it had one foot in a trap. Karim must have faked at least part of his exhaustion so they would give him a shot of stimulants. And when that hadn't seemed to work, they had given him another one. And probably another.

It accounted for the uneasiness he had felt with Karim. The Iraqi had been pretending to be on the edge when the truth was he was actually higher than a kite. Right now he was probably burning energy like it was jet fuel.

There was a noise on the steps below. Morley edged to the railing, looked down and saw Karim's hand sweep along the guard rail, clutching the gun. He jerked back, glancing around. There wasn't time to climb to ground level. And there were no doorways leading off their landing. His shirt suddenly felt damp and sticky where it gathered in his armpits.

Somewhere a Klaxon started wailing. Two flights above he could hear people running down the corridor and shouting.

The turnkey swore and started back toward the basement room they had just left.

"Don't be a fool!"

The turnkey grunted, his reddish eyes indignant at the thought of anyone escaping. Morley dropped to a crouch, steeling himself for the moment when Karim came racing around the corner.

And then Karim, black hair flying, exploded into view. Without hesitation, he braced himself with both hands holding the gun. The roar of the pistol filled the stairwell and the turnkey did a slow pirouette on the steps, his hands automatically clawing at the bloody remains of his face.

Morley dived down the stairs, his shoulders sinking into Karim's sweaty stomach. He locked his arms around the Iraqi's knees, snapped them forward. Karim went with the tug, his knees crushing into Morley's groin.

Morley went down, his head slamming into the concrete. He ducked the foot that kicked at him, grabbed it and yanked. Karim managed to keep his feet under him, frantically trying to maneuver the gun for a clean shot. Morley kept crowding him.

Karim yanked free and danced back a few feet, out of his reach. Morley froze, reading his death in Karim's wild eyes.

More shots filled the stairwell with flying chips of concrete. Morley could hear men on the steps above him.

Karim cursed and bounded past, disappearing into the ground-level corridor on the next landing. Morley ran after him, ramming against the push bar on the metal door and tumbling into the hallway.

The gendarmes were standing at the far end, weapons drawn, hesitating before they rushed into the cross-corridor. Morley spotted the trail of red splotches and wondered why they waited—Karim was bleeding too heavily. He raced into the connecting corridor, following the reddish spatters.

They led him into a whitewashed toilet. There were dark red puddles on the floor and bloody streaks along the walls and the window sill and on two of the window's iron bars.

Karim was crumpled on the floor, one arm around the porcelain bowl. He was hugging it like a drunk who wanted to feel the cool smoothness against his face as he vomited. His eyes half-focused on Morley and his hand briefly left the porcelain and waved. His black hair was matted with blood, his large, liquid eyes almost vacant. He tried to say something. When he opened his mouth, blood trickled out.

The gun was lying on the floor. Morley kicked it toward

the doorway. Karim's lips were moving and he knelt down to catch the words. Something about his mother. He nodded, wondering vaguely what Karim had said. His side started to ache and he felt sick. He could sense curious faces gathering just outside the door but didn't look up.

Karim began coughing and Morley reached out and gently pulled his hand away from the porcelain, cushioning his head with a small stack of paper towels. Karim had almost made it. The drugs had helped but he must have husbanded his strength like a squirrel hoarding nuts. Morley wondered how far he would have gotten under similar circumstances.

Karim was trying to talk again and this time he managed to get several words out in Arabic. *Get out! Leave the building!*

His voice trailed off and the muscles in his face went slack. Morley sat there for a long time, staring at Karim's face, now almost empty of life, and feeling an emotion that he would never be able to describe to van den Haute or Simon. He identified far more with the Iraqi than he ever would with the curious gendarmes pressing in behind him, waiting for the ambulance to arrive.

He sat there, his back pressed against the cold wall, until all the life had finally drained from Karim's eyes. Then he got to his feet and elbowed his way past the guards who stood idly in the doorway, arguing about the Brugeois soccer pool.

twenty-one

IT TOOK AN hour of dancing around van den Haute's questions before he could retrieve his briefcase and guns, which had ended up on the Captain's desk. By then, he'd told him everything he had learned about the seven—everything except his source. He'd be damned if he'd feed Bernadette to Diane.

By the time he was ready to leave, the atmosphere in the office was too tense to risk asking van den Haute anything. He asked anyway. "Who was the seventh man?"

"If I had wanted to tell you, I would have." Van den Haute sat hunched behind his desk, glaring at him. The Captain had lost Karim and someone had to take the blame. That was the only thing bureaucrats like van den Haute were good at—placing the blame for their failures.

"Who visited Karim before me?"

"The list of visitors is *confidentiel*. You know better than to ask."

Morley had his own feelings of bitterness.

"Whoever it was smuggled in the gun."

Van den Haute's voice was ragged. "For all I know, you

did." He controlled his anger with an effort. "I understand your motives. London tells me a few things, too. You have been badly wounded, you don't want to go home. You would like to find out who almost killed you the last time in Brussels so you can leave in a blaze of glory. It is possible you can be helpful in all this. But continue to make my life unhappy and I will have you withdrawn. You understand that? *Bon.*"

He returned to the papers on his desk, his face still white. "You are free to go but not to do whatever you wish. You are a tourist in Belgium, Monsieur, that is the limit of your license."

Morley paused by the pay phone on the landing, dug a *jeton* and a card from his pocket. He'd hit another sore point, his usual luck with the *Capitaine*. But he already had an idea of who the visitor was—or *said* he was. And he knew how he could check. He picked up the phone and when it crackled in his ear, he dialed the number scribbled on Vasiliev's card.

The street outside the gendarmerie was nearly deserted. There were four figures in sight and Morley measured them instinctively, starting with the old woman watching from behind lace curtains across the street, and then the couple pushing a pram toward him on the sidewalk. He stood there, stiff, fingering the Smith & Wesson in his shoulder holster and listening to the faint sounds filtering past the shuttered windows of the conservatory next door.

He concentrated on the fourth figure who'd just stepped out from between some ancient beech trees in the park across the street. He crossed the empty street and made straight for him. The man in the camel's hair coat was now engrossed in the shrubs that lined the curb.

"I thought we could talk about your seventh refugee."

"You've seen the communiqué?" Vasiliev looked curiously at the bruises on his face. "Or did the *Capitaine* tell you?"

"Why don't *you* tell me, Andrei."

Vasiliev looked surprised. "He takes your money and tells you nothing? That's not a very good arrangement, Neal." He studied the four-story building with the double plaque. "The news was released several hours ago. I assumed you had seen it when you called."

Dark clouds had rolled in and the air was filled with a light mist. Vasiliev led the way a hundred feet into the park to a wrought-iron bench by a shallow pond. Morley sat down, straightened out his legs and stared at the giant goldfish surfacing among the water lilies. It was getting chilly and he thought: They'll have to take them in before the water freezes.

"So tell me what your people put out. And especially what they didn't."

Vasiliev settled back on the bench, his gloved hands resting in his lap. "Everything I tell you comes from the Scientific and Technical Directorate—what's left of it."

Morley had the feeling that he not only knew what was coming next but that he should have guessed it long ago. The Sci-Tech Directorate—originally created to steal Western data about nuclear, missile and space research—along with the strategic sciences, chip circuitry and industrial processes—had had one other equally important function: It oversaw Russian science. It had done so with much more stringency than the Kremlin oversaw religion, or stateside computer banks scrutinized credit ratings. The Directorate's officials had not only ruled which scientists would be allowed to experiment or publish or attend international conferences, they had also monitored the entire scientific community both in and out of Mother Russia.

"Who's the defector?"

Vasiliev hesitated. "The official word is that it was a snatch squad. They could be right."

The mist was thickening. There was no sound of traffic from the boulevard and Morley had the impression that he and Vasiliev were suspended in their own private world of gray. For the moment, the rest of Belgium didn't exist.

"Van den Haute said your comrade disappeared in Berlin. What was he doing there?"

"These days, Neal, the word is 'citizen.' He was attending a conference. He was from Academogorodok."

"There were signs of a struggle where he was staying? People saw him resisting on the street?"

"There were no signs of any struggle in his hotel room," Vasiliev said in a strained voice. "But that does not mean he went willingly."

Morley pressed him. "But he still could have defected."

Vasiliev shrugged. "Perhaps. I'm not concerned with the politics of it."

Before the Wall came down, the Russians had been refusing emigration even to waiters and busboys, claiming they possessed state secrets obtained in the workplace. With anyone from Academogorodok, they had meant every word. He had heard stories about the science city that had been built on the white flats of Siberia. It was a total think tank, a scientific Disneyland with all the amenities for the *right* scientists.

"What's his specialty?"

Vasiliev rubbed the bridge of his nose, working his trigger finger through the ready-made slit in his glove. "I can't tell you everything but I can tell you this. The average age at Academogorodok is thirty, the average I.Q. is close to one hundred and forty. Gennadi Troshkin is only slightly older than the average but maybe twice as smart, if that's possible. He's spent almost his entire adult life becoming *the* expert in laser technology. Now he wants to do something else and found—despite this new thing, this so-called freedom—he can't. He's free, all right. Free to be frustrated. To be frightened. Free to be an adolescent all over again, if he wishes, in a world he can't understand and that can't understand him. You know we can't afford to let him go. The new wave of freedom in Russia laps at many shores, but his is not one of them."

Vasiliev studied his face, anxious that Morley believe he was telling the truth.

"The Professor was too valuable where he was. And admittedly a problem. His mother overprotected him as a child. His wife, like many Russian wives, continued the job. She was intelligent and committed; she taught singing to deaf children. He cherished her. She died six months ago and he's been . . . unstable . . . ever since. Understandable, perhaps—but not to the bureaucrats."

He was silent for a moment, trying to decide how much was safe to tell Morley. "More, I don't know, probably couldn't tell you if I did. All that matters is that right now the terror squad has Troshkin and the Directorate wants him back. Badly. So now everybody wants to find the terror squad—us, the Belgians, and you."

Vasiliev didn't know, Morley thought. "Your snatch squad has been here six days and besides going after Cailleau and me, they haven't made a move. It's possible they have another assignment and the Iraqi was the only one who knew it, the only one who could signal the others. But I doubt it. I keep wondering what they're doing."

Vasiliev studied his face. "You know something that I don't, Neal. What is it?"

"I think one of the things they're doing is looking for your Gennadi Troshkin. He's gotten away from them."

It took Vasiliev a second to realize he meant Troshkin had escaped from the terrorists. "Who told you?"

"The Iraqi." Morley shrugged. "Maybe Troshkin never

really trusted his newfound friends. Maybe he realized they never intended to let him go, that they were being something other than idealistic when they helped him run away. Maybe he really *was* kidnapped. Maybe Karim lied."

"We've torn Brussels apart searching for them." Vasiliev's voice was thick with frustration. "Now even if we find them, we still haven't found *him.*"

"He could show up at your embassy," Morley said.

"Or yours." Vasiliev suddenly laughed. "Or neither. Until now, he's been a cautious man. Once having gotten away from the squad, he may have gone to ground, hiding from all of us."

"How long have you been looking?" Morley's mind had clicked into high gear. Even the muted reflections on the pond suddenly seemed brilliant.

"Since four days ago. We tracked them to Brussels and then they disappeared. We thought we had them several times."

Morley lobbed a small stone into the pond and watched the goldfish scatter as the ripples spread toward the banks. "What do you know about the squad?"

"Not as much as you. They're not all Muslim radicals, but they would like to see the Islamic fundamentalists in charge. They've got one thing in common. They don't trust the West, they don't trust us. They believe that both of us have exploited them. From their point of view, they may be right. Neither of us ever gave them anything more than we had to. They were suppliers of oil, customers for arms. They were client states, buffer zones."

Vasiliev was quiet for a moment, studying Morley, trying to read his reaction. "But politics and loyalties change. We've both learned that. Obviously, what we won't give them, they will try to develop for themselves. Or buy. Or steal. Some things we won't let them have, it would be too dangerous. If they obtained nuclear weapons, the Israelis would bomb them, as they did Iraq. Or you would. Or perhaps even we would. There's safety in numbers; in this case, the fewer the better. Gennadi Troshkin would be quite a catch."

Vasiliev shivered against the cold and pulled his coat higher around his neck.

"Science is a valuable commodity, Neal. Troshkin wouldn't be the first scientist to be kidnapped by dissident groups, there have been others. Maybe even some from your country. If the dissidents cannot use them directly, then they are sold to the highest bidder. Since *perestroika* and *glasnost*, Russia has suffered a voluntary brain drain—you're aware of that, Neal. Too many of our top specialists have left, either for your country or those in the Near East. We cannot afford to lose Troshkin, too. There are still secrets and he knows too many of them."

He glanced at Morley. "I'm surprised all of your rocket and computer scientists aren't in protective custody." He smiled at Morley's nod and Morley realized they had just formalized an unofficial mutual assistance pact.

Across the pond, two small boys, their shadowy forms almost hidden by the mist, were feeding the ducks. A dozen feet from them was a wooden hut, no larger than a border guardhouse. Morley could barely make out somebody moving inside, behind the window. He reached for the Smith & Wesson in his shoulder holster.

"The gardener," Vasiliev said. "He has a coal heater and a book of poetry inside. He's quite fond of Eliot." He spent a moment choosing the right words. "We are both survivors, Neal. And for the moment, we need each other. I find I don't mind it that much."

Vasiliev sounded harried, nervous. There were lines under the Russian's eyes that Morley hadn't noticed before and an air of fatigue that clung to him like sweat.

226

"What would you be doing, Andrei, if things had been different?"

"I'd be teaching school in the Ukraine, like my father did." Morley was surprised, the answer came so quickly. "And you?"

"I'm not sure."

"Were you ever married?"

"Once. And you?"

Vasiliev nodded. "She's from Pskov. A doctor. We met on holiday—hers—eleven years ago. She was a teenager but looked older."

Morley remembered the waitress in McDonald's.

"Is she happy?"

"Yes and no—mostly yes. We have a son. I may not always be there, but she has a reason to look at toys and men's shirts when she goes to the department store."

"You don't see each other very often." It was hardly a guess.

"More than I used to. Four months out of the year, maybe."

"That's too little for a woman."

"Yes."

Strange, Morley thought. He had read all the facts about Vasiliev long ago in various dossiers. But right now it all sounded fresh, as if he didn't know anything at all about the man. It occurred to him that he identified with Vasiliev much as he had with Karim.

"What else did the Iraqi say, Neal?"

"About Troshkin? That he had gotten away, that was all."

"You can find out more?"

Morley shook his head. "He's dead."

Vasiliev played with his gloves a moment, then glanced in the direction of the gendarmerie. "From an overdose of 'medicine'?" He sounded bitter.

"Somebody smuggled in a gun. He tried to get out."

"He had guts."

"He left most of them in a toilet on the ground floor." Morley kept his face a blank. "You'd think they could have done better."

Vasiliev considered it for a moment, then dug in his pocket for change. "I'll be right back."

Morley watched him disappear down the path toward the boulevard. He returned a few minutes later, shaking his head. "I called the embassy. Somebody checked—too late. The Iraqi's visitor said he was one of us, that he needed information from Arif about Troshkin. He had credentials and knew about the communiqué so your *Capitaine* believed him. The Embassy never heard of the man. Naturally."

"Whoever he was, he took a risk," Morley said. More important, it meant that the squad had already made contact with collaborators in Brussels.

Vasiliev frowned. "Who took you below?"

"The turnkey."

"An aging prison bureaucrat in a baggy suit, right? I'm sure he confiscated your briefcase and guns. But I'm also sure he didn't strip you down for a full body search. I would guarantee it if you happened to be a very dignified and elderly senior diplomat." He paused. "The Iraqi said nothing more about anything?"

"He was mumbling to himself in Arabic, saying he had to get out of the building."

They walked for a moment in silence.

"Why are they after you, Neal?"

Morley spread his hands. "I swear to God I don't know. Maybe there's a connection with what happened when I was in Brussels before, but if there is, I don't know what it might be."

It was turning colder and his words came out as little puffs of vapor. "I don't know anything that you don't."

Vasiliev turned away, disappointed, and stared across the pond at the vague forms of the beech trees on the other side. "I don't quite believe you and you don't quite believe me. Each of us probably knows something the other doesn't but I doubt that it makes any difference."

He stood up and beat his arms about his chest to get the circulation going. "Troshkin. Everybody is looking for him now." For the first time, Morley could see the fear in his face and realized why he had been so open. "It's my job," Vasiliev continued, his worried voice trailing off in vapors. "I've got to get him back."

twenty-two

THIS TIME, THE door to number eleven was locked. Morley leaned against it and fumbled in his pockets for the passkey, wincing as he shifted his weight onto his game leg. It wasn't so much the pain anymore as the sheer fatigue. The fight with Karim and the emotional aftermath of the Iraqi's death in the gendarmerie had drained him. But then, he had been pushing himself ever since he had returned to Brussels, ignoring the doctors' orders to take it easy, to get as much rest as he could. Now he was paying for it.

He finally found the key and reminded himself for the hundredth time that once inside he could collapse. He twisted the key and the door sprung open, swinging against the inside wall. The curtains had been tied back, letting in the last graying streaks of daylight, but otherwise the room was much the same. The grocery bags and the now-wilted flowers were still on the table, his flight bag leaning against the foot of the bed next to Hannie's red suitcase.

She was sitting in the chair, watching him. "You didn't come back last night." He couldn't tell whether it was an accusation or if she were just hurt.

"Sometimes you have to put in long hours, Hannie." He closed the door behind him, slamming the bolt home before it could bounce free.

"I was worried about you."

Right then, he didn't need her solicitude, didn't want it. "Hannie, you're not my case officer and you're not my wife. I didn't think I had to check in." He regretted it as soon as he said it, but he was too exhausted to care.

Her arms were folded over her breasts, a stack of letters cradled in her lap. She was wearing the wool suit he remembered from the theater and she had pinned her hair up again. He'd forgotten that she had ever worn it that way.

"You're still alive," she said sarcastically. "The day couldn't have been that bad."

He ignored her, yanked off his wet coat, threw it on the bed and limped over to the sink. He felt even more exhausted now than he had in the hall. He just wanted to be left alone, to collapse. He ran some cold water in the sink, stripped off his shirt, then leaned over to bury his face in the chill water.

"Did you stay with Bernadette?"

They stared at each other in the cracked mirror above the sink.

"I had some questions to ask her."

"How was she?"

"Professional."

She was silent for a moment. "And Karim?"

He put down the washcloth and turned to face her. "He's dead. He tried to break out. It was his way of committing suicide. He knew what would happen."

"After you talked to him." This time it *was* an accusation.

He turned back to the mirror, surprised to see his reflection nodding. "That's right," he said in a low voice. "After I talked to him." He had been reminding himself all afternoon that Karim would have tried to break out in any event.

"You broke him. Like you said you would."

He held onto the sink with both hands, seeing Karim on the washroom floor, vomiting blood into the toilet bowl. "Not in the way I wanted." And then, echoing Vasiliev in the park: "It's my job."

"How do you feel?"

He wiped his face with the washcloth. "Why are you so concerned?"

"I don't want to think you're a murderer."

"That's a moral term," he said. He didn't want to argue, he wanted desperately to go to bed.

She put the letters on the table, her face tight. "And you don't have to be moral, is that it? In your world people aren't killed, they get 'hit'—like they had been caught in a bloody car accident. Or they're terminated, like somebody had just fired them from their job."

"I didn't kill him, he killed himself."

"So that lets you off the bloody hook."

He closed his eyes and slowly shook his head. "That's a fucking stupid thing to say." And then he knew why she had said it, what was really bothering her. "You're not responsible, Hannie, not in any way."

"I *am* responsible," she said in a small voice. "I got the information for you." She had probably spent the day thinking it over. Reassessing what she had gotten into, realizing that it wasn't very glamorous after all.

"I can tell you if you'd like, Hannie."

She nodded. "I want to know what happened to him."

First he told her about Troshkin and Vasiliev and how everyone was searching Brussels for the Russian scientist. He told it to her without emotion, as if he were filing a report. And then he told her how Karim had died. When he had finished, she remained silent, her face pinched and drawn.

232

"I think about it a lot," he said awkwardly. "I don't know how to explain it to you. You would have to go through a war for it to make sense, and I'm not sure it would even then."

"You're confusing me," she said, not understanding him. "I can't tell whether you think he was a hero or a villain."

"It would be easier for you if I told you he was one or the other, wouldn't it?" He took a breath. "All right, Hannie, he was a double-dyed villain—dozens of people are probably dead because of him."

"And you?" She wouldn't look at him. "What's the difference between you and him?"

"The Iraqi gave up everything he felt for everything he believed," he said at last. "I feel too much and believe too little and Jesus, there are times when I envy him, when I envy his convictions."

"Everybody believes in something," she said. Her voice was trembling and he knew she wasn't trying to defend Karim, she was trying to defend herself. "It's not a bad thing, to believe in something." And then: "You lost your beliefs while you were in Vietnam, didn't you?"

Morley stared at his face in the mirror above the bowl and tried to keep from shaking. He desperately wanted to talk about it. "When they drafted me, I went in as a conscientious objector— my father really did have this thing about religion. He was a Quaker. I drew all the shit details, I went out with every patrol and carried everything they could pile on me. In two months they broke me. It wasn't the danger. I couldn't stand the hatred of the men in my own unit, I couldn't go day after day with nobody talking to me, I couldn't bear the thought that nobody gave a shit whether I lived or died. So I pulled strings and got assigned to Intelligence and after that it was all down hill."

He turned around to face her. He was closer to tears than he had been in twenty years. "I saw it all, Hannie. I saw eighteen-year-old kids turned into instant quadriplegics, I saw family men volunteer for search-and-destroy missions because they had developed a taste for killing—they wasted kids no older than their own at home. What was even worse, I understood them. I was just like them, I did everything they did."

He couldn't stand the expression on her face and wanted to close his eyes. "I did go back to the States briefly, Hannie. But I no longer fit in—it didn't take long to realize there was no place for me. I couldn't stand my country and my country couldn't stand me, it was a case of mutual contempt. I volunteered to go back to 'Nam. I had forgotten how to live in any other place, I missed the camaraderie and God help me, I even missed the friendly neighborhood gooks."

He wondered if she were going to leave and found the thought terrifying. "This is the only job I've ever had, Hannie. I respect the people I work with. Some of them. Enough of them. We'll lie, steal, cheat and murder so we won't have to go through another war. And if that fails, we'll do our damnedest to win it. Maybe I have to see it that way because I can't afford to see it any other way, but that's the way it is."

He looked down at the bowl and pulled out the stopper. "And maybe I'm lying to myself," he said. "Maybe I've just found a way to take the jungle with me wherever I go. I haven't been back to the States since."

He let the water drain from the sink while he toweled his face. Hannie opened one of the grocery bags and set the table for supper. She had gotten a bottle of wine—a better bottle than the one he had bought—and they drank it in silence while they ate the bread and cheese. By the time they had finished, it was dark outside and cold in the room. He started to shiver and couldn't stop. He had to get to bed.

"You ought to leave," he said. "You're an idiot if you stay, you're a target as long as you're with me." He had to force the words out through teeth clenched to keep from chattering. He stood up. His leg buckled and Hannie had to grab him so he wouldn't fall. She kept her arms around him for a moment and he stiffened, trying to deny that he needed any assistance.

"I don't . . . need . . . help."

She shushed him as she would a child and helped him over to the bed. He collapsed across it. Her fingers skipped quickly over him, undoing buttons and helping him out of his shirt, then taking off his shoes and unzipping his pants and tugging them off. His shorts came with them. She pulled off his socks, then spread the heavy wool blanket over him. He was chilled and held his arms close to his chest for warmth. He wasn't sure whether he was just weak or coming down with the flu.

"I'll be there in a minute," she said quietly. She slipped out of her clothes and undid the clip that held her hair. She shook her head and her hair fell over her shoulders. She looked exactly as she had the first night, her skin a light golden brown with the tan lines showing and a shadowy palm of black hair just below her firm belly.

She slid in next to him and he reached for her, feeling her body and her warmth and for the first time in years, feeling safe. If somebody came in the door, she would have to protect them both; he wasn't capable of it.

His shivering slowed and he dropped his head into the crook of her arm, smelling the faint mixture of sweat and perfume, the last thing he was aware of before falling asleep.

He awoke at what he guessed was three in the morning, lying tensely in the bed, listening. The only sounds were an occasional automobile on the boulevard and the rustle of bedsprings next door. Aside from that, nothing. He gradually relaxed, luxuriating in the warmth of the bed.

Then he became aware that Hannie was awake, too. He moved closer and ran a hand down her side, cupping it gently around the smooth flesh of her buttocks. He felt her hand on his chest and his breathing quickened. It had been different with Bernadette; she had been as professional as the girls in Saigon and he had felt much the same way about her as he had about them. Most of the women he'd had since Vietnam had been like him, professional. . . .

It wasn't frantic this time, there was no haste, he wasn't worried that he might fail. He was in bed with someone whom he liked very much.

It was the first time that either of them had heard the other laugh.

When it was over, he lay on his back, her head resting on his chest, staring at the faded wallpaper faintly visible in the light from the window. The unconvincing festive scene played over and over on the walls. His eyes traced the patterns and he thought how odd it was the things one came to remember.

After a few minutes, he turned back to Hannie. The hospital in London seemed very far away now, and for the first time that night so was Karim. Bernadette was harder to block out, and he felt a tinge of shame. He wondered if he had gone to bed with her as one cripple might with another in the knowledge that since neither one of them was whole, neither would turn the other down.

Then he wondered if there were things she hadn't told him, if she had made love to him to distract him. He hadn't thought so at the time, but at the time he couldn't afford to think so. He'd have to go back and see her tomorrow, check on her story once more, make sure there wasn't anything she had forgotten. Let her know how to get hold of him if she remembered . . .

Then the memory of Bernadette was gone, too, and he was aware only of Hannie laughing quietly in the darkness, her hands teasing his hair and gently touching his scarred back and legs.

236

twenty-three

"*Trois cent francs, s'il vous plait.*"

The taxi had come to a stop in the middle of the wet street, its brakes screeching. The driver turned to collect his fare and for a moment Morley half-expected to see Louis behind the wheel. "How much?"

"Three hundred francs, *service compre.*"

The part of Morley that worried about such things continued to monitor everything around him: the driver's right hand dipping below his line of vision for the wallet lying on the front seat, the other taxi lurching away from the curb just as they turned the corner, one red taillight winking in the mist.

There had to be something more Bernadette could tell him, perhaps had told him two days ago only he hadn't been listening. He had gone over it briefly last night, thought about it more intensely that morning. He had left Hannie with instructions to go back to the Bureau and find out what she could about Teiko and her family. At least it would keep her out of harm's way. He had made another abortive attempt to persuade her to return to London but she had been adamant, as he had known she would be. The Belgians were looking for Serge's murderers, so were the Russians as well as himself. She wanted to be there when they were found.

He hadn't objected enough to her staying. The thought of her waiting at the apartment was too much of a fantasy. He wasn't strong enough to reject it, didn't want to.

He thumbed several bills from his wallet, handed them over to the driver and stepped out of the cab. He glanced up at the little window under the eaves. The lace curtains were blowing out into the rain.

The varnished front door was cracked open and he paused, the hair on the back of his neck stirring slightly.

When he pushed, the door swung open easily on its hinges. He grabbed it before it slammed into the wall and closed it behind him. In the dark vestibule, the stink of last night's brussels' sprouts and sausages hung heavy in the air. He paused on the first landing while his eyes adjusted to the darkness. He was becoming more aware of things now, especially of the silence. What the hell had he expected to hear? The chirp of the bird, somebody moving around upstairs?

The door to her apartment was ajar, a thin crack of morning light streaming across the threshold. He took a few steps toward it and almost stumbled over her body in the gloom of the hallway. Her scarf had been torn off in the struggle and lay on the twisted doormat, next to her keys. Her long legs had bent under her when she collapsed. Her head was at an awkward angle, the marks where she had been strangled still angry in the faint light, the plastic tube jutting an ugly inch from her crushed throat. Her skirt had been pushed up and her red panties were bunched around her ankles.

The cat had been crouching behind her and now ran inside to hide under a chair. Morley walked cautiously into the apartment, holding the Smith & Wesson loosely in his hand. Nobody was there. He made a quick tour of the three rooms.

No drawers had been forced open, no furniture had been tipped over, no clothes were strewn about. He doubted that anything had been taken but then, he knew it hadn't been robbery from the moment he had found her.

He walked back into the hall and knelt by the body. She was still warm. He bent closer. The faint odor of anisette lingered on her mouth. She had probably been to a late party and just returned. How long ago? Maybe only a few minutes. He walked back into the room, glanced around one more time, noted that Noenoesch was still hiding, then closed the door.

They had both been loners, partly by choice, mostly of necessity. She had found it easy to sell or give away her body, but in bed two nights before he had sensed a barrier, knew that there was a part of her that was not for sale.

She had been generous with him.

He knelt again and closed the staring eyes, then started downstairs. Below, the front door was wide open and through it he could see a mover's lorry and a pink baker's van locked bumper to bumper, blocking the street. For a fleeting second, he thought there had been an accident. Then men started jumping out of the vehicles, dozens of them, wearing bulletproof protectors and face shields over their gas masks.

The squads hit the pavement and moved out, clutching MP5 submachine guns and sniper rifles. Morley looked up. Commandos were in position on the rooftops across the street. They would have gotten there first, threading their way through the buildings from the other street.

He stepped out of the doorway. *"Diane! Hold it! Diane!"*

The troops were already converging on the house and he couldn't depend on their discipline. He paused a few feet from the door, his arms held high.

Diane was better trained than he had thought. Nobody fired a shot, although several of them looked as if they wanted to. The lead commandos flung themselves on him, pinning him against the letter box. Somebody tackled his left leg and pain shot through his hip where the doctors had inserted the metal pins.

Another commando signaled the rest of the squad to go upstairs. A radio clipped to his collar suddenly squawked. He listened, then waved the others off of Morley. *"Allons!"* He motioned them to go inside, then pointed toward the black Opel double-parked behind the lorry. "The *Capitaine* wants to see you, Monsieur—over there."

Van den Haute glared at him from the backseat. The Captain had a two-way radio pressed to his ear and was jotting down notes on a pad of grid paper on his lap. He held the radio out so Morley could hear the turmoil, then growled: "Enlighten me, Monsieur—what happened in there?"

"Bernadette," Morley started. "She's—"

The radio erupted in sudden confusion. Van den Haute winced, pulled it away from his ear and spoke into the mouthpiece. "Did you find her?"

"Oui, Capitaine—"

"Bon."

"—dead," Morley finished.

Van den Haute glanced at him. Over the radio, they could hear the sound of wood splintering. "The door," Morley said, disgusted. "It was open—all they had to do was turn the goddamned knob."

"What happened to her?"

"She was strangled."

"How many are inside?"

"Nobody's inside." The radio was exploding again. "Christ, I was just there. Believe me, nobody's inside."

Van den Haute inspected him with distaste. "The whore—she was your source?"

240

He remembered what Schlöndorff had said. "She wasn't a whore, she was a chanteuse." It was as much of a memorial as he could give her.

"We have records on her, she was a whore. What's worse, she was mixed up with you." The Captain looked away, contemptuous. "My God, Monsieur, you have the touch of death."

"She was with Cailleau when he brought them across," Morley said patiently. "She knew them."

"What else did she know?"

"I don't know. That's why I came back."

"You should have come sooner." He inspected Morley's reflection in the window. "She phoned me. She thought I took messages for you. She did know more but she'd only talk to you."

"She doesn't have a phone." Even to himself, he sounded sullen.

"She was calling from a curtain shop on rue Saint Jean Nepomucene. The whore there gave us the address."

"Which shop?"

Van den Haute turned to watch the commandos come out of the building, trailed by two ambulance attendants with a sheeted form lying on the gurney. In his mind's eye, Morley could see through the sheet, could see Bernadette's eyes staring blindly, the piece of plastic jutting from her crushed throat.

"I was talking with your colleagues when the call came through," the Captain said, writing another note on the pad. "Monsieur Tindemans would like you to leave—"

"The girl at the shop," Morley interrupted. "I want to talk to her." He grimaced. "I think I can find out more from her than G.I.S."

Van den Haute swung around, a faint smile on his face. *G.I.S.* A small victory. "I do not care what you want, Monsieur. I have done more than your people could expect me to do. But

I will extend myself one more time. I will give you the whore's name and the address of the curtain shop. I do so only because, as you say, you might be able to find out more than one of my own men. You have this flair for whores."

He signaled to the driver and they pulled away from the curb. He went back to the legal pad. "After that, Monsieur, I am finished with you. When you are through with the whore, you will report to the gendarmerie. You will be there no later than seventeen hundred." He glanced up, his face still flushed. "This is not an exchange, not one of your 'cooperative efforts.' This is an order—to an alien. *Comprendre?*"

twenty-four

"*B*ONJOUR."

"*Bonjour*, Monsieur."

The sensuous young *chat* curled up on the cushiony couch by the window was the first to welcome him. She was the only one to pretend that she meant it. The old woman at the bar mouthed the words and let it go at that.

The younger woman studied his face and went to work. She moved so she showed more of her breasts, flashed a Cheshire smile and jiggled to the sounds of a punk rock tune, her toes tapping to the music from her portable radio. She had energy to burn, but the plastic flowers in the room and the obvious tension under her makeup made the charade seem like a wake.

Morley ordered Scotch and gave in to the girl's plea for champagne. The whiskey the woman at the bar brought him was weak, the "champagne" tasted like cider—for good reason.

He sipped at his drink and sniffed the trace of hash in the dry, spicy air, only half-listening to the laughing girl beside him. Both of them were waiting for the old woman to go back to the bar.

She had just left when Morley caught a movement out of the corner of his eye. He jerked around, slopping some of the whiskey out of his glass. The old woman must have brushed the puppet as she passed. It was a white-faced clown with two eyes like tiny raisins staring blindly from its cocked head. Its orangish hair was pierced with a daisy. Its shoes, several sizes too big, were twisted at right angles to each other. It hung on an otherwise barren wall, dangling from the frayed end of a cord yanked tight around its neck. Its checkered trousers bulged—a silent mockery of every John who had ever dropped his pants in the shop.

"How long are you in Brussels?"

She said it as though, if he had any sense at all, he'd get out yesterday. Morley waited until she'd stopped toying with the bottom button on her blouse.

"As long as it takes to find out who killed Bernadette."

The old woman was back. Both of them stared at him.

"She was strangled after she left here."

The younger woman's eyes narrowed. "You are not a gendarme."

"A friend."

Before he mentioned Bernadette the younger woman had been about to suggest they buy a bottle and take it into the other room. He had seen the old woman's reflection in the window; she had been stabbing at the air, pantomiming that he had paid his money and they should get on with it. Now the girl lay back on the couch, relighting a Thai stick she'd taken from the ashtray. She was deliberately casual, but couldn't quite hide her nervousness. Morley wondered what sort of reputation Bernadette's friends had.

On the other side of the window, a grim-faced middle-aged man in a dark raincoat strolled past. He caught sight of the breast that was playing peek-a-boo beneath the girl's blouse and hesitated. He raised his eyes and she smiled. He glanced quickly away and hurried on down the street.

Before he'd even moved, her smile had vanished.

"What did Bernadette say on the phone?"

"I don't know." Her mind was on the traffic outside. "I was busy."

He watched her while she inhaled again. He could see the joint's glow and her oval face reflected in the glass. Outside, the shadows were starting to creep across the city again. "You were her friend?"

She nodded.

Several cars rolled past, their drivers studying the curtained windows. The man in the raincoat returned, shoulders stooped, hands sunk deep in his pockets. He glanced in again, looking guilty.

"*Smile, damn you,*" the girl whispered between saucy, open lips.

The man outside the glass drifted on. They both followed his reflection in the windows across the way. A few feet beyond the shop, he hesitated, looked back for one last glimpse, then pulled his coat tight around him against the chill and hurried away.

"I hate Brussels in the winter—I hate it all year round." She stared at the joint, then remembered why he was there. "She stopped in to use the phone. Then someone came in and I went in back with him."

"Did you hear anything at all?"

She laughed at the memory, shaking her head. "He was a regular. He always gasps when he loses his breath. And he loses everything very quickly."

"And after he finished?"

"I listened to his troubles. His troubles with work. His troubles with women. He brings all his troubles to me."

Morley was getting impatient. "And when he was finished?" he repeated.

"Bernadette made her calls and left."

"What about *her?*" He jerked his head toward the old woman behind the bar, watching them in the mirror. "Was she here?"

She shook her head. "No. She's angry about that. She thinks Bernadette shouldn't have made her calls from here. She thinks it will be bad for business."

He slid back in the window seat, leaning against the section of wall that jutted out behind him. The girl probably talked her customers into having an orgasm. "How well did you know Bernadette?"

"We worked the same clubs." She made a quick, cutting gesture at her throat. "Men did not look at her the same way after that." She touched her throat again. "That's funny, isn't it? Down *here* she was still the same—but they didn't want her anymore."

She took one last drag from the joint. "I was a good friend of hers. But perhaps not so good a friend as you." She looked at him out of the corner of her eyes, her expression unfriendly. She was jealous, Morley thought. "I think it was *you* she wanted to talk to when she was frightened."

"How did you know she was frightened?"

Her lips twisted in a pout. "I saw her. She was never like that."

"Like what?"

"I told you. *Panique*—nervous."

"What did she say?"

"Only that she had to use the phone."

The old woman coughed and the girl glanced toward the bar. "We should get a bottle. Her palm itches."

He had already wasted too much time. He slipped several

246

banknotes from his wallet, folded them. "Who else did Bernadette trust? Besides you and me?"

She glanced down at the money in his hand and the pout disappeared. "Henri, the mime. He helped her when the butchers told her they had to cut. You can find him at the pub in place Delporte near Prison Saint Giles."

There was another cough from the old woman at the bar.

"She says you must go—that you are no good for business, either."

He slipped the money in her hand. "That's for you, not her."

She looked sour. "The old hag's already counted them."

"She's right," Morley muttered. "She should have been here."

"My name's Elly," the girl said. "You'll come back?" She looked at him hopefully. He had given her money, bought drinks, and hadn't even asked for a hand job.

"I'll remember," Morley promised. At the door, he turned to the old woman. "*Au revoir*, Madame."

Like the aging redhead in the pay box at the Théâtre de Vaudeville, she ignored him.

twenty-five

THE PUB WAS on a narrow, windswept corner opposite a high stone wall covered with tattered circus posters, their faded red and yellow borders worn away by the wind and the rain. Checkered half-curtains brightened the small windowpanes; a tableau of geese winging over a marsh had been etched on the glass door.

Inside, it was all varnished mahogany, stuffed foxes and polished brass. Morley hung his mackintosh on an empty peg and looked around the room. Half-a-dozen tables, most of them empty, a long, dark bar and a door with an enameled sign reading: "Téléphone—Toilette."

La Brasserie de L'Espérance. Despite its promising name, "The Beerhouse of Hope" did little to lift his spirits. He glanced at the pegs holding a score of raincoats. Less than a week in Brussels, and already the smell of damp cloth sickened him.

He cursed the rain, knowing all along that it had nothing to do with his depression, and pushed through the empty chairs blocking his path. On another day, he might even have liked the beerhouse. The tape deck was playing Strauss, every table had a small vase of white and yellow flowers, and the pinball machines in the corner added a lively staccato accompaniment to the waltz.

He settled for the first empty stool at the bar, ignoring the old girls huddled beneath the photographs of ancient bicyclists. They giggled and eyed him over their cherry beers.

The mirror behind the bar was blotchy where the silver had peeled away. He studied its faded reflections, turning his head to catch a glimpse of everyone. He wondered which of them might be Henri. Most of the bar's customers, like the ladies and the bartender, were older—they would have been right at home at Théâtre de Vaudeville. His own face, as pale as the others, peered back at him from behind a display of nylons wrapped in cellophane on the back bar. He fit right in.

He ordered a Pils. When the bartender, a genial sort with an enormous bone-white moustache, had finished drawing his draft, Morley said, "A friend suggested I look up Henri."

The bartender sliced the foam off one stein of beer and filled another. He gestured with his free hand and Morley turned. Four laborers in overalls nearly large enough for Louis were playing cards at one of the tables. Behind them, an old man with a shock of straw-colored hair tinged with gray moved first the white and then the black chessmen across a small folding board.

The bartender shoved the second stein across the mahogany. *"Voor Henri."*

Morley dug in his pocket.

"Nee, nee." The bartender winked at the other customers who'd abandoned their bantering to listen. *"Mijheer* Henri and I have our little arrangement."

Morley was sure of it. From the expectant looks on the faces around him, everybody in the pub was in on their game, whatever it was. Henri saw him coming and nudged the other chair out from under the table with his sandal, pushing the chessboard to one side. The cardplayers were now as preoccupied with watching them as were the old ladies who had abandoned their cherry beers. The Strauss waltz was still playing on the tape deck but even the flippers and bells of the pinball machines had stopped chattering.

Morley set the steins on the table and held out his hand. "My name's Neal Morley. Mind if I join you?"

Henri's handshake was firm. He motioned toward the chair that Morley was already reaching for. Morley turned it to one side, compulsively sitting with his back to the wall so he could keep an eye on the rest of the room. This time, though, the position made him feel as if he were on stage. He picked up one of the steins, holding it by the body so his hand could feel its coolness.

He raised the stein for a toast, hesitating when he realized Henri had done exactly the same. *Exactly the same.* Henri, too, held his stein just so high, gripping it around the full glass so its handle pointed outward. Morley glanced down. Henri had also turned his chair and extended his left leg out just as he had.

Everybody in the room was watching, trying to hide their smiles. He and Henri were the main event. Breaking up the act now would be like smashing the pub's TV set during a soccer broadcast.

"Skoal!"

His toast lacked enthusiasm but they met halfway, then both tipped their steins. His might have hit the table a split second before or after Henri's, the old man mimicked him that closely.

He tried to focus on Henri's eyes and block out the tight expression that he knew was a mirror of his own. "Elly, the bar girl at Sirocco, said that you and Bernadette Schiaffino were close."

Henri didn't answer but leaned over the unsteady table, his

face worried, strained. Then Morley realized it was *he* who looked worried and strained—he had yet to see Henri's real face. He leaned back and straightened his knotted shoulders, watching Henri do the same. He wanted to run a hand across his face to wipe away the tension but stopped himself. He'd be damned if he'd give that to Henri as well.

The cardplayers were urging the mime on. Morley glanced at them, looking back just in time to catch Henri's eyes mocking his. He got angry, then, and Henri caught that, too. The onlookers roared.

Morley ignored the laughter and leaned closer to Henri, shutting out the rest of the room. "It's about Bernadette." He kept his voice low, emphasizing each word. "I'm sorry, Monsieur, but she's been murdered."

The mirror in front of him shattered. The old man stared at him for a full second, not bothering to mimic him when he shifted in his seat. His eyes were suddenly dull, his cheeks sunken. He looked uncertainly over the pub full of customers, coming back to rest on his almost empty stein. It was a stunned, simple gesture that said: *"Forgive me, but you see, this is my job, what I do for my friends, for my drinks. . . ."*

It was then that Morley realized what Bernadette and Henri had in common, the bond that had made them such close friends. Henri was a mute.

The others in the pub were muttering now, confused and angry at him for having spoiled their fun. Henri continued the transformation and Morley watched, fascinated. The eloquent hands tore open an imaginary package, tapped out a cigarette. One hand caressed the cigarette while the other struck an unseen lighter. Morley anticipated what Henri was about to do. The head tossed back, the proud arc of the neck, the smoke blown defiantly at the ceiling . . .

Bernadette.

A moment later, the image flickered away and Henri peered at him questioningly.

He nodded. "A few hours ago," he said in a low voice. "It was . . . sudden." He had almost said "professional."

The pub was silent again, everyone intent on Henri, stunned that the act had changed from comedy to tragedy. Henri sat rigidly still, his watery eyes focussed on a point among the empty chairs. When he finally moved, the motion was small: a slight rotation and snap of the right wrist. Over and over.

Morley stared at the motion, knowing it was familiar. Then he had it. The smack of the riding crop into François' left palm.

"*You* taught her." He didn't try to hide his admiration.

Henri smiled slightly. He reached over to pick up something light between his fingertips. At first, Morley imagined it was a plate. While everyone watched, Henri set it carefully down on a corner of the table. He held his left hand poised overhead, fingers spread wide. He reached down with his other hand, lifted, then swung something in a short arc over the first object and lowered it gently down. He let go, marked a few beats in midair, then tugged nimbly at unseen strings.

> "*You che-ri up-on my knee*
> *No strings for you no strings for me*
> *Just me for* tu *and* tu *for me a-lone. . . .*"

Morley could hear François's boots tapping across the stage, see the elderly audience swooning. . . .

"Henri is too modest!" The barkeep placed two more steins on the already crowded table and smiled anxiously at his other customers. Morley ignored him, studying the broken face across from him. He was seeing the real Henri for the first time.

"The other day I was told Cailleau was a true artist. Now I meet another."

"They talk about marionettes," the barkeep said loudly. "I thought so." He hadn't the slightest idea what had interrupted the game, Morley thought; he was only trying to reassure his customers. "It's true," the barkeep continued, smiling broadly at the others. "There will never be another Cailleau—but there would never have been François without Henri. He brought François to life."

It was the mime who cut him short, aping the barkeep with a fawning gesture. In the split second during which that gesture vanished and Henri's own features rearranged themselves, Morley caught a glimpse of the anger and grief inside the old man. The others in the pub, eager for more sport, broke into demanding laughter.

"Bernadette and I talked late last night," Morley said. "You taught her many things."

The bartender, encouraged by the laughter, interrupted. "Bernadette remembers, Monsieur. She comes often—she was here yesterday afternoon."

"When?"

The question was too sharp and the barkeep looked uneasy. Morley cursed himself for coming on too strong once again.

"Late, I do not know the exact time."

"What did she want?"

"She wanted to find Electro, the magician. He no longer works at the Théâtre de Vaudeville, the customers didn't like him. She wondered if Henri knew where he was." He nodded proudly at the old man. "Many performers come here after hours. "They come to see an artist, they talk to him."

Apparently Henri had a reputation as an entertainer's entertainer. Morley studied the mime, whose attention was once again focussed somewhere beyond the empty chairs, the pain obvious in his face.

"Did she say anything about Electro?"

"Only that he played the same club in Berlin, that Serge had supper with him on their last day there." He half-smiled. "I didn't believe that. Serge disliked few people, but he detested Electro."

Morley looked up with sudden speculation. "Did he tell her where Electro was staying?"

The barkeep turned back toward his bar, suddenly aware that his customers were going thirsty. "He didn't know—he said he'd try and find out tonight, that she should come back."

There was only one question more, and he knew how painful it would be for Henri to answer.

"Who would want to kill Bernadette?"

Henri's face went slack and he turned away. Again, it was the bartender who answered. "A beautiful woman always has disappointed suitors, Monsieur." He grimaced. "Though with her throat . . ."

Morley glanced at his watch. It was almost five, and van den Haute was expecting him. He already knew what the Captain was going to say. The only question was how much time he might have left in Brussels.

twenty-six

THE PAY PHONE in the back room of the brasserie was buried behind a stack of broken chairs. Morley tried to shut out the strains of Strauss and the chatter of the pinball machines but the door to the room wouldn't close. He settled for shouting over the uncertain connection and having Louis repeat the beerhouse's address before he hung up.

He retrieved his mac, nodded to Henri and walked outside, keeping his back hunched to the wind so he could light the cigarette he shook from his coat pocket. For the hundredth time since he had been shot at on the steps of the gendarmerie, he wondered if somebody had followed him, was waiting to gun him down outside. He shook his head. You took what precautions you could; worrying was not one of them.

But of course you still did.

It was raining again, a veiled drizzle. He let his mind wander while he waited for Louis' taxi. *The magician.* He went over what had happened in the last few days, incident by incident, stringing them together like the beads on a rosary. He was still standing there, bemused, when the Mercedes spun around the corner and Louis jammed hard on the brakes, squinting past the wiper blades to make sure it was he.

Morley limped to the open door, pushed the skin books aside and settled into the front seat next to Louis. He told him to drive to the gendarmerie and the big man promptly looked worried.

"Is it serious, Neal?"

"Yes, it's serious."

Louis started to ask questions, then thought better of it. He knew what was happening anyway; he would have heard the entire story from Tindemans.

It was a short ride, stretched out by Louis' sudden insistence on driving as if he were leading a funeral procession. Neither of them spoke until Morley was standing on the curb again. He bent down, the drizzle trickling under his twisted collar.

"Don't wait for me, it may take a while."

Louis leaned out the window, ignoring the rain. "We had good times together, didn't we, Neal?"

Morley reached in and squeezed his shoulder. "You saved my life, Louis. I never really thanked you."

Louis looked sheepish and pulled back inside. "It was nothing, Neal." He goosed the accelerator. The fan belt started to whine and he had to shout. He looked out at Morley and grinned. "Maybe it will turn out all right."

"Sure." Morley straightened up and the water immediately ran down the inside of his coat. "Stay dry, Louis."

"You too, Neal."

He watched as the cab rattled off, remembering when Louis had dropped him off at the galerie his first morning in Brussels. He had done the big man an injustice then. Louis' loyalty was probably as much a commodity as anything else in the world, but still, Louis had once saved his life.

* * *

The walls of the toilet where Karim had died had been freshly painted, the corridor scrubbed and waxed. The gendarme serving as his guide stared straight ahead, his eyes shifting only once and then to stare accusingly at Morley's squeaky shoes and the dirty puddles of water that they trailed. When Morley glanced at the toilet, the gendarme motioned for him to keep moving. It was as subtle as the prod of a nightstick and confirmed everything he already suspected. His tour in-country was over.

The gendarmerie's conference room was opulent, the high wooden beams and burnished, dark-oak paneling superb replicas of some early-nineteenth-century townhouse. The carpeting was thick, the furniture was upholstered in leather, and a white-jacketed cadet stood behind the small bar in the corner. The whole setup made Morley feel as if he was in a posh men's club.

The three of them were seated in armchairs, facing him as he entered. He had heard laughter outside the door, cut short when the gendarme ushered him in. It hung in the dry air along with the cigar smoke. Tindemans and Taca were still smiling; van den Haute looked well scrubbed and recently shaven, politely curious. Whatever it was that had struck the others as funny had apparently not amused him. Morley guessed that the Captain would play the role of an almost-innocent bystander.

"Have a seat, Neal." Tindemans' thin face wore authority with the nervous grace of a king whose crown was much too large. His face was oddly mobile as he searched for the proper expression, one with just the right touch of displeasure mixed with concern. He finally settled for an uneasy look.

Taca had no such difficulty. His watery eyes were large and laughing, his expression one of delight and revenge. Morley knew there wouldn't be any ritual regrets or thanks from either of them.

He heard the gendarme step back and felt the heavy doors close behind him. He eased into a nearby chair.

"Help yourself to a drink, Neal." Tindemans had taken over as host, earning a quick glance of disapproval from van den Haute. He waved at the bar in the corner. "You look like you could use it."

Morley caught the sarcastic undertone and stiffened. "It can wait."

Tindemans cleared his throat. "Euro Tech has a new chief, Neal."

"Congratulations."

"We won't be working together after all." Tindemans started to dry-wash his hands. "I don't have to tell you there will be no more cowboys and Indians." He aborted a nervous smile. "Sabena has a seven-thirty-seven to London in the morning. Flight six-oh-three. It's quick. It leaves Zaventem at seven-forty and arrives at Heathrow the same time. We've already made your reservation."

Taca looked surprised. Tindemans must have failed to consult with him about the time of departure. Not that Taca gave a good goddamn—the fat man must be eager to see him bagged and tagged and shipped back home. Van den Haute seemed disinterested in the proceedings and Morley wondered if there had been friction between the head of Diane and the two men from the Bureau. The whole proceeding had a curiously fragmented air, as if there were really nobody in charge of what to do about Neal Morley.

Cowboys and Indians. That could have been Falk's line. With his muscle behind it, it would have carried some authority. Coming from Tindemans, it sounded absurd.

"Great—I can go right from Brussels to my debriefing."

Taca sniffed. "The subject you were sent to interview was

258

cremated yesterday. I doubt you found out much from the contents of a funeral urn."

"I found out enough." It was a lie but at least it threw Taca off balance.

"You've never been much of a team player, Neal." Tindemans' voice was shrill and Morley was suddenly curious how hard he had worked the cadet behind the bar. He was jumping far too eagerly at the chance to get even. "You never made contact when you undertook your vendetta. You've failed to cooperate with any of us. You've failed at too many things. Moses can't protect—"

Van den Haute interrupted. "I am sure that is between you and Monsieur Morley." There was more than a trace of contempt in his voice.

Tindemans almost stumbled over his words in his haste to back off.

"We won't go into them now but I assure you, they're well documented." He had learned something during all those years after all, Morley thought. "This isn't your private little war. You've been a good operative in the past, one of the best, we don't dispute that. But you've been badly hurt and it's distorted your judgment. You've spent a number of months tucked away between the sheets and things have changed. You will, of course, receive the highest commendation." He looked smug, convinced he had handled it rather well.

Now it was van den Haute's turn. "Your presence is no longer required here, Monsieur Morley." He glanced at the other two, who nodded their heads in agreement. "You are much too concerned with a petty revenge, Monsieur." He looked again at Tindemans and Taca, not smiling. "You Americans have your own interests here, so do the Russians, so do all the others. And so do I. I have a city to worry about, I can no longer let other concerns interfere with mine." He sounded

very pompous. "We split off the leader from the rest of the terrorists; with luck we will locate the others before they can do
any damage. As for locating the Russian defector, that's merely
a matter of time."

So this was how it all ended. Unceremoniously kicked out
of Brussels for a small disability pension back in the States, a
country he hadn't visited since the evacuation from Saigon. His
personal war had ended, and the friends he had left in 'Nam,
the victims of overdoses and betrayals and back alley assassina-
tions, had died in vain. He had gotten too close to some of those
responsible when he had been in Brussels before. They had almost eliminated him then, and they had succeeded now. Bureau
politics had proved to be mightier than the sword after all.

"And the man responsible for bringing in the squad in the
first place?" Van den Haute couldn't possibly believe what he
had said before.

The Captain cut him off. "We are picking up Hans
Schlöndorff, the booking agent. The evidence against him is
overwhelming." He smiled a totally unconvincing smile. "As
you can see, we are doing quite well without your help, thank
you."

Tindemans hurried to step in, not wanting him to forget
who was really responsible for forcing him to leave the country. "As of tomorrow morning at oh eight hundred hours, ETC
will cease to look after you."

"I wasn't aware the Bureau had been looking after me."

Tindemans nodded at van den Haute, who frowned. The
cue was too obvious.

"Monsieur Morley, there have been a number of unre-
solved murders in Brussels—the local police are quite eager to
talk with someone who fits your description. We are firmly
convinced, of course, that you had no real connection with any

of them. Unfortunately, after oh eight hundred tomorrow no one from Diane will be able to intervene for you."

The Captain said it almost as an afterthought, but the three of them had obviously discussed it before his arrival. Without further authorization from London and without the cooperation of Diane, he had little choice but to be on the plane. His last assignment was over. All that remained was to tell Hannie that her assignment was over as well.

His unfinished business in Brussels would remain unfinished.

He stood up to go. Tindemans and Taca were looking at him with varying degrees of mock regret at seeing him leave, but only van den Haute shook his hand in farewell.

"Good-bye, Monsieur, and good luck. I am sure we will meet again under more pleasant circumstances. Until we do, please take care of yourself."

His grip was surprisingly firm, his smile genuine. But all Morley could find in his heart for the Captain was anger.

The window in the front door of the pensione was dark. He had to ring three times before a bare bulb flickered at the far end of the dingy hallway and the silhouetted figure of the concierge shuffled toward him, unlocking the door and handing over the key to number eleven. She said nothing, her irritation at both the hour and him obvious.

No one was in the darkened corridor or the empty room. The note from Hannie was civil, its handwriting familiar. She had already decided to leave, she'd heard that he was being expelled. She had enjoyed their affair, she would never forget him. The note was very cool, very proper. Considering. He buried it in his pocket and limped to the sink, knocking a stack of papers off the table as he brushed past. What the hell had he expected of a four-day affair, undying devotion?

He turned on the tap and soaked his face. The cold water helped, reviving him enough so he could put together some of the pieces. It was all wrong. Schlöndorff wasn't involved, van den Haute was too good a cop to believe that. Morley flashed on Saigon and his job with the White Mice and the Vietnamese stoolies who had fingered and exterminated a lifetime of creditors. He had learned the hard way who was telling the truth and who was setting up their enemies.

Schlöndorff had told the truth when he said he had known nothing about Cailleau's recent trip.

He picked up the phone and asked the concierge for the key to the bath, then made a half-hearted attempt to clean up the room. There were traces of Hannie all over, from the hairpins on the edge of the sink to the dead rose that he found when he rummaged through one of the grocery bags. He could even smell her scent on the pillow when he lay down on the bed to wait for the concierge.

It was after he had taken his bath and was wandering naked around the room, still toweling his hair, that he noticed the multicolored papers scattered on the floor by the table, where he had brushed them off. He stooped to pick them up, holding them carefully by the edges with his damp hands so the ink wouldn't run. A line on one of the pages caught his eye. He immediately sat down and pawed through the rest of the sheets.

None of today had made much sense, and the proof was right there in his hands.

As sure as he'd ever known anything, he knew that Hannie wouldn't have left Brussels without taking along her letters to Serge.

He found the concierge in the long breakfast room behind her office. She was hunched over the first table, sewing.

"When did she go, Madame?"

"Tonight, Monsieur." The needle jerked in and out of the

thick material in her lap. She didn't bother looking up. "About an hour or so ago. Just before you came."

The last plane had left Zaventem for London hours before. The night train was already halfway to Ostend. One thing for sure: London hadn't pulled Hannie out in the middle of the night. With Cailleau dead, they were hardly in a hurry for her report.

"Who did she leave with, Madame?"

"She left with no one—only her things."

It took him a moment to realize that he had asked the wrong question.

"A taxi came for her?"

She glanced up, leaving the needle to plunge through the cloth and reappear apparently all on its own. "I thought it was your arrangement, Monsieur." She now looked disapproving. "I also thought it was unsafe and told her. The taxi made terrible noises and only one rear lamp was working."

Morley stared blindly at the needle flashing before his eyes. Louis's black Mercedes with its loose fan belt and its broken tail light. The same taxi that had pulled away from Bernadette's that morning, though he hadn't been sure at the time because of the haze.

He'd been slow. Fatally slow. And he had made mistakes. Staying two nights in a row at the same pensione was one of them. But trusting Louis had been his biggest mistake, there was no excusing that one. He had spent half a lifetime observing betrayal first hand; he knew how it operated. Only the ones you trusted were capable of it.

His emotions boiled over then, and he bitterly cursed London and van den Haute and himself, not forgetting Hannie. She had wanted to find out who had murdered Cailleau, but she had also wanted the excitement and what she thought was the glamour. He had warned her that it would be dangerous.

Now she was in it up to her sweet little neck. In the morning, they'd find her in an alley and the papers would run a two-inch story about a pretty young *chat* who had crossed the wrong customer.

He groaned and sat down at the table, forcing himself to think. It wasn't her fault, it was his. He had trusted Louis, and had given Hannie every reason to trust him as well. He couldn't blame her for letting him in; Louis would have said he had a message from him. Once inside, he would have forced her to write the note—

He found it in his pocket. The handwriting was uneven, the language stilted. It was Louis talking, trying hard to sound sophisticated.

Then he realized that if they had wanted to kill her, they would have done so right then and there.

Hannie had been kidnapped to serve as bait. For him.

But what worried him even more was the thought of Hannie with Louis. He couldn't forget how the big man had wanted to impress Hannie when they went to Le Couvent, the look in Louis' eyes as he had watched the stage show.

Now Louis had the chance to play the lead in a real-life fantasy in which all the women were willing. What would he do when he realized Hannie didn't want to be his co-star?

Strangle her, like he had Bernadette?

twenty-seven

HE TRIED TO call van den Haute, but the Captain had left for the day. No, the operator would not put him through to the Captain's home; no orders had been left to do so. But he could leave a message for Monday morning. . . . Morley even called the Bureau. He would never have done it for himself, but Hannie was worth his pride. Probably the most that Tindemans would do would be to notify London the next day and report Hannie missing.

The night operator took down his phone number and said he would contact Monsieur Tindemans promptly and no, he didn't know of any address where Louis might be reached. After an hour had passed, Morley knew that nobody was going to call him back.

The Bureau had hung him out to dry.

He went to Louis' apartment house, watching the darkened windows from the street for a few minutes before carding the lock and letting himself in. Without the big man's hulking presence, the apartment seemed oddly barren. A battered wooden table and folding chairs, a small kitchen with a tiny pantry housing mismatched cups and plates, plus a large can of coffee beans and a small Braun grinder. The table and sink were littered with crumpled wads of greasy newspaper and paper plates piled high with stale *frites* and drying clumps of mayonnaise.

The living room was home to a portable television set and a recorder with an umbilical cord camera still plugged in. Both were new and obviously expensive, the latest models. The rest of the furnishings consisted of a recliner and a bookcase that took up half the wall. Most of the books were about sex or popular psychology, with a few dozen sensational volumes on the supernatural thrown in.

The bottom half of the bookcase held a selection of videotapes, all of them apparently homemade, none of them titled. He slipped the last one on the shelf into the recorder and turned on the set, leaving the sound off. It didn't waste much time on romance. Louis starred opposite the Little Bo-Peep from Le Couvent.

The bedroom was about what he had expected. A rumpled mattress and box spring on the floor, a small bedside bookcase overflowing with comic books and pornographic paperbacks. Hundreds of nude pictures had been torn out of skin magazines and pinned on the walls. By the bedroom door was a large shelf for sex toys, plus the others that Louis had found so fascinating: the little wooden acrobats and rope climbers that had kept the big man's hands busy.

He now understood why Louis had settled for driving a cab. He had never been interested in the Bureau as such. Louis's real ambitions involved Little Bo-Peeps and Belindas, his reality was that of the skin magazines and the videotapes.

Aside from the bed and the bookcase, the only other thing in the room was a weight-lifting set. The bar was loaded with more weights than Morley had ever seen in a home gym. The concierge would undoubtedly have complained if she'd known.

266

They wanted *him*, he kept reminding himself, not Hannie. They would know that he would've figured out that Louis had grabbed Hannie and that he would show up at Louis' apartment looking for him. There was no way of contacting him directly, so they must have counted on his figuring out where Louis had taken the girl. But nothing made any sense in all this clutter.

He started, methodically, to take the room apart.

An hour later, he gave up. There were no indications that Louis had even been in the apartment that night. There were no dishes in the sink, the *frites* were cold, the towels in the john were dry. He would wait, Morley thought, then decided against it. It made more sense to check out the obvious holes that Louis might have dived into, then come back. Goddamnit . . . Was Hannie with Louis? Had he delivered her someplace? Or had he already killed her?

He tried not to think about it, knew he couldn't stop. They wanted him, they wanted something from him. Hannie was their way of getting it. Unless . . .

Unless kidnapping Hannie had been Louis' sole and original contribution.

A few hours later, he had come up empty-handed. The manager of Le Couvent denied that Louis had stopped by. And none of the waiters at Roi d'Espagne had seen Louis since the evening when the three of them had been there together.

It was well past midnight when he gave up the search and returned to the beerhouse. Blasts of cold air whipped around the corner as he tugged at the door. It was locked, but a few of the inside lights were on. He tapped on the etched glass, then pounded on it. The barkeep recognized him through the window, threw his dirty bar rag on a table and shuffled toward the door, his key already in hand.

"I was closing, Monsieur, but come in, come in."

A gust of wind whistled around the thick door, rattling it. The barkeep let him in, then slammed the door shut and threw the bolt. It could snow that night, Morley thought. He could feel it.

"A beer or a whiskey, Monsieur?"

He shook his head. "Where's Henri?"

The barkeep nodded toward the back. The mime, bundled up in a thick overcoat, was hunched over his table. Half-a-dozen empty steins and the now-forgotten chessmen kept him company.

"Christ, he's drunk."

The barkeep shook his head, denying it. "He's sick. Over the girl."

Morley unbuttoned his mac and tossed it at a peg. "Is there any coffee?"

"Sit—sit, I'll get it."

He glanced again at Henri. "Better bring us both coffee." He crossed the room, pushing aside some of the chairs arranged in a ring around the mime's table. Henri jerked awake. He reached up and brushed the hair away from his eyes, trying to focus on Morley.

The mime looked sick, all right. Morley wondered how many more steins there had been, then noticed that Henri's coat was dry. The mime hadn't left the pub that night. With all the chairs around his table, he'd probably been a captive entertainer most of the evening.

The barkeep brought two mugs of coffee and Morley watched in silence while Henri fumbled with the handle, then held it with both hands and sipped at it. When the coffee was half gone, Morley asked, "Who booked Electro?"

Henri shrugged. It was the bartender who said, "Nobody

knows, Monsieur. Nobody likes the magician, nobody will admit to having anything to do with him."

Cailleau had had dinner with Electro in Berlin, just before he had told Bernadette of his sudden plans to smuggle in seven "refugees." It couldn't have been a social dinner; like everybody else, Cailleau had loathed the magician. But both of them had been playing the same club in Berlin and both of them had been booked into Théâtre de Vaudeville at the same time.

Electro, of course, knew who had booked them. He had been Cailleau's contact and probably his watchdog. He undoubtedly had known about the smuggling of the terrorists and who was responsible for Cailleau's death. And if he knew all that, he might know where Louis had taken Hannie—and why.

"Where can I find the magician?" Morley watched the mime intently.

Henri's eyes suddenly came alive and his left hand began to flutter. He leaned closer, admiring the way his own hand preened. His other hand fumbled with an unseen latch, opened an imaginary door and reached through it, chasing his wildly darting other hand, finally catching it and soothing it as he drew it under his chin.

"The bird market," the bartender said, trying to talk faster than Henri's hands. "Tomorrow's Sunday—Electro will be at the bird market in Grand'Place in the morning." He took a long pull at his stein. "The doves," he said, wiping his lips on the bar rag. "They say he really crushes them, that he has to go to the bird market often."

The first streaks of dawn came swiftly, outlining the gothic belfry and the laddered rooftops of the medieval guild houses surrounding the square. The cobbled place seemed huge without the flower vendors' umbrellas and with the iron tables and chairs locked behind the shuttered doors of the various cafes. There wasn't a car or another person in sight. Even the pigeons were roosting.

Morley glanced again at his watch, then settled down on some cold cellar stairs to wait. After leaving the beerhouse, he had gone back to Louis's apartment and waited in the dark, flattened at one side of the door, the Beretta in his right hand. But Louis had known better than to come home, and Morley considered the time wasted, like everything else he had done in Brussels.

An hour before dawn, he let himself out of the apartment as quietly as he had broken in and climbed the deserted streets toward Grand'Place. He was running again, like he had the last time he'd been in Brussels.

He tried to sum everything up. Somebody wanted to get rid of him even though he hadn't learned much from Karim and damned little from Bernadette . . . And what had Bernadette wanted from Electro anyway?

His mind swung back to Hannie. He should have forced her to go back that first night; at the least, he could have persuaded London to pull her on the grounds that it was too dangerous. But he hadn't—they would have pulled him as well. Now she was being used as leverage against him. They knew he would come after them; Louis had probably deliberately left a clue in his apartment, and he had passed right over it. For a moment he was tempted to go back and rummage through it again, then realized that what passed for a clue with Louis might escape him completely. He wondered what connection Louis had with the terrorists, how long he had been working both sides of the street.

Church bells suddenly pealed through the gray streets emptying into Grand'Place. Pigeons, sent fluttering from their roosts by the ringing, circled and swooped down on the square. Morley knew his description had been circulated at morning call

270

in all the police stations of the various communes. Soon the gendarmes at Zaventem would report that he hadn't boarded the flight to London.

He stood up, beating his arms around himself to try and warm up. There was always the possibility that Hannie had known something she'd never told him, and that she'd had to be silenced, like Bernadette. Maybe Louis and his friends had decided to get two for the price of one. Paranoia once again. Or maybe not.

Suddenly a stout, humpbacked man scuttled across the cobblestones, a wooden cage tucked under each arm. Almost immediately, others came out from the nearby streets to join him. They set up their cages on short planks or stacked them in tiers.

Morley watched them all—the sellers and the buyers and the swappers—and then there were too many for him to watch from his one vantage point. He stepped out into the square, catching a glimpse of himself in a freshly washed window. He was gaunt, his cheeks and chin dark and stubbled. The commune police might not recognize him so easily after all.

He edged through the crowd, mapping out the rows of cages in his mind. He ignored the clusters of racing pigeons, canaries and peacocks, zeroing in wherever doves were concentrated. Then he circled back into the growing crowd, alert for any sign of the magician or the police.

He had paused in an aisle that offered a view of several of the busiest hawkers and was about to start around for the third time when he spotted two commune police strolling toward him. He crouched down, studying the doves in a bottom cage. He stayed on his haunches, his back to the police, until they had finished joking with a young woman selling canaries and moved on. He slipped away then, taking some comfort in the size of the crowd. It made it easier to avoid the police. Unfortunately, so many people also made it easier for Electro to come and go in the confusion.

And then Morley saw him. At least he saw a greatcoat that looked the same as the one Electro had worn at Théâtre de Vaudeville. The man wearing it seemed too short, but then he was bent over a cage on the ground and Morley couldn't be sure. He elbowed his way through the crowd to get a closer look. Electro. Morley grabbed him by the collar.

The magician was fast. A startled glance, then: "Monsieur! No, no—the bird!" People turned to stare. Electro quickly dipped a hand inside Morley's mac and pulled out a fluttering dove. He held the frantic bird under his chin, cooing to it, then smirked at the crowd and grabbed again for Morley's coat. Morley knocked his hand away—and stared at the broken egg running down the front of his mac. The crowd pushed closer to watch. Morley, still clutching the magician's collar, twisted it tight.

"In Berlin—who sent you to Cailleau?" He held Electro close, his voice a whisper. The answer didn't come quickly enough, and he twisted tighter with one hand while he felt for a knife in his pocket with the other. He found it, worked it open, and a moment later the magician's mouth gaped wide, his watery eyes dilating as he felt the point of the blade slip through his open coat and prick his side.

"*Who?*" Morley whispered again.

" . . . don't know," the magician gasped, his pocked face twitching with fear. " . . . only telephoned . . . "

The rookie policemen had found themselves two attractive peacock fanciers fifty meters away. They were watching the commotion, reluctant to leave their lovely tourists alone with only their guidebooks. Morley had a minute, maybe a little more if Electro didn't start screaming. Time enough. You could do almost anything in a crowd if you were quick.

A jab with the knife, not enough to break the skin. "Tell me."

The eyes were rolling wildly now, and Morley smelled urine; the magician was so frightened he couldn't hold his water. "He goes . . . several names . . . "

"Tell me one of them."

Electro was too terrified to remember any of them. "A fat man . . . he wears thick glasses, sniffles. . . ."

Taca.

Morley almost lost it then. He could feel Electro jerk away and jabbed hard enough with the knife that he knew he had drawn blood. The magician squealed in sudden fear. Morley was frantic. There was no way he could have known about Taca. And he still didn't know exactly where he fit in. And then there was the murder of Bernadette. . . .

"Who booked you into Théâtre de Vaudeville?"

"The fat man—he's one of the owners." A nod and a frightened look at the now-uncertain crowd which had sensed trouble and was edging back.

"He booked Cailleau, too, right?" Another nod. Then the magician caught a glimpse of the police and became mulish.

"I know about you—let me go!"

Morley lowered the knife so he could thrust underhand. Electro felt the point dig into his groin and looked like he was going to be sick.

"What did Bernadette want?"

Another glance at the police, now frowning and working their way through the crowd toward them. "Cailleau's fee for the smuggling—she wanted it. She was frightened, she wanted to leave Brussels."

Bernadette had been running since the night he had met her, when she had hidden Cailleau's Luger in her dressing-room drawer. And then he wondered what Hannie would think. She wouldn't be happy that Cailleau had sold out.

"The girl—where did Louis take her?" Electro looked blank and Morley growled, "The cab driver."

" . . . don't know . . . "

Morley wriggled the knife slightly. He could gut the magician right there and get away in the confusion and the man knew it. *"Liar!"* He pressed the knife harder.

Electro gasped. "They're at the theater . . . my pigeon cage, when I went to get it . . . I saw them!"

They wanted him on their home turf. "You saw Cailleau murdered?"

A sudden, defiant grin. "I was backstage—I saw it all!"

There was the sound of a whistle and one of the policemen started shoving his way through the crowd, motioning to them. He shouted something but Morley ignored him. He'd have to let the magician go, he had to get to the theater. He couldn't let the police stop him.

"We can both get away," he whispered. "The eggs—start shelling them!"

Electro nodded eagerly, the spit running down his chin. He pulled an egg from Morley's mac and popped it into his mouth. He turned, snatched another from behind the first policeman's ear, twirled it and started shelling. The people around them relaxed and Morley slipped away, unnoticed. Behind him, there was a muffled, chirping cry that swelled in volume and then was drowned out by the laughter of the crowd.

He turned once, half a block away, to see if he was being followed. He wasn't. Electro was still holding the crowd with his chirps and shelling. The magician had managed to distract them long enough so he could get away.

And then, like the tumblers of a lock, the pieces of the puzzle started falling into place.

274

twenty-eight

N OBODY WAS AT Théâtre de Vaudeville, not even the elderly concierge with his faded war decorations. But Louis's battered Mercedes was parked in the alley. It wasn't yet ten o'clock, and Morley had to break a lock to let himself in. The lobby was empty and so was the main auditorium. He slipped backstage, feeling his chest start to tighten, knowing that Louis was there, someplace. He wondered about what the magician had said, that Taca owned the theater. If he did, it had to be under a blind—none of the performers had fawned on Taca the afternoon he'd been at Cailleau's performance.

He found the stairs backstage. At the bottom, a single light bulb flared, lighting the steps and the dark mildewed walls. He started down, trying to avoid the inevitable creaking, hesitating on the bottom step to catch his breath. The floor was sagging, the hallway gloomy. What little light there was came from the single bulb—and from an orangish crack beneath the prop room door. He felt for the hinges, checking which way the door would swing if he tried to kick it in, then concentrated on the sounds coming from the other side.

Louis was inside, all right—the crack beneath the door had

suddenly gone dark. He wondered if Hannie was with him, then decided she must be—if she were still alive. He nudged the door, felt it give and then stop short, wobbling slightly. A chair had probably been wedged beneath the knob. But the wood was rotting, the hinges loose and flimsy. One kick and he would be inside.

Inside and facing Louis.

He studied the crack again, sweating. When he first went through, he'd be helpless. There would be a fraction of a second before he could see anything in that black hole and bring the Beretta to bear. And Louis himself might have a gun. Or he might be using Hannie as a shield.

He kicked the door with his foot. "Louis, it's me, Neal."

Minutes passed. Then the door suddenly pushed back as something or someone heavy leaned against the other side. Louis. He could hear him breathing. Jesus. Maybe Louis had been waiting for Taca. Or somebody else.

"They've got the others, Louis. Van den Haute is just a few minutes behind me. We have to talk."

No response—just all that weight pushing back on the other side of the door. Then: "You've got a gun, Neal." Louis said it like one kid talking to another in a game they were playing, one where you make trade-offs and demands, all the time hiding until you saw what happened.

Morley strained to hear if there was anybody else in the room with Louis. If Hannie wasn't inside, where the hell was she? He slowly emptied the Beretta, dropping the bullets into his pants pocket. "Louis, I'm going to slip it under the door. Then open up." He shoved the automatic through the crack, the Smith & Wesson ready in his other hand.

Louis didn't say anything, but Morley could feel the pressure against the door ease slightly. Then he heard the clicks as the Beretta was opened and closed. A moment more of silence. "The Smith & Wesson, Neal. Push it under the door, too."

His shirt was beginning to glue itself to his back. He made his voice sound urgent. "They'll be here any minute, Louis."

"The gun, Neal."

He sensed that he was hesitating too long. It was too risky. Fire through the wood and end it. But he didn't know if Hannie was between Louis and the door, half-smothered by the big man's weight forcing her against the thick panels.

There was sudden anger in Louis's voice. "Don't fool with me, Neal."

"Me for the girl, Louis."

"Sure, Neal." Then: "The gun."

"Give me a minute." He dumped the Smith & Wesson's bullets into his palm and kicked the gun under the door. Again, the small clicks. The door suddenly sagged open.

He stepped inside, moving cautiously in the faint glow from an electric heater on top of a trunk. He glanced quickly around, trying to locate Hannie. To one side of him, the shadowy form of Louis reached up and turned on a bulb. Morley blinked in the sudden light, dim as it was. The prop room was enormous, occupying most of the cellar of the theater. It was also a disaster area. It was filled with old trunks and flats of scenery and rows of costumes hanging on pipe racks. Rain had seeped into one corner of the room, and many of the trunks now lay in puddles of water. Some had popped their iron hasps, their contents swollen by the moisture.

Most of the trunks had been ripped open and their contents strewn around the floor. A number of costumes had been torn off their hangers and were floating in the oil-streaked water. Louis had been looking for something. Or someone?

"Where is she, Louis?"

Something caught his eyes and he turned. They'd moved

Cailleau's trunks and puppets down here and he'd caught a glimpse of some of the life-sized marionettes he'd seen earlier in Cailleau's small dressing room. A policeman and a jester and one in a huge tricornered hat, half-hidden by a trunk.

Louis closed the door and casually bent a metal stool to jam it under the knob. He swung around in a half-crouch, looming up like a huge mechanical bear. The purple veins in his nose and his thick lips gave him a gargoylish appearance. His eyes were very bright. Behind him, barely visible in the dim glow from the light, hung a life-sized ballerina with a delicately-worked tutu. Only the tutu had been ripped away and an arm twisted off. Her exquisite head had been shattered by a blow from the side.

Louis followed Morley's eyes, anxious. "I couldn't tell in the dark, Neal. I thought somebody was down here."

Louis wasn't simple, Morley thought with sudden clarity, he was crazy. He edged away from him, groping around for something heavy, *anything*. There was a crowbar on top of one of the trunks but it was behind Louis.

"Where is she?" he repeated. He backed into a puddle on the uneven floor and could feel the water lap over his shoes.

Louis hesitated. "She's down here with me, Neal. I've got her tied up."

But Louis wouldn't have torn apart the trunks and pulled down the costumes if he had her tied up someplace.

Louis was still coming toward him and Morley kept edging back. A light fixture with a broken bulb dangled from the ceiling and brushed his shoulder. Louis saw it and stopped. He looked sly.

"I'll make a deal with you, Neal. If you help me get away, I'll tell you where she's hiding."

Only Louis didn't know. She must have broken the light

bulb and then hidden someplace in the room. He could imagine what Louis had done next. The big man had blundered around in the dark, looking for her, and stumbled across the ballerina. He had ripped it apart, furious. Then he had found another light fixture to turn on and went searching through the cellar for her. He had mangled the flats and knocked them over, torn apart the trunks and then, in a rage, had broken everything he could get his hands on. The backdrops were trampled, the painted flats smashed, every crate Morley could see was in splinters.

He now had a very clear idea of what Louis would do if he caught Hannie. Bernadette's purple, crushed throat was suddenly sharp in his mind. He felt something heavy in the water and stooped to pick it up: The magician's collapsible bird cage. It was the only heavy thing he could reach that was still light enough to pick up.

Louis said quietly: "Drop it, Neal." Then he lunged.

Morley swung the cage around his head and threw it. Louis grabbed it out of midair, hugged it against his chest and squeezed, crushing the wrought-iron cage as if it were an empty cigarette pack. Morley dodged behind a stack of broken trunks, working his way toward the door where the solitary bulb dangling from its cord cast shadows over the life-sized marionettes perched on top of Cailleau's storage boxes.

"Tell me if I have it right, Louis." Where the hell was Hannie? He had circled the entire basement, looked behind every battered flat and backdrop. "After you dropped me off at the gallery, you parked the cab and hung around Théâtre de Vaudeville until Cailleau came on. It was easy for you to get backstage—you had dropped Taca off so many times everybody knew you. While they were watching François, you killed Serge with the ice pick. Your timing was off there; Cailleau was supposed to be removed before I had a chance to talk to him at all."

"You came in early, Neal. You weren't supposed to."

"Bernadette was next—she knew who had set up the deal, too, and Taca was afraid she'd tell me."

Louis grimly shouldered aside the boxes and came steadily at him. "Something like that, Neal." He sounded unhurried, and Morley swore quietly to himself. It was three hours to showtime, it would be at least another hour before anyone showed up and heard them down there.

"Tell me about Bernadette, Louis. Did Taca set her up for you, too?" And then he had a terrifying thought. "Or did he promise you Bernadette if you would take care of her afterward?"

Louis shook his head, his expression one of chagrin. "She wouldn't let me touch her, Neal." He smiled, almost boyishly. "She didn't know what she was missing. She should have talked to the scag." And then: "You knew about the tube in her throat? She couldn't talk very well. She couldn't scream at all."

Louis was standing with his back to the light; he was outlined in the glow, his face in shadow. A man in an alley standing in front of a streetlamp would look just like that, Morley thought.

And then another tumbler dropped into place and Morley remembered what had happened six months before in Brussels. He and Louis had gone for a meet, discovering when they got there that the address was an alley remarkably like the one where he had met Leather Jacket. He had been surprised, but Louis hadn't, reaching in the shadows for a bat and catching him offguard. The beating had been savage, it had been meant to kill.

Somebody had started screaming then and he didn't realize until later that it was himself. Afterward, he had remembered nothing.

"I'm going to kill you, Louis!"

"I don't think so, Neal."

Morley threw something then, he didn't know what, and Louis grabbed for him, pushing aside trunks as though they were empty cartons. He could feel Louis's hand brush his arm before he slipped away. The crowbar—he had to get it. It had been next to the electric heater on top of a trunk. It wasn't there now.

He dropped to his knees, groping frantically in the puddle around his feet and coming up with handfuls of dripping costumes and draperies. He felt around on the floor, then sensed something above him and rolled—a reflex action, there wasn't time for anything more—kicking out from under Louis, who was straddling him, the crowbar clutched in his hands.

Still rolling, his clothes soaked, Morley dragged himself out of the water, using a nearby box for leverage. He stood up and wrenched the stool free from under the doorknob. He swung it sideways, putting his entire body behind the blow. Louis took it on the shoulder, grunting. Morley dropped the stool lower and shoved it into Louis's stomach, scrambling backwards to stay away from the big man's hands. His feet slipped on a soggy costume, still trying for a purchase on the slippery floor.

He fell on his back in the water, trying desperately to roll away from Louis, who was taking giant steps toward him. Then the big man was standing over him, holding the crowbar above his head as if he was holding a spear about to impale a fallen gladiator.

Morley held up one hand to ward off the blow. "Why'd you stop, Louis? When we were in the alley?" At the end of it all, that was the only question he had.

"The gendarmes came too soon. I told them that we'd been set up, that we'd been jumped." Louis's face suddenly went wooden and his shoulder muscles tensed. Morley caught his breath for the final scream.

There was a sudden noise behind them and Louis whirled. His eyes opened wide and his lips curled back over his teeth, giving him a feral, savage appearance. He shouted with sudden, frightened rage, Morley temporarily forgotten.

Morley staggered to his feet, watching as Louis whirled around with the crowbar, staring at the wall where they'd piled Cailleau's trunks. The life-sized marionette with the large tri-cornered hat had stood up and taken a step toward them, its movements oddly jerky as if Cailleau's ghost were pulling its strings.

Louis backed away, then suddenly charged forward, swinging the crowbar. Morley climbed on a trunk and grabbed for the electric heater, the nearest thing handy.

"Louis! Watch out!"

He had to yell twice. Louis glanced back and Morley threw the heater with all his strength. Louis caught it, holding it against his chest to crush it as he had the pigeon cage.

There was a crunch and a shower of sparks and a faint whimper from Louis. Morley stared, not understanding, then realized the heater had been on an extension cord. It was still plugged in when Louis, ankle deep in water, had smashed it against his chest.

The big man's face froze in an expression of childlike astonishment. He teetered for a moment, then collapsed into the water on the floor. He had remained standing just about as long as François had before falling over the body of Cailleau.

They had lucked out, Morley thought; neither he nor Hannie had been standing in the water. He limped over to Hannie, who sagged into his arms, the tricornered hat slipping off onto the floor. She was crying, and he held her for a long moment, gently stroking her hair.

She sobbed into his shoulder. "I didn't think I could fool him but I did. He lost control when he realized I had been there all along."

Morley let her go, knelt down and swiftly ran his hands through Louis's pockets. A few francs, a small metal puzzle made of rings, a package of gum and a set of keys.

And in his shirt pocket, damp from the water on the floor, a ticket to the circus.

"He was supposed to meet Taca there," Hannie said.

Something in her voice caught him and he glanced up. Her face was drained of emotion.

"I wasn't as brave as Bernadette," she said in a low voice. "I didn't scream at all. I didn't even try to."

twenty-nine

THE ARENA WAS packed. Morley spotted several gendarmes scattered through the crowd and pulled Louis' cap lower over his forehead, tugging at the strings of the balloons he'd bought so they floated closer to his face. The cap was too big, but it fit better than the ski sweater he'd stolen from the theater's prop room. He'd bulked up with clothing, at a distance looking far more like Louis than his slim, haunted version of the original Morley. It was unlikely that any members of the gendarmerie would recognize him.

Taca was sitting in the reserved section. The seat next to him was empty and Morley slipped quietly into it. Taca noticed him out of the corner of his eye, turned toward him thinking he was Louis, then realized with obvious shock that he wasn't.

"I hope you didn't leave Louis in pain like you did the boy from the theater."

"If you're asking, can he testify against you, the answer is no." Morley slid his arm around the back of Taca's seat so the balloons blocked their view from the gendarmes.

"I'm impressed." Taca, his face perspiring, stared at the woolen cap. "Your recovery—it *is* remarkable."

The throb of organ music and the screams of the crowd made them both look down. An elephant waltzed into the ring followed by performers in spangled tights. Morley leaned closer so Taca could hear him over the noise.

"I could kill you right now," he said. His left hand held the balloons, his right the Smith & Wesson hidden under his bulky sweater, its barrel pressed firmly against Taca's pudgy side. His right hand was trembling; it took an effort to control it.

Taca turned away and looked down at the ring. "I rather doubt that you will." He pointed with his rolled-up program. "Relax and enjoy the show, Monsieur Morley. Neither of us is going any place for the moment."

There was a troupe of jugglers in the ring now. Morley recognized the woman Schlöndorff had coached. The act worked surprisingly well. She wasn't good, but the more professional members of the troupe anticipated her mistakes and stepped in, effortlessly saving the balls. She was comic relief as well as a reminder to the audience that the juggling *was* difficult. The occasional nearly dropped ball looked intentional on her part, a demonstration of skill rather than ineptitude.

"It's not your sort of performance, I know," Taca said, studying him from behind his thick lenses. "You'd prefer three rings and an orchestra but then, you miss the point. With only one ring and *everyone* watching, you have to be very good."

His hint was unmistakable. Without turning around, Morley counted six gendarmes in the stands nearby. He suddenly realized he was the only one not applauding the jugglers and perfunctorily beat his hand holding the balloons against the arm of the seat. "I underestimated you. It won't happen again."

"I'm not offended." Taca looked smug. "After twenty centuries of occupation, we Belgians have developed our own sort of genius. Caesar learned—he called us Gaul's bravest people. Our little mannikin pissed on the best of Napoleon's soldiers.

The members and lobbyists attending the meeting of the European Union will learn. Even ITT will learn."

"Europe for the Europeans, Belgium for the Belgians," Morley said bitterly.

"More accurately, for the Walloons, the Flemish are really intruders. I never deceived you, Monsieur Morley. You knew my ideology from the start."

"You're part of the terrorist network," Morley accused. He couldn't keep the surprise out of his voice.

For the first time Taca looked away from the circus below. "I wondered what you would call it. The 'network.' " His thick lips caressed the word like it was a brioche. "I like that, it has a certain ring. But terrorism has a point, Monsieur Morley. It is not really random, without a purpose, as you and your compatriots would like to think. The goal we seek is freedom. I am constantly surprised that your country would argue with that."

Again, the hacking cough and the sniffles. "Forgive me if I point out that all my associates are dedicated people. Like the Zionists, they'll—"

Morley was finding it difficult to control his anger. "Your associates want to carve out their own little Israels, only with a lot less justification. The Basque separatists, the Portuguese Maoists, the Red Brigades, the Islamic Extremists, every so-called freedom movement willing to murder—"

It was Taca's turn to interrupt, his watery eyes blinking angrily behind his thick lenses. "I'm glad that you're aware of them all. But I should point out to you that there's nothing wrong with wishing to preserve one's political and cultural—or religious—heritage. Here in Belgium, we've had quite enough of your Coke culture and your high rises. As for the casualties that will inevitably result, wasn't it one of your patriots who said the tree of libery was watered with the blood of martyrs?"

"Actually, it was a Frenchman." Morley was calm again.

"De Vieuzac. He also said that it is only the dead who do not return."

"Referring to yourself," Taca sniffed. "Or perhaps to your unfortunate affair with Louis. If only you believed what you preach, Monsieur Morley. But then, you've never been the type to question. 'Of the people, by the people.' Did you ever ask yourself just who is meant by 'the people'?" He tapped Morley's knee with his program. "Last month at Schepdaal, there was a ball for Belgian and German SS officers, their collaborators and sympathizers. There was a fine Bavarian orchestra, 'Edelweiss,' but it was very difficult to dance—the floor was too crowded."

They were wasting time; he had to get Taca out of there, Morley thought. But they couldn't move, not yet. "What was your plan? A new force on the world scene?"

Taca half-smiled, his gold caps flashing.

"Now, that is a *very* good idea. The industrialized nations are so strong, so powerful. You control the wealth of the world, you control the natural resources, the oil. You also control a vast pool of scientifically talented people. Or think you do. There are those scientists who do not agree with the purposes to which their discoveries are put. And there are those who would simply like to leave. Like Gennadi Troshkin. I decided to help in distributing that talent pool more equitably."

"And as an analyst, you knew where all the little Troshkins were and how to get them. And what price they might want." Morley's voice was ragged. He'd been up all night, and it was now early Sunday afternoon. His body ached for rest.

Taca's smile was sly. "I diligently read all the journals and printouts. It's my job. But certainly your government has always been aware of scientists elsewhere who would like to defect. Those who could be persuaded, those who could be bought.

And, of course, those who have become disenchanted, who have devoted their lives to a particular line of research only to see that research discontinued or cut back."

He turned back to watch the circus. "The large group of rocket experts in your own country, for example, when your space program was all but dismantled. And your technical specialists now out of work because of your military cutbacks. Have you any idea how bitter some of them are? A lifetime devoted to specialties your government said were vital to the country, then suddenly they are unemployed, possessors of a talent for which there is no market. They have to eat, Monsieur, they have to provide for their families. Who could blame them for looking for opportunities elsewhere?"

He coughed and wiped at his mouth with a wadded-up handkerchief. "There are countries—never mind which ones—that are willing to be hospitable." He stared at the activity in the ring below, his mind elsewhere. "But perhaps I overemphasize the importance of science. Have you any idea how fragile modern society has become? Not long ago, if you had wanted to black out a city, you would have had to smash every street lamp. Today, all it requires is a defective relay in a power station." He sighed with feigned regret. "The vulnerability of modern technology."

"An interesting way of describing terrorism," Morley said slowly. "But the scientist was hardly your main intent. Your network intended to blow up the Berlaymont Building, right?"

Taca shrugged. "Big nations use big weapons, little nations use little ones. It's amazing, isn't it, to think that a few plastic bombs set off on the same day could ground all the world's airlines. Or a large one could bring down an entire building in a major city. Or that a single well-placed shot could leave an entire nation leaderless."

"And countless people would have died—clerks, typists,

288

passersby, and maybe a few of the finance ministers. But none of that would have bothered you."

"A small toll," Taca said casually. "For a major gain. The casualties would have been only a fraction of those who die daily in one of the African famines."

"You forgot drugs," Morley said in a tight voice. "The casualties are somewhat larger when you consider them."

Taca laughed.

"Oh my, no, Monsieur—you can't consider them a weapon, they're a vice. We didn't invent the trade, we merely profit from it. The wheels of any organization can't function without the grease of money."

Morley remembered the stacks of coins on Taca's desk, his fascination with money. He had misjudged the Belgian right from the start, he had underestimated Taca's parochialism, his enormous appetite, his desire for power. . . . Taca had found the perfect sea in which to swim. Surrounded by so many others just like him, who would ever suspect him?

"You're the banker," Morley said quietly.

Taca's eyes glittered behind his glasses. "You'd have to prove that, and I doubt that you can."

Morley counted the gendarmes again and cursed under his breath. "What happened to Schlöndorff?"

Taca shrugged. "They let him go, of course. He's guilty of nothing and he's a Belgian."

The jugglers were winding up their act; the clowns were waiting off to one side.

"And the other members of the terror squad?"

"You can hardly expect me to tell you, though I understand two more were picked up this morning." A sigh of regret and a smile. "We don't always win, but that's hardly your problem. Everybody is looking for you now."

"And Troshkin."

"And Troshkin." The amusement in Taca's voice made Morley turn, but the fat man was only studying the clowns.

"The two they picked up won't have Karim's strength."

Another shrug. "They know nothing. Only Karim knew who to thank for his mission."

Morley had a flashback to Karim collapsed over the bloody toilet bowl. "And me."

Taca nodded in agreement. "And you. Of course."

Morley took a firm grip on the Smith & Wesson. "You're right, this isn't my thing. Let's go somewhere and talk."

"*Mister* Morley, I've already been taken to the little boy's room. I have no intention of leaving here with you. Besides, you can't possibly go now—you'd miss the best part." Taca jabbed with his program toward the arena. "That ridiculous clown, the shy little man with the tragic face. Isn't it amusing how so many of the other clowns are hovering around him, almost as if they were protecting him?"

Morley stared at the hesitant, tense clown below.

Taca buried his face in his handkerchief. "Of course," he wheezed. "Why else would I go to a circus that didn't have the decency to stay in a tent? All Russians love the circus. The posters were plastered all over Brussels. It was only natural that he should try and hide here."

He waved Morley away. "Go ahead, take him. If you don't take him now, you never will. Your Russian friend has gotten here before you. The other clowns, they are not very funny, are they? Maybe it's because they're not clowns. I think perhaps your friend will succeed, and Citizen Troshkin will leave the country as anonymously as he entered, with van den Haute none the wiser."

Morley studied the ring. The clowns around the one Taca had pointed out as Troshkin were surprisingly drab. Perhaps they *were* Vasiliev's men, taking the scientist into custody in a foreign country, a thousand miles from home.

"Him for you, is that it?"

Taca nodded, hugging the haversack in his lap. "The price is surprisingly small—for both of us. Job security for you, anonymity and a new beginning for me. Besides, you have no choice."

"How do I know that's him?"

"Trust me." Taca roared with sudden laughter. "What else can I say? But I *do* appreciate the irony."

"I'd rather have you than Troshkin."

Taca's voice was icy. "Monsieur Morley, you still don't understand. Nobody's left. Cailleau is dead, the Iraqi is dead, the whore is dead, and I'm afraid our magician friend has disappeared—I can assure you they won't find him for days and when they do, he'll be able to say no more than the whore. You can shoot me here if you wish, but it will be quite impossible to walk away as you might if we were on one of your back streets. I am a respected Belgian, one who was deceived by your government. The papers would be full of your deviousness here in Brussels. Nothing would save you from prison. And I doubt that you would consider your freedom for mine a fair trade, no?" He smiled, his porcelain teeth giving his face an oddly mechanical appearance. "The girl—you found her alive?"

Morley nodded, his throat dry with fury. "I sent her to a doctor."

"No doubt he'll patch her up almost as good as new, if not quite. You should send her back to working in a bar or a massage parlor, something pure and sweet and wholesome. Or as you once said about poor Hans, she should make an interesting Sister."

Taca heaved to his feet. His voice was sly, insinuating.

"You lost Cailleau, but you can still leave Brussels a hero.

Who knows what secrets that Russian clown possesses, how valuable he might be to your country. And how grateful it will be if it is you who finds him and helps him defect to the West."

Taca roared with laughter, his great belly heaving. He shuffled up the aisle to the exit, not bothering to glance back, not at all worried that Morley might actually do what he desperately wanted to—empty the Smith & Wesson into the fat man's back.

thirty

IT WAS DRIZZLING again. Avenue Louise was almost empty except for an occasional stroller oblivious to the rain. This time Morley didn't bother to ring. He took advantage of the deserted street to quickly pick the lock and slip inside the building that housed the Bureau. It was Sunday; the chances were that nobody would be at work.

Almost nobody.

He avoided the lift—the noise of its operation would serve as an early warning—and climbed the stairs. At the top landing, he paused to wipe the sweat off his face. He was pushing himself dangerously far. His left leg was quivering, the muscles protesting painfully. For a moment he wasn't sure he was up to it, and for the first time in days remembered Leather Jacket in the alley. It wouldn't be as easy this time, not unless he were very lucky.

But he couldn't turn back now. He had waited too long.

Another lock to pick, then he walked quietly past the silent printer and down the long hall. He listened outside the library door, heard nothing, turned the knob and eased it open. The room was deserted, but there were signs that Taca wasn't far away. A mini-Schimmelpennick smouldered in the ashtray. A few crumpled bits of gold foil littered the desk around the cannister of Godiva chocolates, next to several neat stacks of coins. The haversack was on the floor, open, and beside it a stack of papers. Taca had no intention of handing in his resignation personally.

Morley walked back into the hallway, pausing when he heard the sounds of the toilet flushing. He limped down the corridor, stopping outside the washroom door. He wondered if he would catch Taca with his pants down. He gripped the Beretta firmly in his hand, then kicked the door open.

Taca squinted up at him from the sink, his face wet, a bar of soap clutched in his thick hands. His gold, wire-rimmed glasses were on the small ledge above the bowl, his suit coat on a hook by the door. He filled the far end of the narrow room, his stomach pushing out between the top of his pants and the bottom of his pin-striped vest.

"We hadn't finished talking," Morley said.

Taca put the soap down and methodically wiped his hands on a paper towel. "I thought we had made an agreement—the scientist for me."

"Your agreement, not mine," Morley said. "I made arrangements to have Troshkin picked up before coming here. It didn't take long." He could waste Taca right there, wanted to do it badly.

Taca managed a smile. "Your Russian friend may lose his job." The smile turned to a sneer. "Your countries remind me of Louis's comic books. It's really rather amusing watching such superpowers dwindle."

"You haven't told me everything I want to know." It sounded stupid to Morley even as he said it. All the fat man would do was confirm what he already knew. But it would make a difference to hear him say it.

Taca thoroughly dried each finger. "If there's anything you wish to ask . . . " He finished with a shrug.

"You own Théâtre de Vaudeville," Morley said.

"My interest in our national heritage, as I once said. I'm a quiet stockholder, it's not well known."

"You book the acts. That's how you met Cailleau."

"He wanted to work again. The pensioners are hardly critical—I knew he would have an audience, it wasn't quite an act of charity."

"You own Le Couvent, too."

"A little pleasure with business. I won't pretend you weren't aware of that."

"You sampled the acts, didn't you?"

"Is that what Louis told you? His major failing—he judged everybody by himself. Yes, I frequently booked the acts there as well, if that's what you mean."

"That was how you got to know Bernadette." A wary nod. "And you introduced her to Cailleau."

Taca slowly buttoned his cuffs. "He was a lonely man, one didn't have to be clairvoyant to see that."

"Compassion was never your motive," Morley said grimly. "You fixed him up with Bernadette because you wanted her to persuade Cailleau to work for you. And she did."

There was a sudden glitter in Taca's eyes. "You're insinuating I deliberately planned a love affair for Monsieur Cailleau. Perhaps I did, but grant me some credit. He was old and pitifully grateful. For Bernadette, he had to be both. She was sensuous on stage, but the illusion faded rather quickly once she was off. You're aware of that, of course. In any event, it was a cheap favor. It cost me nothing."

Morley had his own memories of Bernadette. "You didn't figure that she might develop something for Cailleau in return. If not love, perhaps respect."

"There is no way we can know the answer to that, is there, Monsieur?"

"Did you promise Bernadette to Electro, too? Or did you offer him the Little Bo-Peep you used to control Louis?"

Taca moved away from the sink, edging toward the rear of the washroom. Morley found himself in the doorway, automatically trying to keep the same distance between them.

"Louis had a large appetite, but hardly a taste for quality."

"I once thought Louis had saved my life," Morley said wryly. He felt like he was back in Vietnam, dealing with one of the French black marketeers who had stayed behind to profit on the American occupation. They were just as evasive, just as dangerous. He could feel the same gathering rage, the same desire to cut short the conversation and simply waste him.

"If you really thought that, you repaid him rather badly," Taca laughed. He took another step back. "I first met Louis when he came to Le Couvent two years ago. He was very useful to me."

So far he could have guessed everything that Taca had told him. But there were some questions that had been on his mind from the moment Electro had fingered the fat man.

"The terrorists," Morley said. "You really brought them in for the European Union meeting, didn't you?"

Taca looked surprised. "Isn't that obvious? My associates and I were prepared to go to great lengths to disrupt that meeting. Assassinating the finance ministers would have been one way. Destroying the building another—it would have made a larger statement, if you will. We want no international super-governments in Belgium. We wanted to discourage them."

"And Troshkin?"

Taca smirked. "Forgive me for what I told you at the arena. It was necessary to divert you from me, though I couldn't help but enlarge on what was basically your idea. Kidnapping

Troshkin was the result of serendipity—he happened to be in Berlin. I knew he was unhappy, I offered him a chance to get out, I knew he would be worth a great deal of money to the right parties. He came very willingly. I had thought he would be more grateful."

"What went wrong?" Morley asked.

Taca wiped at the soap in his eyes. "I'm not sure I follow you."

"You couldn't have been relying on Cailleau to bring out your squad. He was too old, too inept, he lived too much in the past. He never would have fooled the border guards, he never could have smuggled them past the infrared detectors. He couldn't have been part of your original plan."

Taca bowed slightly. "Once again, you're very astute. The poor old man's schemes were pathetic. It was all he could do to fool the aging matrons at Théâtre de Vaudeville. But the original plan had fallen through, and Mossad was too close to the Iraqi. I had to improvise an alternative, and both Cailleau and Electro were there."

And then Morley had the entire picture.

"Cailleau was an excuse," he said slowly. "You bribed the guards to look the other way. But once the alarm was sounded, they could always say they had been deceived by Cailleau."

The gold gleamed in Taca's gaping smile.

"It was absurd, ridiculous. But it was also inspired. And it worked."

"Electro tried to persuade Cailleau to help but failed. Bernadette succeeded."

"You *are* clever, Monsieur. A combination of love, nostalgia, money . . . It was irresistible."

"And the magician was another distraction, just in case."

He was seeing more of the real Taca now, the hatred and rage beginning to peep out from behind the thick lenses.

"Of course."

Then Morley remembered.

"And Falk?"

A small smile.

"A suspicious man. He had to be eliminated. Louis made the bomb. It was primitive, but effective."

Morley had only one more question.

"You were the other partner in the import-export firm, weren't you?"

Taca showed his porcelain teeth in a short laugh that quickly faded. The hatred and fury were fully present now, undisguised.

"Pierre Faure, Edgar Mollett, Leon Lavisse—you remember the names?—were my friends, my colleagues if you will. You murdered them six months ago because of some ancient vendetta dating from Vietnam decades ago." He shook his head in mock wonderment. "You hold your resentments a long time, Monsieur. Mine are more recent. Pierre, Edgar and Leon had become friends of mine. I swore personal revenge. The patriots whom Monsieur Cailleau helped bring into this country owed me a favor."

Taca paused, his voice soft.

"I asked for you."

Morley took another step into the washroom, then found himself fighting to keep his footing. The Beretta popped from his hand and flew across the small room. The floor near the door had been covered with a slime of soap and water. He dropped to his knees, scrambling for the gun. He almost screamed when Taca stepped on his hand.

"You're not nearly so quiet as you think," Taca grunted. "The floor boards in the hallway creak, you should have noticed." Morley caught him by the ankle and the fat man went down. A moment later, he almost had the air knocked out of him as Taca rolled across his chest.

He had once thought of Taca as an aging weightlifter gone to flab. He hadn't been far off the mark. He grabbed Taca by the tie and collar but the fat man reached up and effortlessly peeled off his fingers. Then they were both on their feet. The gun had slithered behind the washbowl stand; neither of them could get it without turning his back on the other.

Taca grabbed a bottle of mouthwash from the sink and knocked the neck off against the washbowl. He held the broken bottle with the jagged edges pointing toward Morley. It was a scene Morley had played in a dozen Saigon bars.

"There'll be nobody here until tomorrow, Monsieur," Taca murmured. "I'll have disappeared by then."

Taca thrust at him and Morley felt the cloth of his coat rip. The fat man was faster than he had thought possible. He gripped his hands together and swung them like a club at the florid face in front of him. The broken bottle cut into his upper arm. He didn't feel any pain, only the sudden, sticky warmth of blood. It was like being in a fire fight in 'Nam, where you didn't feel the wound until it was all over.

Taca backed against the door, still holding the broken bottle, watching him, waiting for an opening. Morley gripped his upper arm and groaned. Taca lunged for him. He jerked to one side and tripped the fat man, then leaped for the door and slammed the bolt home. The two of them were locked in the small washroom now, there was no way either he or Taca was going to leave unless the other were dead.

Taca read the message in his face. His own face turned a mottled red. Morley grabbed for him and Taca abruptly spun and caught him in the kidney with his foot. Morley went down, holding onto the arm with the bottle and dragging Taca with him. Taca fell heavily to the floor, momentarily stunned. Morley pulled him over to the toilet bowl and pounded the right arm holding the bottle on the edge of the bowl. Taca screamed and his grip loosened. The broken bottle fell into the pink-tinged water.

Then Taca caught him in the stomach with a foot and Morley doubled. He'd been slow again, too slow. He could no longer control the quivering in his left leg and could feel his muscles growing weak with fatigue. He gagged and tried to straighten up and Taca threw a body block, forcing him against the wall. The fat man kneed him in the groin and he slumped to the concrete floor. He could feel the cool porcelain of the toilet bowl next to his head, then Taca's fingers had tightened around his throat. The fingers with a life all their own.

He arched his back but couldn't push the fat man off. He reached up and grabbed Taca's thick fingers to pull them away. Taca was sweating heavily; the odor made Morley sick. He yanked again at the fingers. He felt like he hadn't taken a breath for minutes.

The hands around his throat tightened even more.

"Good-bye, *Mister* Morley."

They would find him with a throat like Bernadette's, crushed and purple, his eyes staring as blankly as hers had.

Desperate, Morley thrust a knee upward, felt it sink into the thick pillow of the man above him, heard a grunt. He rolled, tearing at the hands, kicking out with his knees, then was on top of the fat man. The thick fingers loosened slightly and he grabbed a frantic chestful of air and forced himself up into a squatting position, straddling Taca.

The big man's hands felt for his throat again and closed directly on his windpipe. Morley was no longer quite sure where he was or who he was fighting. Brussels and Saigon were suddenly interchangeable, Taca's face that of a hundred black marketeers and assassins back in 'Nam. He grabbed Taca's head by the ears and brought it down, hard, on the edge of the ceramic bowl. Again. The room was starting to swim. He dragged Taca over the toilet bowl itself and caught the pull chain with his shoulder. The fingers on his throat loosened as Taca turned, trying to get away. Morley forced his head into the turbulent water boiling up in the bowl.

The water turned a bloody pink. He felt Taca go limp and thought that he had probably killed him. He was too exhausted to feel triumph, too tired to feel much of anything, but he continued to batter Taca's head against the edge of the toilet. The black marketeers in 'Nam had had a dozen lives. . . .

There was a splintering sound behind him and the door suddenly crashed open. A distant voice said, "Somebody call an ambulance for the pig. And open a window—*mon Dieu*, how can anybody stink so much when they sweat?" Morley felt a hand touch him on the shoulder and the same voice said gently, "Don't flush him, Monsieur, we have our own little score to settle."

The voice sounded remarkably like that of Captain Willy van den Haute.

thirty-one

Mᴏʀʟᴇʏ ᴘᴀᴜꜱᴇᴅ ʙʏ the rack of dripping raincoats to listen to the celebration. The old girls were back, sipping their cherry beers, and Schumann had replaced Strauss on the tape deck. The pinball machines were chattering again, but losing ground rapidly to the crowd gathered around Henri's table. Hannie was there, her attention caught by the mime and his new chess partner.

The greasepaint and the gaudy costume were gone, but he could still see traces of the tragic clown in Troshkin's face. The Russian was wearing a suit two sizes too big and a frayed shirt; both had obviously come from the rack of worn clothing behind Henri. The two men were bent over their chess pieces while everybody else clustered around them was kibitzing.

The barkeep was the first to spot Morley and immediately motioned his wife to draw their friend a beer. Then Hannie noticed him and hurried over. She threw her arms around him. "You're all right?" She studied him, anxious.

He assured her that he was and nodded at Troshkin. "How's *he* doing?"

"See for yourself." She sounded as proud as a mother at

her son's first birthday party. Morley smiled, then concentrated on Troshkin. His short brown hair had been recently trimmed, his moustache waxed. His glasses had small round lenses; the clear plastic frames that rode the permanent crease of his broad nose had long ago darkened to amber. His hazel eyes were bright as well as nervous. Troshkin was reading the faces around him, listening to the tone of the conversation and tracking its flow by following the eyes of the speaker. He had a full laugh, surprisingly vibrant for such a slight man. It was triggered by the smiles of the others and encouraged by their laughter, and it was always the loudest of all.

Hannie wasn't the only one taken with him. Henri watched over Troshkin like a mother hen, launching into a mime routine whenever the Russian seemed confused.

"They've been like that ever since we got here," Hannie said. She was still watching him closely, trying hard to keep her voice light. "The bartender didn't have any more vodka, so he gave him a tumbler of jenever. Gennadi tried forcing it down, but we could see he thought it was pretty awful." She laughed, tentatively touching his arm. "But he does like the beer. We may have to pour him out the door."

Morley glanced again at Troshkin, then back to her. "I didn't think you could do it." He paused, as tentative as she was. "I didn't want to ask you so soon after . . . "

Her voice was shadowed. "I couldn't have gotten him away by myself. Monsieur Schlöndorff helped. He had the other performers gather around Gennadi so the Russians couldn't get close to him. They walked him out."

Morley thought of the woman the booking agent had taught to juggle. Schlöndorff had lied to him—he'd never really stopped being a *fluchthelfer*.

Troshkin looked up then, sensing he was being studied. His face lit up and he crossed the first and second fingers on each hand and snapped them apart quickly. Morley didn't know much Russian, but he recognized the universal sign for prison and everything associated with it. One Russian word came to mind—*druzhba*, the word for friendship—but he couldn't bring himself to use it. The scientist would think he was a bastard soon enough.

Troshkin pulled himself up from the table, grabbed hold of Hannie's hand and then, smiling at both of them, reached for Morley's. Morley guessed by the sudden quizzical look on his face that he sensed things weren't quite as they should be. He broke the grip and patted Troshkin's shoulder, suddenly aware of how sweaty his hand had become. The barkeep showed up with more beers, and he grabbed one and handed it to Troshkin.

The bartender was grinning. "He wanted to know why we had all the clothes, and Henri had to explain that Prison St. Giles is just across the street, and the first thing a man wants when he's set free is something to drink and clothes of his own." He reached down and tugged Troshkin's cuff over his thin wrist. "See? Now he's no different than the rest of us."

Hannie drew Morley away to another table where she had two Scotches waiting. They clinked glasses and she whispered, "I've been watching you. What's wrong?"

He leaned back in his chair, feeling the wood creak as he took a deep breath. Once again he was aware of her scent. She'd been through hell, but she looked better to him than ever. He picked up his glass, tasted the liquor, and wondered how long the bartender had hidden the bottle of Johnny Walker Black.

"I had to make a phone call," he said casually. "They'll be coming soon."

"They?"

He was tired of many things, but most of all, he was tired of having it always come down to this.

"Everyone knows he's here. Officials from the embassies

want to talk to him. Simon wants to talk to him. So do the Russians, and the Belgians are hardly going to stop them. I can't, either."

He had nothing more to say and she stared at him.

"Two hours of freedom and then a clown again. Is that it?" She gave up struggling to control her anger. "Doesn't he get a choice?"

"Sure." But he couldn't face her, and knew that gave the lie to both the freedom and the choice.

Morley stood by the airport terminal window staring out at the rain. In the downpour, the sky and the wet tarmac and the two airplanes on the apron below were all the same indiscernible gray—as washed-out as the beige-colored room they'd been locked in for hours.

"You spent a long time with him, Andrei." His voice was barely audible over the sudden rumbling of jet engines on the strip below. He cleared his throat and spoke louder. "How'd it go?"

"All right." Vasiliev stepped to the window and looked down at the planes. "In Russia, we call this a 'mushroom rain.' " He glanced sideways at Morley. "You know, in this drizzle I can't tell which plane is which."

Neither could he, Morley thought. One of them had been readied for flight, the result of a decision reached in another part of the terminal. He followed Vasiliev's eyes and glanced through the glass partition at Troshkin, sitting in the next room. Two gendarmes stood on either side of him.

Vasiliev said, "I don't think he likes me very much."

"He thinks no better of me."

Morley checked his watch and shifted his weight to his other leg. Nearly three hours had gone by since the two delegations had arrived at the conference room in the terminal—

both sets of first secretaries from the embassies had burst through the door simultaneously and hastily drawn their experts into tight circles at the far ends of the long room. The two groups had taken turns talking in hushed tones to Troshkin, who had said very little, seldom raising his eyes.

Vasiliev had been the last one to talk to him and after that, Troshkin had reluctantly agreed to return to Russia.

There was a minor commotion in the next room, suddenly filled with a dozen gesturing officials. Morley watched through the glass as the gendarmes nudged Troshkin and he got up to leave. He didn't glance at either Vasiliev or Morley.

"He'll readjust soon enough, Neal."

Morley felt irritated. "I expect that kind of crap from somebody in pinstripes. You know better."

"Catch up, Neal," Vasiliev said quietly, watching Troshkin disappear under a black umbrella. "His work is all he's got. We both can understand that. He never would have felt at home with the language, acquired a taste for bourbon, gotten a really good cup of borscht or made one close friend who wasn't an expatriate as miserable and homesick as himself."

Morley said nothing. Vasiliev continued talking as Troshkin walked up the steps to the hatchway and disappeared inside. A moment later, the plane's door was closed and the steps wheeled away.

"Back home, he has his notebooks, his assistants, the lab apparatus that he designed himself. What would you have done with him in the West? Debriefed him for six months and tossed him on the rubbish heap when you discovered you already know everything he knows? The only real secret is whether something can be done at all. After that, it's just research."

"So much for the Cold War being over," Morley murmured.

Vasiliev was surprised.

"You think Troshkin was wanted for weapons research?" He shook his head. "I'm sure Gennadi knows something of military value, but that's not why we wanted him back. Russia has to have new industries, and what Troshkin knows could be the basis for a very healthy one. We need the foreign exchange, Neal—very badly."

Vasiliev looked bemused.

"What I told Troshkin is that he would, of course, own a healthy share of the stock and five years from now, he could be a very wealthy man. There is also a young female laboratory assistant who is quite fond of him, and more than willing to help him forget his recent tragedies. In a short time, I think he will be willing to speak to me again."

Morley felt a sudden surge of bitterness. His tour of duty in Brussels had been one-third tragedy, one-third farce and one-third useless.

Vasiliev turned away from the window, not waiting to watch the plane lift off. Morley picked up his briefcase and Vasiliev slipped into his camel's hair coat.

"Where do you go from here, Neal?"

Morley shrugged. "I'm due to see van den Haute in an hour. After that, I'll probably be on the next plane back."

Vasiliev suddenly said, "Does it seem to you that much of what we do these days is like a dream, Neal? That it touches us, but not the heart of us?"

Morley looked at him questioningly. Vasiliev was in a black mood, not so strange considering they were in Brussels. But it went deeper than the city or its weather.

"I'm sure you've heard the saying, Neal, that every generation has its war. Vietnam was yours; you were more deeply involved there than I was. Afghanistan was mine—you must ask me to tell you about it someday." The expression on his face suddenly became one of deep sadness. "Better yet, do me a favor and don't ask."

He shook himself and stooped to retrieve a newspaper from a nearby chair. He turned and held out his hand and Morley took it.

"What are you going to do now, Andrei?"

"Go back to Moscow. This was my last tour of duty, Neal. I hope to buy a small shop or perhaps teach . . . history. Grow fat on my wife's cooking, play with the children, and sit on a park bench and watch the pretty girls walk by. And you?"

Morley really hadn't thought about it.

"I don't know," he said slowly. "I really don't know."

Vasiliev touched him lightly on the shoulder.

"You're very good at what you do, Neal. But I think it's time to go home."

Morley shrugged. "I don't know where home is; the States certainly aren't."

Vasiliev tapped his head. "I meant up here, Neal. Please think about it. Sitting in the sun and playing with your grand-children is not all that bad."

And then he was gone.

thirty-two

THE CAPTAIN'S OFFICE was warm, the hiss of the radiator familiar. Van den Haute pressed a buzzer on his desk and when the cadet came in, said politely: "Coffee, black—right, Neal?"

Morley nodded, wary. Van den Haute's sudden affability was a warning sign. Then he remembered that Troshkin was gone, the terrorist squad had been rounded up and Taca was in custody. In another few hours, he himself would have left.

"A farewell cup, *Capitaine?*"

Van den Haute cocked his head, the perfect picture of a relaxed bureaucrat. "It's a shame you can't spend a holiday in Brussels, Neal—you may not realize how much our city really has to offer." He looked apologetic. "But I understand you have to report and get a final medical check from the doctors."

"You're too kind," Morley said dryly. "You've always been too kind."

Van den Haute looked at him politely. "I'm not sure I understand."

"You could have thrown me out of Belgium any time. And

Simon could have recalled me, *should* have recalled me. Neither of you did."

The Captain looked uncomfortable. "I think you make too much of too little."

Morley sipped his coffee. "I can get the story from London—eventually."

Van den Haute leaned back in his chair, lacing his fingers behind his head. "My responsibilities are different from yours, Neal. They're different from your associates' and they're certainly different from the Russians'. My concern is for Belgium, my concern has always been for Belgium." He looked thoughtful. "Other countries with whom we cooperate sometimes forget that and consider us . . . parochial. More coffee?"

He refilled Morley's cup and helped himself to a small cake from the silver tray. "The terrorists frightened Cailleau—deliberately—and he ran straight to his friend in London." He looked up. "Cailleau was actually bait for you, Neal. I'm surprised you never realized that."

It was Morley's turn to look blank and say, "I don't understand."

"No offense intended," van den Haute soothed. "After Cailleau's complaint, London notified E.T.C. that they would be glad to send an out-of-country operative over here to handle it. Their reply to an obvious request by Cailleau."

"Cailleau knew Taca was with the Bureau," Morley objected. "He would have asked that his request be kept private, that the Bureau not be notified."

Van den Haute nodded. "You're right, particularly in view of what he really wanted to tell London—that their Bureau here had been compromised. It's the sort of information you pass along in person, not over the phone. Unfortunately nobody in London believed his story about the terrorists any more than you did, and some minor clerk automatically notified E.T.C.

310

Both London and myself were shocked, of course, when M'sieurs Tindemans and Taca requested that the assignment be handed to you. I was well aware that you had been hospitalized, that you were probably not up to anything even minor. I'm glad I was mistaken. You sure you won't have a cake?"

Morley shook his head and van den Haute helped himself to another.

"The request was an early warning signal. We knew there was a radical movement in the city, we suspected that somebody in E.T.C. was involved. The request that you be sent made us even more suspicious, and we checked into the incident of six months ago once again. The actions of both Taca and the cab driver were suspect, but we could prove nothing." He wiped his fingers on a tiny paper napkin. "I was delighted you volunteered—it saved me from forcing your man Simon to give the assignment to you. The devil, of course, was Monsieur Taca—your man Tindemans is merely an incompetent, you agree?"

It occurred to Morley that he had underestimated van den Haute far more than he had underestimated Taca.

"You said Cailleau was bait for me?"

"Because you had—ah—removed the two consular officials and the import-export executive. As you know, they were all associates of *Docteur* Taca, members of his crusade. You survived the attempts to kill you six months ago, and fortunately for Louis and Taca you remembered nothing of the assault itself. But Monsieur Taca still wanted revenge. Cailleau was due to be murdered in any event—he knew too much—but he also presented an opportunity to get you back in Brussels. Risky, of course. Taca had Cailleau killed, and no doubt would have removed you immediately as well. But you remember the meal at Comme chez Soi? You gave no indication that you knew of

Taca's connection, so there was no hurry. You were now in the country and within Taca's reach."

"And the attempt outside the gendarmerie?"

Van den Haute shrugged. " 'No hurry' is a relative term. There was a timetable of sorts. The terrorists were in the country, but shortly they would be preoccupied by the European Union meeting. Taca took advantage of their 'down time,' so to speak."

"And Bernadette."

"The chanteuse." Van den Haute lingered over the word for a moment. "She undoubtedly considered herself safe at first; she'd been useful to Taca a number of times. He assumed she would be silent but he hadn't counted on her fondness for Cailleau. She chose to tell you a little and apparently decided the next day to talk more fully. She tried to contact you through us, failed, realized she had compromised herself and then tried to blackmail Electro the magician for the money to leave Brussels. An unwise thing to do. Electro, of course, told Taca, who sent Louis after her."

Van den Haute looked up from behind his cake.

"I'm sorry her timing was off, I know your feelings for her. I was harsh in judging her. She was not a whore, as I once called her. Our profession is not a pretty one, and sometimes women on both sides have to do things they would not ordinarily do. But one should not confuse them with the women of the curtain shops." He was watching Morley closely. "I would not blame myself, Neal."

Morley looked away. "I thought that Louis had saved my life."

"The man who drove your 'taxi.' Monsieur Tindemans tells me he was a good employee. But with that type, you have to beware when they change employers."

"And Hannie?"

312

"It was time to eliminate you. The girl was an obvious means by which to decoy you to the theater, though I understand you had your difficulties in finding where they had taken her."

The last tumbler clicked into place.

"You knew what was happening all the time but you left me out there," Morley said, trying to smother a sudden surge of anger. "So did Simon. Cailleau was bait for me. I was bait for Taca."

Van den Haute looked faintly embarrassed.

"I would be lying if I denied it. But I cannot honestly believe you expect compassion from a government. Yes, we used you. You are a tool—a superb tool—and we borrowed you for a while to act as Taca's rabbit. The world is very much a stage, as Shakespeare once put it. A puppet's stage, if you will. Each of us takes his turn at being the puppeteer. This time it was my turn." He grimaced. "In times past, I've had someone higher up pull my strings. You've reminded me of that upon occasion." He smiled. "Besides, Neal, you rather desperately wanted to stay in Brussels. It is not my fault that Monsieur Taca found you before you found him. But I believe it all worked out to your satisfaction."

"Who pulled Taca's strings?" Morley suddenly asked.

"I don't know, though I think we'll find out soon enough. There's still the man who managed to get the gun to Karim." Van den Haute finished his coffee and stood up. "We did our best to watch over you, Neal. Please don't criticize us for having arrived late this last time. Be grateful we arrived."

"You did your homework," Morley murmured.

Van den Haute nodded modestly. "What we do not know, we shall soon find out. *Docteur* Taca is in custody. The interrogators failed with Karim but"—cynically—"they continue to benefit from the latest researches in science."

Morley was at the door when he suddenly remembered and said, "I made a promise to Karim."

"To tell his mother? I understand your concern. I'll see to it." Morley had taken another step toward the door when van den Haute cleared his throat and said: "I want to officially extend the gratitude of my government."

Morley waited in silence while the Captain struggled for words. "This is not the best of all possible worlds, Neal. It never will be. What you do—what we do—extends the life of this farce we call civilization for a few more years. I am not sure the price we pay is worth it, but I have seen the alternative. In these cynical times, I realize it is not always a compliment to be called a patriot. Perhaps it's because we've forgotten that a true patriot is one who believes in his country more than the politicians who run it."

He smiled. "What I am trying to say, Neal, is that what you do is a thankless job. So do not expect any."

"I never have," Morley said.

Van den Haute nibbled at one of the small cakes.

"Neal." He said it hesitantly, not looking at him. Morley realized he was about to be offered advice and automatically resented it in advance. "Have you ever been to a class reunion?"

Morley shook his head.

"I used to go. And then I realized I was tired of spending time with people for whom the world had stopped revolving. Too many of them lived in the past, unaware that time was passing them by, that the world was changing. For them, the past was like a tar pit in which they were mired. I did not wish to be mired along with them, and so I stopped attending. Some memories should be given a decent burial. The French who were in Vietnam before you finally realized that. Perhaps it is time that you should, too. From one friend to another, Neal."

He suddenly changed the subject.

"You'll be leaving soon, I understand?"

"There's a flight this afternoon," Morley said stiffly. "I don't imagine you'll be sorry to see me ago."

The Captain shrugged and smiled. "I would not lie to a friend," he said.

Thirty-three

"**M**AKE OUT YOUR expenses on the plane . . . "

It was absurd, he thought. He had so much he wanted to tell her, and here he was talking about expenses.

"You're budgeted for a per diem . . . " He tried to keep his eyes on the pad in front of him and concentrate on the figures, but all he could think about was the softness of her hair and the golden glow of her body when she had stood in the light streaming through the window—how long ago?

" . . . whether they told you or not, you're entitled to a lot more than you spent. Triple that—put it down to 'client relations' or 'sources,' whatever you want. You'll get it."

They were sitting in a small cafe, at a tiny table by the windows. For the first time in days, the sun was peeping through the sullen overcast, and he could feel the warmth through the glass.

"You're not coming, then," she said.

He looked up, trying to ignore the hurt in her eyes. "My bag is still in the room."

"So? They won't give it away."

He smiled, remembering her half-buried in the feather bed. "Who told you that?"

"Once I went to a hotel with a complete stranger. He told me." She turned away, studying the clock on the wall. She was obviously fighting her emotions. "You should do something about your nightmares, the ones where you're still in Vietnam—"

He shrugged. "They'll go away."

"I think I'm beginning to understand you," she said. "I'm sorry it took so long."

The images that flashed through his mind, of Karim and Louis and Bernadette, were painful. But the memory of lying in Hannie's bed, exhausted and sick and for the first time in years totally dependent upon somebody else, was a comforting one. He understood himself a little better, too. He held her hand for a moment, then reluctantly let it go.

"You'll stay in touch?"

She nodded, then suddenly looked him full in the face and burst out: "We're lying, aren't we? We'll probably never see each other again unless it's 'duty,' and then we'll be oh-so-formal and polite. . . ."

He didn't answer, but settled for looking mildly unhappy.

She fumbled in her purse. "This is my card—call me when you're in London." She hesitated. "You could help me pack."

He glanced at the card and slipped it in his pocket. "I have to make a call, Hannie—time to check in."

She looked at him for a moment, then stood up quietly and walked to the door. She didn't look back.

He waited until she had disappeared up the street, then walked outside to one of the small tables in the sunshine. His rescheduled flight left around five—he'd have to call London before then—which meant he could sit in the sun for a while longer and pack at leisure. Hannie would probably leave him a note, but at least there wouldn't be the pain of saying good-bye.

He picked up a newspaper from one of the nearby tables and settled in the chair, facing into the sun so it hit his face. The first sunshine in . . . how many days?

"Monsieur?"

The waiter was looking at him expectantly.

"Just some Perrier."

He was halfway through the front page article praising the success of the European Union meeting before he realized he hadn't really read a word. He smiled, then glanced overhead at the shimmer of a jet high in the bright blue sky. Hannie would be almost packed by now, waiting for the concierge to call for a cab. He took her card from his pocket. A second address and phone number had been written on it. Her apartment number. He'd be welcome any time, he was sure of that.

There was no future in it, of course. There was a gulf between them, of both age and experience, and no way could it ever be bridged. But there was no way he would ever forget her, either.

He sipped at the Perrier and once again thumbed through the paper. There was nothing in print—van den Haute had made sure there wouldn't be. He wondered idly if he'd run into Vasiliev again, and whether or not Andrei would really retire. Vasiliev's last words had been meant as a show of personal friendship. The Russian had been the only one who had understood him.

Which wasn't quite true. Toward the end, Hannie had understood him as well as he understood himself. And van den Haute probably always had. All three of them had given him the same advice, and he had resented it from each of them. He had chosen the life he led and it was much too late to change it.

He finished the last of the Perrier and closed his eyes,

leaning slightly back in his chair to let the sun warm his neck and chest. There was time, he could afford to doze off for a few minutes, even if he risked once again seeing the crowded embassy roof and hearing the beat of the 'copter blades and the shouts of the embassy personnel as they fought for a place on board. . . . Or if not that, then the nightmare of the small huts and the flames beyond and the crumpled figures. . . .

He moved uneasily in the chair, then relaxed. Hannie was very sharp in his memory, curled up in the huge feather bed, the covers around her neck, her eyes closed and the hair tumbled about her face. In his mind's eye he watched her as she woke up and walked over to the window, the soft light dappling her golden skin. . . .

He frowned and tried to force his mind to recall the embassy roof and the flaming hut but the figures were vague, the sounds merely a muted hum. Then they dwindled and disappeared completely, and what filled his mind was the image of Hannie, her breasts moving slightly as she breathed in her sleep.

His eyes shot open and the legs of the chair hit the walk with a thud. The embassy roof had refused to appear; so had the flaming huts. He realized suddenly that they were part of a past he no longer quite remembered, a past that wasn't nearly as sharp as yesterday or the day before, and would be even fainter tomorrow.

All the sutures were out, all the strings cut. The men who had sold poisoned narcotics in Vietnam were long gone, those who had tried to kill him in Brussels were either dead or languishing in prison. It was all over, part of another life. He had gone to his last class reunion. . . .

He stood up and pressed a banknote in the waiter's hand, then hurried inside to the phone. It took him a moment to get through to van den Haute.

"Twenty-four hours," he said urgently. "You owe me."

There was a long pause on the other end of the line, then he could hear the Captain's suspicious voice: "Business or pleasure."

He smiled. "Not business."

Another pause, then a resigned sigh: "Enjoy your holiday in Brussels, Neal."

Morley hung up, then ran outside to hail a cab. London could wait—Tindemans had undoubtedly filled them in hours ago anyway. What was important now was that Hannie wouldn't have finished packing, not yet. She'd be sitting at the little wooden table writing him a note, and probably scratching out two words for every one she wrote down. She might know him as well as he knew himself, but it was also true that he knew her better than she knew herself.

A cab squealed to the curb. He opened the door, squinting his eyes against the sunlight, and laughed.

A sunny day in Brussels. . . .